W. A Zeller

Complete City Directory of Huntington, Indiana

W. A Zeller

Complete City Directory of Huntington, Indiana

ISBN/EAN: 9783741187513

Manufactured in Europe, USA, Canada, Australia, Japa

Cover: Foto ©Andreas Hilbeck / pixelio.de

Manufactured and distributed by brebook publishing software
(www.brebook.com)

W. A Zeller

Complete City Directory of Huntington, Indiana

COMPLETE

CITY DIRECTORY

—OF—

Huntington, - Indiana,

1897-98.

COMPILED AND PUBLISHED BY
W. A. ZELLER, Jr.,
HUNTINGTON, IND.

DIRECTORY

OF THE

CITY OF HUNTINGTON.

1897=98.

———◆———

County Officials.

Court House, n Jefferson, between Court and Franklin

Hon. C W Watkins, Judge 56th Judicial Circuit

John R Day, Prosecuting Atty

William P Moffett, Clerk

William F Swaim, Auditor

Jacob W John, Treasurer

Jefferson J Sprinkle, Recorder

Thos J Ruggles, Surveyor

J R King, Coroner

Henry D Shideler, Supt of Schools

Dr C L Wright, Health Officer

John M Smith, Commissioner 1st District

Isaiah M Strouse, Commissioner 2d District

Samuel H Eviston, Commissioner 3rd District

Hart & Hart, County Attorneys

Huntington Circuit Court.

January term begins second Monday, 12 weeks

April term begins second Monday, 12 weeks

September term begins first Monday, 15 weeks

Huntington City Government.

City Building, sw cor Cherry and Market

Council meets second and fourth Tuesday nights in each month

S T Cast, Mayor

E Q Drummond, Clerk

O S Bay, Treasurer

A A Crandal, Marshal.

J Fred France, City Attorney

Frank Guthrie, City Civil Engineer.

Wm. Schwartz, Supt of Water Works

Richard Gardner, Street Commissioner

W T Whitelock, Commissioner

Isaac E Fisher, Commissioner

Louis G Trixler, Commissioner

J M Wright, Commissioner

Jacob Stults, Commissioner

William Dimond, Councilman 1st Ward

Jacob Speaker, Councilman 1st Ward

Chas S Gibson, Councilman 2d Ward

Chas Mader, Councilman 2d Ward

Marion G Wright, Councilman 3rd Ward

Anthony A Weber, Councilman 3rd Ward

Thos Buchanan, Supt of Electric Light

W A Berry, Health Officer

Dr Chas L Wright, Health Officer

Mat Highland, Chief of Fire Department

Thos Brady, policeman.

W H Stewart, policeman

Wm Riley, policeman

Sun Ross, policeman

Wm Millen, deputy city marshal

Edwin B Ayres, Metropolitan Commissioner

John Q Cline, Metropolitan Commissioner

H D McClelland, Metropolitan Commissioner

Alonzo A Crandal, Captain Metropolitan Police

William Millen, Sergeant Metropolitan Police

J M Boyd, Metropolitan Police Officer

Henry Kohlenberg, Metropolitan Police Officer

Clarence Bilger, Metropolitan Police Officer

Post Office.

Post Office I O O F block, e Franklin st Office hours, 6
a m to 7:30 p m; Sundays, 9 to 10 a m

New Post Office building 12 w Market.

J F Fulton, Post Master.

Scott Cole, Post Master elect

Schools, Public and Parochial.

Marion B Stults, member Board of Education

John Minnich, member Board of Education

John C Altman, member Board of Education

Robert I Hamilton, Supt Public Schools (6 in number)

John Renn, Supt Lutheran School

Rev Dr J H Hueser, Supt SS Peter and Paul's Catholic
School

Rev Father Quinlan, Supt St Mary's Catholic School

Churches.

Christian Church, se cor Guilford and Franklin. Rev.
H C Kendrick, pastor

Evangelical Assc of N A Church, 86 Front street. Rev
Howard Steininger, pastor

First Baptist Church, 35 e Market. Rev H F McDonald,
pastor.

First Presbyterian Church, nw cor Tipton and Warren.
Rev H L Nave, pastor.

German Reformed Church, nw cor Henry and Etna ave.
Rev J F Winter, pastor

Methodist Episcopal Church, nw cor Market and Guilford Rev F M Stone, pastor

St John's English Evangelical Lutheran Church, nw
cor Foust and Second. Rev M H Hockman, pastor

St Peter's Evangelical German Lutheran church, the
Unaltered Angsburg Confession, 76 Lafontaine st
Rev W J Kaiser, pastor

SS Peter and Paul's Catholic Church, 97 Cherry Rev
Dr J Hueser, pastor

United Brethren in Christ Church, sw cor Matilda and
Poplar Rev J W DeLong, pastor

German Baptist Church, ne cor Guilford and Washington

Episcopal Mission, 33 Poplar.

Christian Chapel Church, cor Court and First Revs C
V and Mary A Strickland, pastors

Tabernacle Baptist Church, cor Condit and South. Rev
C S Winans, pastor

Etna Avenue U B Church, cor Etna ave and Olinger.

St Mary's Catholic Church, 174 n Jefferson Rev Father
Quinlan, pastor

Societies.

Catholic Benevolent Legion, meets second and fourth
Tuesdays of each month in Roche block

Knights of St John Com'd No 156, meets in Roche block
first Monday of each month

Ancient Order Hibernians, meets first and third Tuesdays in each month in Roche block

Knights of the Maccabees of the World, meets every
Monday night over 62 n Jefferson

Lime City Council No 267, National Union, meets first
Wednesday night of each month over 83 n Jeff'son

James R Slack Post No 137, G A R, meet second and
fourth Mondays in each month over 9 n Jefferson.

James R Slack Corps, No 42, meets in G A R hall first
and third Thursdays afternoons of each month

Brotherhood of Locomotive Firemen, meets every Wednesday evening over 55 n Jefferson.

Ladies' Society to the B of L F, meets every Wednesday
afternoon at 2:30 in B of L F hall

Order Railway Conductors, Division 120, meets every
Sunday afternoon over 58 n Jefferson

Ladies' Auxiliary to O R C, meets first and third Thursday afternoons in O R C hall

Brotherhood of Locomotive Engineers, meets every Sun-
afternoon over 56 n Jefferson

Good Will Lodge, Auxiliary to B of L E, meets first and
third Wednesday afternoons in B of L E hall

Brotherhood of Railroad Trainmen, meet over First National Bank first and third Sundays of each month

Ancient Order United Workmen, meets second and fourth
Friday nights in each month over 62 n Jefferson

Royal Arcanum, meet every Tuesday night over 83 n
Jefferson

Knights of the Golden Eagle, meets every Thursday
evening in G A R hall

Improved Order of Red Men, Mishinewa Tribe No 81,
meets each Tuesday evening in Griffith block

Supreme Court of Honor.

Modern Woodmen of America, No 3116, meets second and fourth Fridays of each month in Griffith blk.

Haymakers, meet first and third Friday nights in each month in Griffith block

Mystic Lodge, No 110, F & A M, meets first and third Thursdays of each month in room opposite court house

Amity Lodge, No 483, F & A M, meets first and third Mondays in each month in Clayton block

Huntington Chapter, No 27, R A M, meets in Clayton block on second Friday in each month

Huntington Council No 51, R & S M, meets in Clayton block on fourth Monday in each month

Huntington Commandery, No 35, meets in Clayton block on second and fourth Thursdays of each month

Floral Chapter, No 75, Order Eastern Star, meets second and fourth Tuesdays of each month in Mystic hall

Lafontaine Lodge, No 42, I O O F, meets in Odd Fellows' block every Tuesday evening

Silica Fons Encampment No 88, I O O F, meets in Odd Fellow block on second and fourth Thursday of each month

Charity Lodge No 261, Daughters Rebekah, meets in I O O F blk on first and third Thursday evenings of each month

Huntington Lodge, No 93, K P, meets every Wednesday night in Castle Hall over 2 c Market

Huntington Division No 16, U R K of P, meets second and fourth Tuesdays of each month in Castle hall

Rathbone Sisters, K of P, meet in Castle hall

Huntington County Medical Society, meets at Exchange Hotel second Tuesday in each month

Walther League, meets every first Monday in each month at 48 Polk

Dr Martin Luther Young Ladies' Society meets every second Sunday in each month.

Frauen-Verein, of the St Peter's Lutheran church, U A C, meets every third Sunday in each month

Huntington Humane Society, meets first Tuesday of each month at the law office of Spencer & Branyan

W C T U, meets every two weeks at the homes of members.

EXPLANATION:—This Directory includes the names of all citizens of Huntington as completely as the enumerators were able to secure the same. The name of the head of the family is given in full; the name of the wife will be found in brackets, thus [Elizabeth], and the names of children follow.

The star (*) indicates names of persons residing outside the city limits.

The dagger (†) indicates names of persons residing in the disputed annexed additions.

Names overlooked or omitted in the original canvass will be found in the supplemental list.

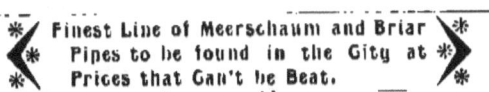

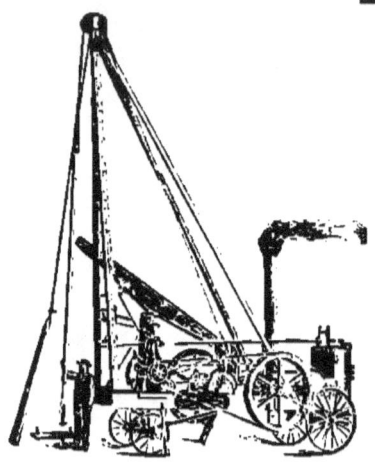

A

Abbott, A C, cond Erie, res 28 Fruit [Maude] May and Ruth

Abendroth, David C, saloon, 92 N Jefferson, res 62 Oak [Hannah] Tillie, Katie

" Albert, clk, res 62 Oak

" Emma, bookkpr, Democrat, Marion, O, res 62 Oak

Achey, Anna, (wid Wm A) res 69 Court

Ackerman, Geo, emp Lang's brewery, res 34 Marshall [Florence]

Ackerman, Chas, stone mason, res 115 Cherry [Mary] Frank

Ackerman, Frank, saloon, Echange hotel, res 157 Guilford [Margaret] Frederick E, Eugene F, Maureen, George E, Lucile A

" Chas. jr, emp Lang's brewery, bds 64 Marshall

Ackley, David, carpenter, res 31 Bingham [Ida] Blanche

Adams, A J, eng, Huntington Mill Co, res 15 Front [Nancy A] Amos R, Josie, William, Boston G, Lulu L

" Benton, plasterer, res 7 Erie [Mattie] Carl, Harry

" Harvey, tender lamp tower Erie, res 73 South [Emma F] Guy

" William, lab, res 77 S Jefferson [Mary]

" Elizabeth, (wid Cyrus) res 73 South

" H E, agent, res 96 Whitelock [Mary E] Edith Blaine Henry C

Ady, I J, student, bds 54 First

Agan, Laura E, teacher public schools, res 64 E Franklin

Ager, Daniel F, carpenter, res 94 William [Lena] Frank B

" Elmer B, painter, bds 60 Whitelock

" Mary, res 69 W State

Ahlschwede, Elizabeth (wid Fred) res 90 W Matilda

" William, barber, res 90 W Matilda

* " Geo, lab, res W on Wab Ry [Alice] Louisa

Ainsworth, Clara (wid G W) res 29 Iowa

" Chas. lab, res 29 Iowa

Alberts, Chas (col'd) brk and stone mason, res over 26 Front
    Harold

Alexander, John T, attorney, over 6 W Market, res 226 N Jefferson [Mattie M]

*   "   Wm, sawyer, Withington factory, res Stringtown, E Fair Ground [Nettie] Flora Chas Arthur

    "   Jasper S, lab, res 32 Mayne [Susan] Leota Harl Carrie

Allen, E E, insurance, real estate and loans, over 46 N Jefferson, res 58 S Jefferson [Jennie E] Harry, Hazel

Alleman, Chas E. clk Frash. res 44 S Jefferson [Anna B]

Allerton, Asa, emp shoe factory, res 13 Simon [Sarah] Gottie, Harry, Fay, Fern, John

    "   Ezekial, teamster, J Kenower & Sons, res 4 Gay [Lena]

Alles, Jacob J, wagon-maker W Washington, res 103 W Tipton Cassie, Emma

    "   Joseph W, lab, res 103 W Tipton

    "   Jacob, jr. clk. res 103 W Tipton

    "   Sisters (Cassie, Emma) dressmakers, 103 W Tipton

Allison, W Fred, lab, bds 80 Whitelock

    "   James, emp lime kilns, res 91 Broadway [Rosanna] Bessie, Vernon, Virgil

    "   Lawrence, emp Briant stave factory, res 91 Broadway

    "   Henry, lab, res 91 Broadway

    "   Arthur, emp lime kilns, res 91 Broadway

Allman & Bash, (Ed O Allman, C E Bash) flour, feed and seeds, 11 E Washington

Allman, Edward O, (Allman & Bash) res 3 Whitestine [Maggie] Agnes, Carl

    "   Jane S (wid Tipton) res 70 E State

    "   Geo J, lather, res 14 Railroad [Lillie] Geo J

Allman & Boos, (Chris Allman, Conrad Boos) saloon, 13 E Franklin

Allman, Christian (Allman & Boos) res 80 First [Elizabeth] John, Lena, Bertha, Nicholas, Edwin

Allman, D F, plasterer, res 8 Byron [Margaret] Laura
" Bessie, clk, Frash, res, 8 Byron
" Enos, plasterer, res 68 Frederick [Rebecca J] Clara
    L
" Mary A (wife of Frank) emp. laundry, res 32 William
    Harmon E, Malie B, Fred H, Florence, Chal-
    mer E
Alpaugh, E K, res 116 Guilford [Sarah]
Altenhoffer, Mary, domestic at 223 N Jefferson
" Joseph, emp boiler shops Erie, res 113 Poplar
Altenbach, Simon, carpenter, res 45 Sabine Anna, William,
    Henry, Emma, Lewis, Oscar, Leo
Altman, Reuben M, (Dickover & Altman) res 45 Henry [Belle]
" John C, res 47 Henry [Buena V] Cora D
Altom, Adaline (wid Hezekiah) res 2 Bechtol. Clarence, Del-
    cina, Ethel, Homer
Altstadter, Albert, boots and shoes, 76 N Jefferson, bds Ex-
    change hotel
Amen, John, emp Western Lime Association, res 57 Grayston
    ave [Mary] Charles
Anaway, S D, brakeman Erie, res 65 Webster [Ada]
Anderson, D C, confectionery, cigars and tobaccos, 31 N Jef-
    ferson, res 5 Fredericka [Jennie E D] Agnes D
" Peter, cond Erie, bds Star restaurant
" Margaret (wid Jos L) res 288 N Jefferson Sarah
    Jennie B Josie L
" Sisters (Sarah, Josie L) dressmakers 288 N Jeffer-
    son
" O E, emp Erie shops, res 26 Madison [Jennie]
    Russell
Andrews, Chas, lab, res 60 Condit [Vera] Marie
" Flora (wid Geo B) res 144 Condit Jesse, Samuel,
    George
" Daniel, emp Erie shops, res 144 Condit
" George, lab, res 160 Byron
" Jacob, lab, res 160 Byron

Anglemyer, David D, clk, Bridge, res 1 Arthur. [Almira] Don, Adam
"   Thaddeus, teacher public schools, res 1 Arthur
Anglemyre, Jacob (Thompson Ice Cream Co) res 77 E Market [Hattie] Ethel
"   Levi, (Thompson Ice Cream Co) bds 77 E Market
"   Samuel, carpenter, bds Windsor hotel
"   Wm F, car repairer Erie, res 51 Whitelock [Axie]
Annan, Thos, machinist Erie, res 107 Lincoln ave [Francis] Thomas jr
Anson, F C, stone dlr, res 35 Buchanan [Belle] Mary, Bessie
"   John, bookkpr, res 35 Buchanan
"   Fred, clk, res 35 Buchanan
"   Bert, lab, res 35 Buchanan
Applegate, Ralph, emp Erie shops, res 72 E Market
Arick, Geo E, emp Erie shops, res 57 South [Ida A] Marshall N, Melvin R
Armstrong, Mary A, (wid George) res 76 Etna ave
"   West, eng Erie, res Hotel Eastern
Arnold, H H & Son, (Mrs H H, Chas) dry goods, carpets, notions, etc, wholesale and retail, 48 N Jefferson
Arnold, Anna (wid Henry H) res 223 N Jefferson
"   Chas (H H Arnold & Son) res 223 N Jefferson
"   Isaac N (Huntington Mill Co) re 193 N Jefferson [Susan L]
"   Elizabeth, bookkpr Huntington Mill Co, res 193 N Jefferson
"   Jacob, res 137 Poplar [Katherine]
"   Jacob jr, carpenter and contractor, res 76 Poplar [Catherine] Lizzie, Celia, Herman, Joseph Mary
"   Geo W, carpenter, res 76 Poplar
"   Henry E, emp M B Stults, res 76 Poplar
* "   Christian, emp Erie shops, res E end Tipton
Ashley, Chas C, barber, emp Kintz, res 15 Milligan [Mary E] Ethel B, Harold J, Mark V, Neil C

Ashley, Carrie (wid Samuel J) res 37 W Market   Bessie
Ashbaugh, John C, sawyer Briant, res 201 E State [Belle]
Auer, Anna, servant, 36 W Tipton
Auker, Daniel, postal clk Wabash Ry, res 64 Webster [Eureka] (child not named)
Aumock, Susannah (wid Philip W) res 90 Etna ave
Ayres, Edwin B (Huntington Co Bank) res 46 W Matilda [Belle] Porter, Katherine

B

Babb, Etta (widow) seamstress, res 87 Clark. Mabel, Samuel, Clark. William
  " Clarence, emp fair ground, res 87 Clark
  " Bert, emp shoe factory, res 87 Clark
Bach, Michael, emp Martin brick yard, res 9 Koeher [Mary] Frank, John E
Bacher, Mary, res 96 Poplar
Bahr, Julius, painter, res 31 S Briant
  " Laura, (wife of Julius) res 101 Guilford
Bailey, J A, (Bailey & Ham) res 84 Etna ave [Ella] Charles, Frank, Minnie
Bailey & Ham (J A Bailey, John Ham) meat merchants 21 s Jefferson.
  " W J, carpenter, res 39 Condit [C V]
 * " Perry, lab, res S Etna ave [May] Lucile
  " John B (Fisher, Keefer & Bailey) res 27 Milligan [Mary C] Grace A
  " Maude M (Fisher & Bailey) res 27 Milligan
  " Frank H, emp A O Kenower, res 27 Milligan
  " Geo, ret, res 162 E Franklin [Leona B]
  " T H, cond Erie, res 141 E Market [Viola]

Bain, Eli, lab, res 119 Elm [Sarah] Ethel
"   Henry, res 30 Olinger [S E]
"   James, lab, res 13 Green
"   Elizabeth C (wid W J) res 13 Green

Baines, John, car inspector Erie, res 20 Poplar [Minnie]
          Edwin A

Bane, Wm, carpenter, res 21 Green [Hattie] Cora, Paul,
          Ruth

*Bare, Edward, teamster, res W end William [Anna] Bert,
          Elma, Elmer, Dessie, Inez, Ina

Bare, Frank, emp Withington factory, res 55 S Briant [Emma] Eva

*Bair, Aaron J, teamster, res 173 Front [Sarah]

*Baker, J F, teamster, res S of Buck [E L] C H, M M, R
          D V

Baker, W H, retired, res 260 E State [S E] A E

Baker, A O, teamster, res 260 E State
"   Edward F, lab, res 20 Jackson [Mary] Irene C
"   A J, clk, res 1 Lee [Mary] Lota
"   E W, clk yard office Erie, res 1 Lee
"   Wm B, fireman Erie, res 58 Webster [Rella] Ziopha
          M
"   J C F, brakeman Erie, res 128 First [Lida E] Geo H,
          Fay
"   J W, emp car dpt Erie, bds 154 E Franklin
"   Mrs Mary C, (wid Samuel D) res over 123 N Jefferson
"   Roberta D, clk, Miles, res over 123 N Jefferson
"   Ila H, clk P O news stand, res over 123 N Jefferson

Balfour, John, cond Erie, res 47 Leopold [Anna]

Balzer, Conrad, lab, res 70 Olinger [Hannah] Anna, Mary,
          John, William
"   Ed H, compositor Herald, res 70 Olinger

Banks, Lucetta (wid James) res 14 Salamonie ave
Barber, Mary, (wid) res 44 Cline (Nelson Mohn)
Bare, Sadie, tailoress, res 78 Front

Barker, Roscoe, lab, res 127 Etna ave [Rose] Myrtle, Herbert, Mabel, Herman, Marie, Harold

" J M (Fotterall, Barker & Brown Co) res 3 Salamonie ave, [Jane S] James M, Zua

" Fred H, emp shoe factory, res 3 Salamonie ave

" James, clk, Hurd & Smith, bds 71 Elm

*Barnes, Geo W, blacksmith Erie, res Stringtown, e fair ground, [Lillie] Charles

" Benj, carpenter, res 38 Everett [Eliza]

" Avery, carpenter, res 38 Everett

" Elmer, lab, res 35 Mayne [Melissa] Nelson, Ora

" Elzie, emp Perrine & Bartlett, bds 35 Mayne

" Amos M, boiler maker Erie, bds 15 Garfield

* " John, lab, res Stringtown e fair grounds [Melinda E] Samuel J

* " Thomas A, emp Briant, res Stringtown, e fair ground

* " James, lab, res Stringtown, e fair ground

Barnhart, Mary (wid George) res 20 Buchanan

Barrett, John B, stone mason, res 49 Elm [Mary]

" Geo E, stone mason, res 49 Elm

" James R, stone mason, res 49 Elm

Barrick, Ruth (wid Ed) res 195 N LaFontaine Jesse Loulie A, Howard L, Everett M

Barrow, H P, carpenter Erie, res 43 Sabine [H A] Clayton, George D

Barsh, Mrs John, res 32 W Market Mamie

Bartchore, Ellen (wid) dressmaker, res 16 Mayne George

Barter, Geo, boiler maker Erie, res 27 E Sabine [Mary] Susie, Willie, Leona

Barton, Elizabeth, (wid W H) res 97 Poplar. Herbert

Bartlett, B J, bookkpr Perrine & Bartlett, res 92 Front [Francis S]

" Mary (wid T P) res 179 N Jefferson

". Wm P (Perrine & Bartlett) res 3 Allen [Luna] Charles, Grace

Bartram, Mary (wid John) res 65 Hitzfield

Bash, Catharine (wid) res 112 Guilford
"   C E F (Allman & Bash) res 38 E Washington [Eliza-
              beth] Kenower, Henry
"   F S, city editor, Herald, res 41 Etna ave
Bashong, Lafayette, porter Grand View, res same
Bately, M J, (wid) res 68 Grayston ave
*Batram, Andrew, res 26 Brawley. [Louisa]
*   "   Jacob, lab, res 26 Brawley [Anna] William
Bauer, John, res 149 N LaFontaine [Elizabeth]
† "   Chas, lab, res Gephart add [Lena]
"   Cora, servant, 156 N Jefferson
Bauer & McCarty, (P Bauer, J M McCarty) groceries, 129 N
              Jefferson
Bauer, Peter G (Bauer & McCarty) res 33 Oak [Francis] John
              E, Virgila, Cornelius, Julius P
Baughman, Wm, gardener, res 269 W Matilda [Isabella]
              Ervin, Hulda, Charles.
Baumgartner, John, bartender, Max Baumgartner, res 123 W
              Tipton [Emma H] Fred M, Rose V, Gertrude T
"   Roman, res 7 German [Mary]
"   Mary, domestic, 17 Bingham
"   John, clk, Lininger & Mentzer, bds 26 William
"   Max, saloon 63 N Jefferson, res 107 Cherry
              [Rosa] Katie
Bay, O S, city treasurer, res 70 Henry [Laura A] George H,
              Mabel A
Beal, Carrie (wid) res 125 First
"   Chas, baker, Lininger & Mentzer, res 33 Milligan [Led-
              die] Donald
"   W A, brakeman Erie, res 34 Front   [Flora]
"   Frank, emp Nichols, res 78 Elm
"   David, emp Nichols, res 78 Elm [Martha]
Beard, Isaac F, (Congress Bicycle Wrk) res 44 S Jefferson
              [Louisa] Ada, Carrie
"   Edwin, teamster, res 19 Milligan [Mary] May Eva
*Beaver, Samuel, lab, res S end Etna ave [Mary] Clara

Beaver, Henry, blacksmith, res 77 E Franklin [Susanna] Ella
" Frank, clk Erie freight office, res 77 E Franklin
" D G, blacksmith, 30 E State, res 70 E Market [Mrs D G] Mayme
" Albert A, eng Erie, res 26 Byron [Emma K]
" Ed, (Beaver & McCarty) res 127 E Franklin [Bertha] Lewis, Ruth, Clarence
Beaver & McCarty, (Ed Beaver, Pat McCarty) blacksmiths, 14 Warren
Beaver, Wm J, eng Perrine & Bartlett, res 26 Garfield [Louisa]
Bechtol, Chas, machinist Erie, res 60 E Franklin [Mary E] Harmon
" Chas O, student, res 60 E Franklin
" Mary, res 286 N Jefferson
Beeching, Grant, emp Briant, res 98 Whitelock
" Geo, stave jointer Briant, res 17 Grayston ave [Fredericka] Mamie
" J E, emp Briant, res 27 Sabine [Cosie]
" C H, eng Erie, res 128 E State [Ida] Nina, Ella, Cossetta, Mildred
" Eugene, eng Briant, res 14 Kocher [Louisa]
" Andrew M, emp Briant, res 76 Lindley [Lillian] Aaron L, Archie W, Marion R, Jera B
Thos, eng Hawley lime kilns, res 61 Lindley [Sarah] Osa, Clarence, Mary
" George, emp Briant, res 61 Lindley
Beck, Adam L (Western Lime Assn) res 41 s Jefferson [Elizabeth] Marshall, Magdalena.
† " Lawrence, emp shoe factory, res 27 Catharine.
† " Joseph, res 27 Catharine. Edward C, George, Agnes L, Alice W
" Elizabeth (wife of Geo W) res 86 Henry. Leonard E, Bertha
" Mary, res 25 Faust.
" John L, electrician Huntington Light & Fuel Co, res 106 Poplar [Mary] Edith, Ethel

Beck, Chris, fireman Erie, res 137 First [Anna]
" Mary (wid Christian) res 137 First. Minnie
" John, eng Erie, res 139 First [Matilda] Lizzie, Sophia, Clemens, Carl
† " Albert, janitor William St School, res 112 Henry [Cora] Charles, Howard
" V H, emp Wabash Transfer, res 23 Grayston Avenue [Eliza A]
" W R, physician and surgeon over 80 n Jefferson, res 78 c Market [Nanetta] Lucile.
" Cassie, canvasser, res 104 e State.
" Mary, canvasser, res 104 e State
" Daniel, fireman Erie, res 106 e State. [Ottie]
† " George, teamster, res 5 Swan [Celia] Anna, Nora, Charlie, Harry, Ernest
" Adam (Western Lime Assn) res 83 w State [Mary E] Harmon S
Becker, Michael J. marble and stone dealer 29 w State, res 131 Oak [Margaret] Ferdinand, Carl, Hilda, Marcellus, Leo, Bertha
Becker, Peter, emp M J Becker, res 111 Oak
Beckstein, Jacob J, lab, res 89 Lincoln Ave [Johannah] Minnie, Fredericka
" John, machinist, res 89 Lincoln Ave
" Adolph, clk Heaston & Dumbauld, res 89 Lincoln Avenue.
" Paul, baker A Pastor, res 81 e Washington street [Louisa]
Beeber, Alice J (wid W P) res 26 w Market
Beehler, L E, machinist Erie, res 53 Kintz [Rinda A] Anna, Clara
Beekman, Carey, lab, res 70 Frederick [Minnie] Ora
Beel, Carrie, res 150 Etna Ave
" Thos, lab, res 24 Monroe.
" John, emp Perrine & Bartlett, bds 70 Frederick

Beggs, Robert, emp shoe factory, bds 61 e Market
Beghtel, Mary, res 190 Guilford
Beiber, J C, fireman Erie, rms over 54 Guilford
Beitenman, John, cashier C & E freight hs, res 32 w Market
Beitler, Sophia, clk H H Arnold & Son, res 95 Oak
   "   Emma, tailoress, res 95 Oak
   "   Jacob, res 95 Oak
Bell, W M, bookkpr C E Briant, res 119 Railroad   [Lavinta J]
   "   W S, mail carrier, res 8 Superior   [Cornelia A]
   "   Otto M, emp Briant, res 8 Superior
   "   Harry B, eng Western Lime Assn, res 8 Superior
   "   William H, student, res 8 Superior
   "   Wm E, emp H V Peden, res 11 Warren   [Mary E]   Iva
Belton, Catharine (wid James) res 26 Randolph
   "   Robert, veterinary surgeon, res 26 Randolph
Benn, Paul, fireman Erie, res 90 Wilkerson   [Sarah]
Bennett, Etta, domestic 122 Guilford
   "   Homer C, eng Erie, res 133 e Market   [Francis E]
       Ethlyn   Homer jr
Bensing, Elizabeth (wid Nicholas) res 155 Poplar. Henry,
       Lulu, Ruth, Gertrude
   "   Eva, servant, res 155 Poplar.
   "   William, clk W A Zeller, res 155 Poplar
   "   George, clk Pottlitzer, res 155 Poplar
Benward, Joseph S, res 65 Grayston Ave   [Mary A]
Berg, Chas, emp Erie Section, res 51 Dimond [Sophia]
       Bertha, Minnie, Elma, Lola
Berkfield, Jacob, tonsorial parlor 12 w Market, res 104 e Frank-
       lin [Maria] Lillie, Chas, Ada, Clarence,
       Elmer, Frank
Berothe, Mary (wid Quint B) res 91 e Market
Bernhart, Eliza (wid) res 23 Salamonie Ave
Berry, C (wid G E B) res 43 e State. Dot, Edwin E.
   "   W V, emp J Kenower & Sons, res 51 Leopold [Mary I]
       Thos E, Francis M, Minnie.

Berry, W A, feed yard 60 Warren, res 74 w Market   [Mary R]
"   Robert M, emp W A Berry, res 74 w Market
Best, George W, attorney over 72 n Jefferson, res 21 Olinger
       [Mina]   Georgia M
"   Harley, printer, res 21 Olinger
"   Harry, emp W D Brown, res 33 e Tipton
Beuner, W A, student, res 34 Front
Beverly, James, lab, res 74 Bingham, [Lavina]   Merrill,
       Howard,   Mary,   Porter
Beyer Bros, poultry dealers s bank Little River near Charles
       street   Joseph Lautzenhauser, mgr
Bickel, John, lab, res 98 Buck   [Lydia]   Susie
"   Wm, lab, res 98 Buck
"   Emmett, machinist Erie, res 98 Buck
"   Dora, emp shoe factory, res 98 Buck
"   Thos S, emp shoe factory, res 98 Buck
Bicycle Club Rooms, 32-34 e Market
Biglow, Jane, res 57 Frederick
"   Elizabeth (wid A A) re - 123 Cherry
Bilger, Clarence E, emp Perrine & Bartlett, res 207 e Market
       [Cora]   Gladys,   William
Biliter, Ben F, publisher Farmers Guide and general printing
       16 s Jefferson, res 59 William, [Elizabeth]
Billiter, Chas F, res 120 Etna ave
"   Mrs Catharine, res 120 Etna ave
"   Wm M, prop feed yard 5 Frederick, res 59 William
Bippus, John, clk Huntington Light & Fuel Co, res 191 n Jeff-
       erson [Eunice]   Theodore
"   Geo J (Huntington Light & Fuel Co) res 166 n Jeffer-
       son [Anna]
"   J Fred (Huntington Light & Fuel Co) res 235 n Jeffer-
       son [Myrtle]   Bernice,   Dorothy,   Geo jr
Bir, Xavier, blacksmith Erie, res 144 Oak   [Theresa]   Frank,
       Joseph,   Herman,   Paul,   Henry
Bir, Leo, boiler-maker Erie, res 126 e Sabine   [Rosa]   Jacob,
       Mary,   Edward,   Laura,   Anna,   Eveline

Bischoff, William, lab, res 108 Walnut [Caroline] Rudolph,
    Luella, Christian
"   Christian, teamster, res 106 Walnut [Ida] Mollie,
    Hugo, Mata, Adolph.
Bishop, Hubbard, emp Griffith & Son, res near end w Matilda
    [Fannie] Hazel, Agnes
Bitner, Sherman, fireman Erie, res 33 High [Capitolia]
"   H L, carpenter, res 228 e Market [H E] Levi
Bitzinger, John, job compositor Herald, res 106 Oak. [Han-
    nah] Irma, Marguerite, Arnold, Carl
Bixler, Wm, emp Erie round hs, res 59 Marshall [Ella]
Black, Harriett, res 58 e Franklin
"   Robert, res 100 Etna ave
"   Joseph M, with H C Black, res 77 Henry [Rachael M]
    Fay A, Pearl E, Starr E, Lulu I, Frank C
Black, Harvey C, abstractor over 56 n Jefferson, res 50 Front
    Burnice
"   Morris W, res 50 Front
Blackburn, Lalla (wid Will J) res 97 n Lafontaine. Katie,
    Robert
"   Frankie, amanuensis, res 97 n Lafontaine
"   Charles, apprentice Erie shops, res 97 n Lafontane
"   Matilda (wid Thos) (Pomeroy & Blackburn) res 67
    w Matilda.
"   Robert F, baker Ed Willis, res 14 Canal [Mary]
    Bessie, Herbert, Frank, Francis.
Blake, Elmer, res 20 Garfield
Blaugh, Elmira (wid) res 110 Etna ave
Blickenstaff, E A, insurance, etc, I O O F building, res 277 N
    Jefferson [A A] Eva, Ethel, Carl
Blocker, E S, eng Erie, res 36 Frederick [Addie M] Marcia,
    Lloyd S
"   Ray V, machinist Erie, res 36 Frederick
Blockson, H H, res 198 Cherry [Cecelia]
Blum, Harmon, clk McCaffrey & Co, res 83 Frederick [Eliz-
    abeth]

Blum, Fred, emp F Blum, res 82 Oak [Carolina] Louisa
Blum, F H, boots and shoes. 77 n Jefferson, res 82 Oak
Blum, John, tinner Bridge, res 82 Oak
"   Albert R, emp F H Blum, res 82 Oak
"   Kate, dressmaker, res 82 Oak
"   Bena, compositor Democrat, res 82 Oak
Blunt, Scott, blacksmith, res 85 Condit [Abbie] Etta B
Board of Trade, H L Wells, mgr over 72 n Jefferson
Boehner, Chris, shoemaker, res 43 Buchanan [Charlotte]
"   Fred, barber, res 43 Buchanan
"   John, lab, res 43 Buchanan
"   Chris jr, emp Griffith & Son, res 43 Buchanan
"   Geo, car inspector Erie, res 43 Buchanan
Bohanon, John, car repairer Erie, res 12 Mayne [Ollie]
            Louis
*Bolanz, Fred, lab, res Stringtown e fair ground [Mattie]
            Edgar, Magdalena, Gladys, Mary
Bolinger, Sarah E (wid Simon) res 3 Lee Melinda H, Edward
Bond, ——, lab, bds 137 e Market
Bone, H, brick-mason, res 144 Cherry [Kate]
Bonebrake & Bonbrake, (Emsy S, Grant) barbers, 4 w Market
Bonbrake, Grant (Bonebrake & Bonbrake) res 24 n Lafontaine
            [Faira]
Bonebrake, Emsy S (Bonebrake & Bonbrake) res 4 Whitelock
            [Minnie] Mildred
"   A S. student, res 54 First
*   "   Milo, teamster, Perrine & Bartlett, res e Front
            [Etta] Flossie
"   Simon H, res 19 Garfield [Matilda]
"   Mary (wid Eli) res 96 s Jefferson Harley
Bonewitz, Orlando, clk Boston store, res 33 Elm [Lydia]
            Garl
Boone, Robt A, stationary eng Erie, res 28 Etna ave [Eliz-
            [beth] Leslie
*Boos, Conrad, (Allman & Boos) res 181 e Tipton
"   Katie, res 19 Leopold

Boos, Jacob, (Huntington Co Bank) res 23 W Matilda [Caroline] Katherine, Clara, Francis, Agnes, Herman
" John, prop Oak saloon, Oakland ave, res same
" Jacob jr, clk Oak saloon, Oakland ave, res same
Booth, Chas E, fireman Erie, res 61 s Jefferson [Hattie]
*Bortz, Daniel, lab res N Jefferson
Bowers, Amos, photographer, res 325 e State [Mary] Minnie, May
" Orlando, carpenter, res 329 e State [Ella] Clarence Ira A, Chas B, Herbert
" George, emp lime kilns, res 333 e State [Clara C] Harley F, Martin, Wm A
Bowlar, Ed, switchman, Erie, bds Windsor
Bowman, Samuel, carpenter, res 27 Bingham [Ella]
" Rev R S,evangelist, res 29 Bingham [Lillie] Myrtle
" Fred E, clk H L & F Co, res 84 e Market
" Henrietta (wid J R B) res 94 e Market
" J W, blacksmith, 131 e State, res same [Anna]
" Henry H, janitor e State st school, res 278 e State [Grace] Thurston
Ephraim, lab, res 52 Jackson
Carey, emp Briant, res 52 Jackson
John W, car repairer Erie, res 20 Gay [Sarah] Lena, Mary
" Norval V, clk Postoffice, res 20 Gay
" Harry O, emp Erie, res 20 Gay
" Thad, emp Briant, res 20 Gay.
† " Ruth C, res s Salamonie ave
" Arthur W, emp Erie, res 20 Gay
Bowser, E W, switchman Erie, bds Windsor House
" E E, brakeman Erie, res 115 e Franklin
Bowsher, Thos, lab, res 37 Mayne. [Letta] Rosa
" Hiram, emp Perrine & Bartlett, bds 35 Mayne
Boyd, Lena, res 28 Warren
" Chester, lab, res 68 Olinger. [Maggie] Cecil

Boyd, A, carpenter Eric, res 134 Etna ave
" J M, lab. res 134 Etna ave [J C] Nora, Norman
" James A, teamster, res 167 Wilkerson [Emma] Theo, James, Charles
Boylan, E S, carpenter Eric, res 46 Byron [Olive J] Clara, James
Boyle, Maggie, res 145 First
" Frank, switchman Eric, res 126 First. [Kate] Mildred,- Arthur
" George, lab, res 126 First
Braden, V M, lab res 127 n Lafontaine [Rosannah] Goldie Clarence Elmer
" Walter, lab res 127 n Lafontaine
" Maude, domestic, res 127 n Lafontaine
" Delia May, domestic, res 127 n Lafontaine
Bradford, Duzell R, lab, res over 32 Cherry
Bradley, O E, druggist, cor Jefferson and Franklin
Bradshaw, Samuel (col'd) porter Trixler's barber shop, rooms same
Brady, Johannah (wid M B) res 98 Cherry
" Thos, policeman, res 144 Guilford [Mary] Mary E
" William, boiler-maker Eric, res 144 Guilford
" John, painter, res 144 Guilford
" Peter, carpenter, res 19 s Briant
Brahs, Fred, lab res 71 German [Christiana] Edith, Clara
" Chas, emp Griffith & Son, res 71 German
" John, emp Griffith & Son, res 55 German [Marie] Anna, Martin
" John F, jr, clk Strodel, res 55 German
" Fred, emp Griffith & Son, res 55 German
Brandt, Chas F, plasterer, res 77 e State [Maria]
" Ralph V, plasterer, res 77 e State
Branyan, Branyan & Branyan, (J C, J S, E C) attorneys I O O F building
Branyan, J C (Branyan, B & B) res 95 Etna ave [Emma R] Wilbur E

Branyan, John S (B. B. & B) res 124 Etna ave   [Ella]   Mary H
     "   E C (B. B. & B) res 97 Etna ave |Lulu J| Bessie A,
           Harold B
     "   W A (Spencer & Branyan) res 150 Guilford   [Margaret M]   Hugo,   Hazel

Bratton, Fredericka (wid James M) res 48 s Jefferson
     "   Mat, carpenter, res 48 s Jefferson
     "   Mrs. Ida, dressmaker, res 96 s Jefferson.   Ray,   Edith

Brawley, L J, res 143 Etna ave   [Mary W]
     "   L C, res 143 Etna ave

Brebach, Katharine (wid Justus) res 123 Dimond
     "   John, tailor over 65 n Jefferson, res 123 Dimond
     "   Gus, tailor over 65 n Jefferson, res 170 George street
           [Anna]   Clarence, Ada, Herbert
     "   Henry, steam fitter Erie, res 61 Dimond   [Elizabeth]
           Harmon,   Eddie
     "   William, machinist Erie, res 70 Esther   [Maggie]
           Harry,   Eva

Breen, Mary, res 106 e Franklin

Bresenhen, Benj, emp Huntington Light & Fuel Co, res 163
           Cherry   [Johannah]   William,   John,   Mary,
           Edward

Briant, Cyrus E, stave and bending works e of Webster st to
           Little River, res 89 Webster   [Julia]

Briant, John M, clk C E Briant, res 89 Webster
     "   Wm T, mgr Briant bending works, res 76 e Market st
           [Flo]   Ben
           Chas O, emp C E Briant, res 39 Superior   [Ida F]
           Arthur D
     "   Mrs Adelia A, res 98 Lincoln ave.   Leland,   Clarence.

Bridge, Lewis, hardware, stoves, etc, 67 n Jefferson, res 50
           William. [Lenora] Mary R,   Wilbur
     "   Orlo, clk L Bridge, res 50 William.
     "   Rev. Henry, res 133 Court   [Maria]   Herbert, Katie
           Delbert.   Gertrude

Bridge, Levi, emp Withington, res 24 Randolph [Liona]
   Vilas, Griffith
" Miss L C, res 33 e Matilda
Briggs, W J, operator Erie, res 76 s Jefferson [Mamie]
" Chas M, emp fire dept, bds 59 Mayne
" J M, dry goods peddler, res 264 n Jefferson [Eliza A]
   Clinton, Arthur, Chas, Estella
" William R, clk M B Stults, res 80 Poplar [Cora]
Brightmire, Lydia (wid Simon) res 20 Whitelock. Elizabeth,
   Minerva
Brineman, M D, architect over 7 s Jefferson, res 81 Henry
   [Mary E] Clara E, Allen G, Jesse L
" Harry F, res 81 Henry
" Laura M, cashier Harris, res 81 Henry
Brinneman, Dora, teamster Griffith & Son, res 126 Railroad
   [Anna] Virgie
Britton, Dora, emp shoe factory, res 83 e Market
Broaders, Ella, res 41 e Franklin
" Wm, emp Erie shops, res over 112 n Jefferson
" Mary (wid James) res over 112 n Jefferson
Brobst, M N, brakeman Erie, bds 85 e Market
Brock, Harry, boiler-maker Erie, res 46 High [Della] Hazel,
   Clifford
" Geo, boiler-wiper Erie, res 10 Mayne [Elizabeth]
Broderick, Daniel, section foreman Wabash, res 114 e Frank-
   lin [Therise] Bonaventure
Bronkar, J M, lumber, lath and shingles 67 e Washington,
   res 75 e Washington [Lydia A] Lucile, Francis
Bronkar, Hannah, emp Hoosier laundry, res 75 e Washington.
Brooking, James, carpenter, res 42 Fredericka [Ida] Willie.
Brookover, Eliza (wid G W) res 17 Randolph. Mary A, Daisy
Brooks, W H, clk engine dispatcher Erie, res 82 Wilkerson st
   [Bertha]
Broomer, Hannah, res 76 William
" Wm, machinist Erie, bds 119 Court

Brown, W H, agt Singer Sewing Machine, res 27 n Lafontaine
    [Salome] Ethel
"   John F (Lime City Cigar Co) res 92 w State [Alice]
    Cecil M
"   Mabel, res 92 w State
"   Elma M, res 56 Elm
"   Frank (Fotteral, Barker & Brown Co) res 35 Henry
    [Ella]
† "   R Z, insurance, res s Salamonic ave   [Orvilla]
"   Frank, carpenter, res 126 Front
Brown, J L, agt Pabst Brewing Co, res 132 e Market [Mary]
    Harry
"   Mrs Mary, clk C Mader, res 17 e Market. child
"   W W, brakeman Erie, bds Windsor
"   Alzina P (wid Wm B) res 69 e Franklin
"   Ed T, nursery dlr, res 65 e Franklin [Sarah J]
"   Chester L, res 65 e Franklin
"   James H, cashier Wabash freight hs, res 42 Whitelock
    [Mary] Otto
Brown, Elmer E, livery, feed and sale stable 32 Cherry, res
    over same [Rosa]
"   George J, eng Erie, res 51 First [Jennie]
"   F A, foreman composing room Herald, res over 20 s
    Jefferson. Joseph, Paul
"   Mrs Amelia, res 49 Sabine
"   Samuel, machinist Erie, res 49 Sabine
"   James F, painter Erie, res 51 Mayne [Hannah M]
    Minnie G, Ida M, Rosa B
"   C A, painter Erie, res 41 Whitelock [Della] Mabel,
    Cleo, Donald
"   Wm R, res 209 Guilford [Sarah M] Emma M
"   Wm E, clk P O news stand, res 55 Wilkerson
"   John, clk, res 55 Wilkerson
"   Nehemiah, res 209 Guilford [Sarah] Emma L, Mary
"   George, brakeman Erie, bds Hotel Eastern
Browne, A O, ex-prop Osborne hotel, res same

Brubaker, Maude, domestic 87 Clark
   "   Thornton, painter, res 44 Indiana st [Mary A] Emery
Bruce, W H, eng Water Works pumping station, res same. [Orville A] Wm S
Bruder, Wm, res 81 Esther [Mary]
Brumbaugh, John, carpenter, res 4 Grayston ave [Susan B]
   "   Noah, boiler shops Erie, res n end Harris [Rebecca] Lloyd S, Lavina M, Carl J
   "   J H, car shops Erie, res 22 Wesley [Ida]
   "   Wm, carpenter, res 9 Bingham [Anna]
   "   Clara, cashier Boston store, res 9 Bingham
†   "   Isaac jr, carpenter, res Wright st [Ida B] Harry W
   "   Fred, carpenter, res 17 Mayne [Amanda]
   "   Jas, carpenter, res 17 Mayne
   "   Jefferson, carpenter Erie, res 17 Mayne
   "   Bertha, emp shoe factory, res 17 Mayne
   "   Wesley, cond Erie, bds 139 e Market
   "   Geo, cond Erie, res 75 e Matilda [Mary] Katie, Chas, Agnes
   "   John jr, fireman Erie, res 136 e Market [Dixie] Agnes, Mabel, Hazel
   "   Isaac, carpenter and contractor, res 2 mile s city.
Bruner, Elizabeth, domestic 207 n Jefferson
Buchanan, Samuel, contractor and plumber 11 w Market, res 132 Poplar [Catharine] Lillian, Johannah E, Charles L, Gertrude A, Paul M, Isabella, E Eugenia
   "   Thos J, machinist, res 132 Poplar
   "   Bridget (wid) res 50 w State
   "   John J, lab, res 50 w State
   "   Joseph W, emp fire dept, res 50 w State
   "   Thos F, eng electric light works, res 157 Cherry
   "   Matthias, res 157 Cherry [Catharine] Elizabeth
   "   Wm J, machinist, res 157 Cherry
   "   Mrs B (wid Henry) res 161 Poplar. Mary

Prices Always Correct, at MALIN'S

Bucher, Chas, driver S P Stults, rms 63 e Market

Bucher & Weber (W A Bucher, A A Weber) feed barn s w corner Matilda and Warren sts

Bucher, W A (Bucher & Weber) res 7 Marshall [Mary] Earl, Roy

" Samuel, res 20 Marshall [Eliza]

Buchheit, Louis J, bkpr Western Lime Assn, bds 110 Cherry

Budg, John, lab, res 47 Walnut

Bullerman, F W, emp Erie shops, res 56 n Lafontaine [Mary] Rebecca, William

Bump, Silas, emp city, res 58 Superior [Nora] Chas, Chester

Burdg, F T, brakeman Erie, res 110 Lincoln ave [Laura] Florence

Burgenheuler, Gerhart, lab, res between river and Wab Ry, w end State [Minnie] Baby

Burke, Edward, boiler-maker Erie, res 33 Marshall [Catharine] Chas, William, Nellie, Edward, Catharine

Burket, Eli, res 40 Salamonie ave [Martha]

Burket, Adna, clk Colter, res 33 Grayston ave

" Joseph, carpenter, res 33 Grayston ave [Eliza] Carl Allie

" Chas, carpenter, res 33 Grayston ave

Burnison, Alex, eng Erie, res 95 e Market [Mary]

Burman, Frank, emp Erie, res 103 Dimond [Minnie] Bertha

" Carl, emp Western Lime Asn, res 63 German [Sophia]

" Harmon, lab res 63 German

" Wm, emp press room Herald, res 63 German

" Paul, cigarmaker, res 63 German

Burn, William, teamster, res 150 Etna ave [Kate] Harmon, Herbert, Minnie

Burns, Thos, cashier Citizens Bank, res 117 Guilford [Emma B] Flora

" A L, eng Erie, res 1 Harrison ave [Rachael] Carrie M, Alice O, Gertrude, Howard, Walter D, Thomas J

Abstracts prepared with care, at **BLACK'S ABSTRACT OFFICE.**

Burris, Isaac, lab, res 16 Glenn [Nancy]
"   Harry L, lab res 16 Glenn
"   Aurelius, clk Fisher and Snider, res 16 Glenn
Burt, John, emp Malins, rooms 46 E Market
Burton, D S, miller Minnich, res 70 w Matilda [Jane] Jessie
Bush, Harry, wagon maker, 7 Front, res 41 s Briant [Elizabeth]
"   Lewis, res 70 W Market [Agnes,] Edward
"   Geo, eng Erie, res 48 Oak [Mary] Erva, George jr,
          Lewis, Laura
"   Chas R, machinist, Erie, res 48 Oak
Bussard, Thos, cond Erie, bds 28 Guilford
Butcher, John, emp Griffith & Son, res 77 Swan [Cloa] Grace
          Lena, Ervin
Butler, Thad, managing editor Herald, res 10 Randolph
          [Kate S] Robt A Jean J
"   Chas A, sea post clk, res 10 Randolph
"   Mark, compositor Herald, res 73 Frederick [Vinnie]
          Mary L, John A, Glenn, Frank   .
"   Clinton, eng Erie, res 30 Henry [Etta] Kenneth D,
          Mildred G Benj E
*Butt, A J, fireman Erie, res e Front [Henrietta] Everett,
          Mary, William, John
*Buzzard, John, (Hedge Fence Co) res 315 Etna ave s [Rebecca] Ervin, Ora, Bert, Ethel
"   John, emp Lushing, res 47 Walnut
"   L S, clk P O, res 68 Elm [Lurana M] Bruce
"   Anna (wid) res 36 Milligan. Grace, Lillie, Jeus
"   Chas H, timber buyer Withington, res 23 Lehmeyer
          [Jennie] Esther M, Bertha F, Inez
Byler, Christian, clk Schaefer & Schaefer, res 77 Whitelock
          [Nina]

C

Cable, B F, carpenter, res 77 Frederick [Mary A]

Cady, Edwin, nursery agt, res 47 Leopold

Cahalane, Patrick, eng Erie, res 165 e Franklin

Cain, Wm E. brakeman Erie, res 41 Kintz [Hattie] Blanche R, Gladys M, William E

" Amanda (wid Freedom) res 10 Wesley

" John, brick mason, rms Citizens Bank block

Caldwell, Sophia, teacher Orphans Home, res 72 Poplar

" Axie, res 72 Poplar

Calhoun, Mary, domestic at 225 n Jefferson

" D S, miller Huntington Mill Co, res 138 Cherry st [Addie] Carl, Gale

Callahan, Jesse, shoemaker 7 Front, res 25 Mayne

" Lyman, lab, res 25 Mayne

Calonkey, Mary L (wid Constantine) res 16 Garfield

" Leon R, emp Democrat, res 16 Garfield

Calvert, O W (Kenner & Calvert) res 36 Webster [Nellie] Ola

" Will, clk Dickover & Altman, res 36 Webster

" Alvah, machinist Erie, res 36 Webster

Cameron, Newton, res 18 Warren [Laura]

Campbell, Anna, artist, res 87 e Market

" Sarah (wid Wm I) res 96 Etna ave

" James, res 96 Etna ave

" Maggie, teacher, res 96 Etna ave

" Dallas, lab res 188 Guilford

" George, carpenter, res 188 Guilford [Mary] Dessie V

" Calinda (wid E) dressmaker, res 20 Whitelock

Canfield, James, prop Eastern Hotel 122 e Market, res same [Lottie] Walter D

Carey, Cyrus, carpenter, res 79 e Market [Mary]

" Wm F, clk McCaffrey, res 104 e Washington [Jennie] Bruce

Carey, James, emp Erie shops, res 97 e Franklin [Bridget]
        Eugene, Agnes, Ralph, Paul
    "   John, stationary eng, res 27 Gay [Mary C]
    "   Joseph, porter Osborne, res same

Carll, Jason, carpenter, res 221 e State [Margaret] Harry,
        Clarence, John J
    "   Chas, teamster, res 221 e State

Carney, Florence, res 125 First

Carr, Jasper A, foreman Nichols mill, res Joe street [Anna]
        Laeuna, Chas, Geo, Cecil, Hazel, Ruth
    "   Jasper A jr, brakeman Erie, res Joe st
    "   Bert, lab, res 135 Etna ave [Nora] Harry

Carroll, Joseph A, insurance, res 105 e Franklin [Grace] Jos
    "   Thomas A, boiler-maker Erie, res 105 e Franklin

Carson, W F, physician and surgeon over 76 n Jefferson, res
        15 William [Mrs W F] Lena, Grace

Cassaday, O A, emp Malin, res 100 w Matilda [Rachael]
        Lewis

Cust, Simeon T, mayor of Huntington, insurance and loans
        over First National Bank, res 33 Frederick. [Jen-
        nie] Fred, W B

Cast, William H, clk Collins Ice Cream Co, res 134 Etna ave
        [Elizabeth]

|Castledine, Laura (wid) res s end Briant. Clarence

Cawley, Elizabeth (wid Phineas) res 131 Court

Central Union and Long Distance Telephone Co (Heaston &
        Dumbauld mgrs) 47 n Jefferson

Chafee, Wm C, physician and surgeon over 78 n Jefferson,
        res 52 w Matilda [Anna S]

Chamberland, Jacob E, carpenter Erie, res 88 Superior [Cora
        V] Mary

Chamblin, Chas, res 40 Green [Clara] Earl

Chambers, Mattie, elocutionist, res 93 Oak

MATHIAS LUBER,

Tobaccos. Pipes, Cigars, &c.

19 E. Franklin St.   HUNTINGTON, IND.

MARTIN MINDNICH,

—Manufacturer of—

Huntington ❀ White ❀ Lime.

BUILDING STONE A SPECIALTY.

OFFICE:—Two and One-Half Miles E. of City.

❖L. C. MITTEN,❖

Contractor and Builder,

11 S. Lafontaine Street.

Huntington, · Indiana.

❂——W. ✳ R. ✳ MARDENIS——❂

DEALER IN

GROCERIES, PROVISIONS, Etc.

——FRESH AND SALTED MEATS.——

Cor. State and Condit Streets.   HUNTINGTON, INDIANA,

Cash Paid for all Kinds of Country Produce. Full Line of
Teas, Coffees, Cigars and Tobaccos.

Chapman, B H, emp Hoosier laundry, res 16 Allen [Rosella] Fay
†   "   Henry, employ shoe factory, res 7 Catharine [Katie]
  "   William, res 46 Mayne
Cheesman, H C, barber Trixler, bds 6 e Market
*Chenoweth, L O, carpenter, res s Etna ave [Viola] Pearl, Harry, Mary
*   "   Arthur, lab, res s Etna ave
†   "   John A, plasterer, res s end Henry [Ida B]
  "   T E, res 29 Sabine st [Dora] Hope
  "   Edwin, machinist, res 23 Faust [Ethel M]
  "   Cora, dressmaker, res 71 Henry
Chesterman, Joseph, emp round house Erie, res 152 e Sabine [Ellen] John, Hayden
  "   Chas, emp Erie, res 152 e Sabine
Christian, Blanche, waitress Star restaurant, res same
  "   Harvey H, machinist Erie, res 34 Marshall
  "   Ellen (wid) res 34 Marshall. Edith M, Harry G
Chubb, Sarah E, (wid J J) res 63 Henry
Churchill, Daniel, lab, res 57 Dimond [Hattie] Claude, Clyde
  "   B F, shoemaker, bds Midway restaurant
Citizens' Bank, (E T Taylor and F Dick props) 41 n Jefferson
Clark, Wm F, lab, res 63 Mayne [Lucy] Mary, Emma, Sylvester, Cora, Irene
  "   Chas, lab, res 63 Mayne
  "   R E, fireman Erie, bds Hotel Eastern
  "   Dora, teamster Briant, res 15 e Sabine [Mary] Geo, Etta, Walter
*   "   Chas S, lab, res s end Buck
  "   Michael, emp lime kilns, res 61 Division
  "   Margaret, (wid D P) res 38 Elm
  "   Albert, emp Erie round house, res 89 e State [Elizabeth] Elwood
  "   Mary L, teacher public schools, res 26 w Matilda
  "   Robert, eng Erie, res 10 Wesley [Nellie] Blanche, Mabel, Calvin, Helen

Clark, Myron, emp Griffith & Son, res 2 Lee [Kate]
    "   Emma, res 32 w Market

Class, Elmer, emp Withington, res 64 Grayston ave
    "   Chas, lab, res 64 Grayston ave [Mary E] Pearl,
        William, Eddie, Howard, Hazel
    "   Daniel, emp Briant, res 36 Grayston ave [Mary]

Clause, Amelia, domestic 126 n Guilford
    "   William, emp Withington, res 14 Sherman [Mollie]
        Chas

Claybaugh, Thos, blacksmith Erie, res 111 Oak [Margaret]
        Emery, Vernon, Chas jr
    "   James, coach builder Erie, res 115 e Franklin
        [Catharine]

Clayton, E K, res 32 W Matilda, [Anna] Elizabeth
    "   John, prop Clayton's Household Furnishing Store,
        res 33 w Tipton [Maggie]
        Will E, blacksmith Erie, res 97 First [Rosannah]
        Ruth

Clayton Household Furnishing Store, (John Clayton prop)
        16-18 w Market

Clem, Allie, teacher garment cutting, res 14 Henry

Cleveland, Phoebe (wid Thos) res 219 n Jefferson
    "   Henry, clk H H Arnold & Son, res 35 Frederick
        [Adda] Tom

Cline, J Q, attorney, I O O F building, res 26 Fredericka [Ola
        A] Carl, Claude, Grace, Pearl, Clair
    "   Wm W, lab, 94 Cline [Charity]
    "   Isaac H, emp Briant, res 239 Etna ave [Mary A]

Click, Samuel F, butcher, res 105 e Washington [Flora I]
        Bertha

Clow, Phoebe (wid Thos) res 13 Kocher
    "   Wm D, emp stone quarry, res 13 Kocher

Cobb, B M, attorney over 16 w Market, res cor Elizabeth and
        Kintz [Nancy C] Jessie M, Francis E, Oscar
        H

Coblentz, Henry, emp Erie, res 27 Canfield [Minerva] Bessie M

Colclesser, David, fireman Erie, res 23 Gay [Cora]

Cole, Scott, justice of peace over 9 n Jefferson, res 146 William [Lida] Grace, Abel, Paul, Burnham

* " Chas, emp Western Lime Assn, res e fair ground

" W R, fireman Erie, res 12 Superior [Bertie] Goldie

Coles, Chas K, fish dlr, res 8 Mayne [Sarah J]

" Arthur E, carpenter, res 8 Mayne

Collins, Julia A (wid John) res 56 Frederick

Collins, E A (Collins & Son) res 90 Etna ave [Matilda]

Collins, Mrs Mollie, res 90 Etna ave

" W H (Collins & Son) res 117 Etna ave [Anna] Russell

Collins Ice Cream Co (E A Collins, W H Collins) 90 Etna ave

Collins, W H, painter, res 229 William [Lydia A] Cordelia, Andrew

" Henry H, painter, res 229 William

Collins, Timothy, dlr in hard and soft coal, sewer pipe, etc, near Wab freight hs, res 179 Cherry

Collins, Ellen, res 179 Cherry

" Eliza, teacher, res 179 Cherry

" William, emp Griffith & Son, res 89 Webster [Mary] Martin, Edon, Earl

, Ida (wid Patrick) res 162 Poplar. Elizabeth

" Albert E, eng Erie, res 44 Sabine [Mary] Corning

" Agnes, clk P Scheiber, res 162 Poplar

" Mary, trimmer Mrs C H Immell, res 162 Poplar

" Frank, emp Democrat, res 162 Poplar

" William M, painter, res 229 William

Colter, Chas, groceries and provisions 241 e State, res same [Lucinda]

Coltrin, Mary, teacher public schools, res 47 e Tipton

Comer, Hiram E, boiler-washer Erie, res 85 Sabine [Anna B] Albert, Charles, Mary, Harvey

" Murray, lab, res 60 Condit [Phœbe] Alfred, Henry

Comer, John, emp Perrine & Bartlett, res 26 Nebraska [Irena M] Eva M, Mary A, Minnie, Willard, Dessie, Roy, Effie

Commerdinger, Chas, carpenter, res 59 South

Commons, Robert, laborer, res 270 e State [Nora] Sophia, Hazel, Ernst

Comstock, B A, township trustee over 9 n Jefferson, res 68 High [Celia]

Conarty, Walter, brakeman Erie, res 20 Leopold

" Edward, cond Erie, res 21 Leopold [Ella] Patrick, Helena, Edward jr, Walter jr

" Sarah (wid E C) res 20 Leopold

{Congress Bicycle Works, s Salamonie ave

Conley, John, boiler-maker Erie, bds Windsor hotel

Conn, Wm, emp Briant, res 46 Buck [Sarah]

Connelley, John J, lab, res 235 n Jefferson

Connon, Fred, eng Erie, res 48 s Jefferson

" Caroline (wid Lawrence) res 48 s Jefferson

Conover, Henry, cond Erie, res 111 First [Anna]

Cook, S H, lab, res 116 Railroad [Clara]

† " Eugene F, telegraph operator, res s end Henry

" Samuel E (Milligan, Whitelock & Cook) bds 9 e Tipton

" Samuel, blacksmith J J Stoltz, res 116 Railroad

" Edward M, emp lime kilns, res 116 Railroad [Laura]

" C W, emp lime kilns, res 116 Railroad

Cooley, Mrs Olive, res 93 w Tipton

Coolman, W H, clk Whitelock & Son, res 20 Purviance [Ida E] Lulu, Russell

Cooper, Geo, lab, res 22 Guilford

" John, lab, res 22 Guilford

" John J, lab, res 117 George

" Jonathan, lab, res 117 George [Mary] Ota, Vadie, Geo.

Corell, Peter, shoemaker W A Zeller, res 86 Frederick [Kate] Lizzie, Lulu, Edward

" Emma, clk Economy store, res 86 Frederick

Corell, Jacob, emp shoe factory, res 86 Frederick
"   Henry, emp Huntington Mill Co, res 41 Milligan
        [Cora] Marie, Baby
"   Daniel, emp Briant, res 15 Walnut [Mollie] Hazel
        M, Donald
Cornell, Clark, carpenter Erie, res 154 e Tipton [Della] Geo
        Harry
Corlew, George, res 3 Oak [Anna]
Cornelius, Clem W, emp Perrine & Bartlett, res 6 Mayne st
        [Mary]
Cory, H W, physician 4-5-6 I O O F building, rms same
Couch, Rev B L, pastor Wesleyan Methodists, res 71 Elm
        [Sarah E] Lillie J
Couch, Hartwell, tailor, I O O F building, res 37 Salamonie
        ave [Minnie] Grace, Carl, Earl
Coughlin, Jos B, clk Coughlin, res 118 Cherry [Bessie] Alice,
        Joseph jr
Coughlin, Sue A, boots and shoes, 62 n Jefferson, res 118
        Cherry
"   Mary, res 118 Cherry
Covey, Herbert, emp Briant, bds 1 Bechtol
Cowgill, Rose (wid) res 59 Mayne. Cluster LeVon
Cox, W G, eng Erie, res 77 First [Katharine] Florence N,
        Gilbert K
"   William, blacksmith, res 128 Byron [Mary] James C,
        Isaac, Luella, Buehlah, Dulah, Bertha
"   Mary B, teacher High school, res 88 n Lafontaine
"   Josephine M, teacher High school, res 88 n Lafontaine
"   Cyrena (wid Wm G) res 88 n Lafontaine
"   Stephen C, carpenter, res 88 n Lafontaine
"   Winfield S, boiler-maker Erie, res 47 Elm [Clarissa]
        Ethel, Eldon, Floyd
Coy, Reuben A, janitor court house, res 39 Franklin [Alice]
        Ray O, Shirley E
"   Abraham, res 77 Frederick
"   Harvey, car inspector, res 13 Third [Dessie]

Craft, Elias, brick layer, res 66 Esther [Cora] Jessie
Crandal, Samuel, res 51 e Sabine [Dorris]
"   Anna, res 51 e Sabine
"   A A, city marshal, res 19 n Lafontaine [Mary M]
            Viola M, Chas C
"   Mrs Belle (wid Samuel) res 53 Warren. Allen, Virden
Crane, J E, fireman Erie, res 167 e Market [L L]
Crane, J E, tobaccos and confectionery, 167 e Market
Crawford, Noah, emp Briant, res 98 Grayston ave [Anna]
            Dallas, Chas
"   Thomas, res 17 Cline [Elizabeth W]
"   Harry, lab, res 17 Cline
"   Nelson, emp Briant, res 151 Broadway [Lizzie]
            Joseph E, Laura, Emma
Creider, David, machinist Erie, res 17 Salamonie ave [Rose]
Creiger, Howard, emp round house Erie, res 156 e Franklin
            [Maggie]
"   Albert, emp shoe factory, bds 154 e Tipton
Creamer, J N, cond Erie, res 193 e State [Lucretia]
Creviston, Jacob L, section Erie, res 110 Grayston ave [Dena]
            Edna, Harry
Cribb, George, cond Erie, res 132½ e Market [Mattie B]
"   James, emp Erie, res 28 Gay [Hannah] Edith G,
            Irene G, Myrtle R, Inez B, Fred
†Crill, Harvey C, blacksmith Erie, res Catharine st [Lizzie]
            Mary
†Crill, Chas, boiler-maker Erie, res Catharine st
Cripe, James, lab, res 89 Lindley [Laura] Ernest, Vergil,
            Mary
Cripe, David, carpenter, res 89 Lindley
Crist, Geo W, fish dlr, res 4 Leopold [Nancy] Harry O,
            Clinton
          N H, cond Erie, res 74 e Matilda [N A] Walter, Her-
            bert, Raymond
"   Edward, lab, res 17 e Tipton
"   LeRoy, machinist Erie, res 7 Kintz [Clara] Laura B

Crist, John J, fish dlr, res 15 Division [Mary]
" James L, moulder, res 17 Division [Dora] Clifford, Carl
Crites, Alexander, bakery 106 n Jefferson, res 39 e Tipton st [Florence] Marion, Dora
Croker, James W (col'd) stone mason, res 15 Cline [Carrie] Meryl
Crosby, Michael, emp Erie round hs, res 24 Leopold [Susan] Henry, John
Cross, Mace, emp Erie, res 80 First
" C A (wid) res 31 w Matilda. Grace A
Crouch, Pathania (wid) res 16 Salamonie ave
Crow, A D, eng Erie, res 130 Condit
" Linda J (wid Joseph) res 130 Condit. Minnie
" Mrs Sophia M, dressmaker, res 104 Court. Anna F, Chas V, Lizzie R, James A
" John C, plasterer, res 104 Court
" Thomas D, brick mason, res 104 Court
Crull, A U, teacher high schools, res 70 e Market
" A B, carpenter Erie, res 26 Henry [Lizzie] Lawrence E, Fay N
" Harley R, student, res 26 Henry
" John L, butcher, res 114 First [Emma] Fern
Cull, John J, eng Erie, res 103 e State [Louisa] Mamie, Frank, Fred
Cull, James, emp Erie shops, res 80 Wilkerson [Anna]
Culler, Stephen, night watchman Briant, res 57 Webster [Nettie]
Culp, Lavina, (wid Daniel) res 22 Mayne
Culp, J D, stone dlr, res 24 Mayne [Jennie] Gertrude. Chas Harry, Ruth, Dean
" Glenn, lab, bds 10 Mayne
" John T, lab, res 22 Mayne
Culver, Ellis, tinner, Dickover & Altman, res 26 Mayne [Anna]
" Nelson N, tinner, res 48 Mayne [Sarah]

Culver, Daisy, clerk. res 48 Mayne

Cummings, Luther, res 59 William

Cunningham, Thomas, boiler-mkr Erie, res 78 e State [Alice]
          Otto, Fern

Cunningham, Mrs C F (wid) literary writer, res 58 e Franklin

Cunningham, James, lab, bds 40 Grayston ave

Cupp, Uriah, carpenter, res 115 Railroad   [Mattie]

Curran, L, cond Erie, res 85 e Market

Cushman, David, lab, res over 53 Guilford

Cutshall, Mrs M J, res 63 Frederick
  "   Florence M, music teacher, res 63 Frederick
  "   Charles H, reporter Herald, res 63 Frederick
  "   Foster E, compositor Herald, res 63 Frederick

D

Dages, Will, electric light tender, res 82 Webster st [Agnes]
          Monica

Dahne, Eda, domestic 15 e Market

Dailey, Maggie, librarian city school, res 22 w Matilda

Dailey, Anna A (wid D O) res 22 w Matilda

Dairs, Richard, lab, res 14 Hasty [Mollie]

Daltry, Thomas, foreman blacksmith shop Erie, res 45 e Sa-
          bine [Carolina]

Daltry, John, blacksmith Erie, res 16 Iowa [Florence] Thos

*Danhauer, Chas, emp Erie shops, res n canal e of city

Daniels, T E (Kitch & Daniels) res 52 Oak   [Naomi]

Danielson, Rose C, teacher public schools

Darr, J W, eng Erie, res 56 e Market [Mavine] Nellie

Darr, I W, fireman Erie, res 105 Lincoln ave [Susan] Bernice

Darrow, Ned, emp E E Brown, rms over 32 Cherry

Daugherty, Richard, brick mason, res 31 Iowa [Mary] Clara E, Mary J, Richard L, Clarence F

Daugherty, John, contractor and stone mason, res 23 s Briant [Caroline] Cecelia, Lucy, John L

Davidson, Duncan, merchant police, res 9 Allen st [Anna] Julia, Johnnie, Willie, Josephine, Mabel, Alice

Davies, Joseph, tile merchant 43 e Market, res 111 Etna ave [Sarah] Lorene M, Winifred, Jesse, Leslie

Davies, Harriet, res 36 w Tipton

Davis, James L, blacksmith 7 Front, res 16 Whitelock [Jennie] Clyde, Floyd, Eva, Fred

" Guy W, fireman Erie, res 44 Indiana [Chloa]

" James F, emp Catholic church, res 101 Cherry [Christina]

" Chas, eng C Fulton, res 69 Cline [Ola]

" H C, engine dispatcher Erie, res 70 First [Ida May]

" Hubert, res 100 Cherry

" Caldwell, clk L Levy, res 58 e Franklin

" C H, domestic 52 w Matilda

" Richard, emp W M Billiter, res 12 Hasty [Mary]

Day, T M (Dad) cond Erie, res 28 Guilford

" Everet M (L J Day & Son) res 53 Mayne [Olive V] Sylvester F

" John R, prosecuting attorney, res 94 s Jefferson [Matie] Irl M, Ocle

Day, Samuel F, livery and feed stable 23 Cherry, res 32 w Market

Day, Robt J sr, res 32 w Market

" Chas, painter, res 16 Mayne

" Edmurd, res 16 Mayne [Sarah Ann]

Day & Elser (R J Day jr, Geo Elser) hippodrome, headquarters fair ground

Day, R J jr (Day & Elser) res 126 Guilford [Bertha]   Donald
"   L J (L J Day & Son) res 102 s Jefferson [Adelia M]
        Pearl,   Beatrice
Day, L J & Son (L J, Everet M) groceries 23 s Jefferson
Day, L E, clk L J Day & Son, res 102 s Jefferson
*DeArmitt, Mrs Florence, servant Orphans Home, res same
DeArmitt, J B, teacher, res 121 Byron [Anna] DeVoe
Dearwester, George H, cond Erie, res cor Elizabeth and Mar-
        garet [Sarah] Blaine, George, Celia, Sadie.
Dearworth, C W, operator Erie M M office, res 64 Frederick st
        [Margaret]
     "   Russell, emp Erie oil house, res 119 Court
Decker, Henry, emp Hoosier laundry, res 4 Herman [Alice]
Deeds, O O, plumber, res 29 South [Amanda] Glenn E,
        Ethel M
Deemer, W H, emp Erie shops, res 8 Erie [Martha E] Harry
        O, (child unnamed)
Deighton, Selina, prof nurse, res 7 Elm. Arthur, Amy M,
        Hilda, Daisy
Deighton, Percy, musician, res 7 Elm
Dellinger, Jacob H, emp Erie round house, res 12 Nile [Cath-
        arine] Ernest
DeLong, Rev J W, pastor Matilda st U B church, res 23 Poplar
        [Emma] Fred W, Leo
DeLong, A W, res 57 s Jefferson [E C]
Delorme, Bertha (wid Edward) res 66 w Matilda. Adela, Ed-
        ward
Delvin, Della, res 58 e Franklin
     "   William, carpenter Erie, res 134 Elm st [Rachael]
        Mary
     "   Chas W, street sprinkler, res 117 s Jefferson [Eliza-
        beth] Goldie, John H, Robert, Ethel, Louis.
DeMoss, John, machinist Erie, res 60 High. [Alice] Edna
DeMuth, L L, eng Erie, res 109 Lincoln ave [Emma] Donald
Denis, Frank, fireman Erie, res 11 Iva [Minnie] Mildred

Denius, Ed, emp Briant, res 73 e Sabine [Esther] Waveland
" Sophrona (wid) res 47 Elm
" William, bridge carpenter Erie, res 21 Harris street
[Louisa] Edith, Maybelle
" Clark, emp Erie shops, res 21 Harris
Denton, John, emp Briant, res 26 Wagoner [Sarah Ann]
" Chas, lab, res 15 w Market
Deville, Peter, carpenter, res 174 Cherry [Matilda] Mary
† " Nicholas J. carpenter, res s Salamonie ave [Mary A]
Laura, John, Mary, Rose, Joseph
DeVoe, Jennie, housekeeper 19 Salamonie ave
DeWitt, Fremont, emp Erie, res 16 Harris [Mollie] Bud,
Clinton, Ada
Dial, John, lab, res 2 Bechtol
" Jackson, carpenter Erie, res 104 Lincoln ave [Sarah]
Dora
" W F, inspector Erie, res 146 Condit [Sarah] Jennie,
Clara
Dicer, John, switchman Erie, res 10 Simon [Lena] Fred,
Veronka, Carl, Bernese
Dick, Julius (F Dick & Sons) res 197 n Jefferson [Frank]
" Jacob (F Dick & Sons) res 207 n Jefferson st [Susan B]
Fred
" Fred (F Dick & Sons) res 29 Frederick. Amanda
Dick, F & Sons (F Dick, Julius, Jacob) clothiers 49 n Jefferson
Dickinson, J R, eng Erie, res 1 Jacob [E M] Darke D,
Sarah E, Ralph, Marshall, Cortland
Dickover & Altman (W H Dickover, R M Altman) hardware 5
s Jefferson
Dickover, W H (Dickover & Altman) res 47 High [Martha]
Arthur L, Mabel L
†Dickover, Jacob, carpenter, res s Henry [Lydia] Jennie,
Emma
Diefenbaugh, Margaret (wid Peter) res 153 Court
" William, lab, res 38 Halstead
" Ed, machinist Erie, res 38 Halstead

Diefenbaugh, Mollie (wid Martin) res 38 Halstead.   Flora,
    Clara,   Lulu
"   Allen, emp Erie, res 63 High [Maggie]
"   John, cook Allman & Boos, res 57 Warren
"   Lewis, butcher, res 57 Warren [Sarah] Lizzie,
    Chas, George, Lewis jr, Harry, Lulu, Nettie
Dill, W W, pianos, organs etc, 30 s Jefferson, res 101 Etna ave
    [Etta] W Aubrey, Susan
Dille, Icabod, res 45 Etna ave [Rebecca]
Dinius, M F, res 96 Etna ave [Mertie E] Theresa W
"   E E, emp Briant, res 66 Grayston ave [Jennie F]
    Vergil E, Emma
Dinius, Harvey, grocery 106 Etna ave, res 110 Etna ave
    [Jennett] Loyal L, Ethel E, Ruth R, Burnet B
Dinius, A Link, caller Erie, res 106 Lincoln ave [Minnie]
    Bernice, Ruth
"   W F, attorney, res 11 Monroe [Clara] Vera, Marie,
    Bertha
"   Rev W O, pastor Etna ave U B church, res 28 s Jeffer-
    son [S V]
"   John, cond Erie, res 121 e State [Anna] Essie,
    Nellie, Robert
"   Lillie M, teacher public schools
Dillon, Martha (wid James) res 4 s Lafontaine
"   W K, emp Erie shops, res 76 Superior [Sarah] Hat- •
    tie, Edgar, John
"   Mahala (wid) res 77 e State
Dimond, Joseph, carpenter, res 17 William [Flora] Joseph,
    William, Blanche, Arthur, Ruth
"   Frank, electrician, emp city, res 17 William
"   George, emp shoe factory, res 17 William
Dimond, William, horse shoeing and repair shop 44 Cherry,
    res over same [Maggie] Harry, Hazel
Dodson, Lola, domestic 26 n Lafontaine
Dohle, John, hostler Dr F S C Grayston, res 74 Cherry street
    [Minnie]

Doell, Wm, lab res 61 Clark [Bertha] Frederick

Dolan, Seymour J, clk Ackerman, res 102 E Franklin

" Lena, clk Arnold & Son, res 102 e Franklin

" Edward, res 102 e Franklin

" Josephine, clk Arnold & Son, res 102 e Franklin

" Lewis A, emp Stults livery, res 102 e Franklin

" J R, asst yardmaster Erie, res 102 e Franklin [Elizabeth] Henry, Bart, Leo

" J H, brakeman Erie, res 13 Third [Ida]

Dolby, Grant, timber cutter, res 24 Monroe

Doudna, B F, brakeman Erie, res 84 e Sabine [Allie]

Doudna, Mrs L (wid) res 84 e Sabine

Donk, Geo, emp shoe factory, bds 60 Whitelock

Donley, John, shoemaker, res 53 Warren. Jessie

Doolittle, J A, eng Erie, res 9 Superior. John M, Geo A

Dorn, Matthias, plumber W F Dorn, res 108 Hitzfield street [Martha]

Dorn, F William, foundry and machine works 44 e Matilda, res 104 n Lafontaine [Mary] Bertha, George

*Dorsch, Fred (Stults & Dorsch) s Etna ave [Nora] John W, Baby

Doty, Clara, res 69 e Franklin

Doub, G H, clk McCaffrey res 60 e Matilda street [Melvina] Mary M

" J W, baker 123 n Jefferson, res 34 Poplar street [Myra] Harold, Maida

" John M, lab res 64 Zahn [Lizzie] Charles, Harry, Marshall

" Henry, lab res 64 Zahn

Douglas, Mrs Sophia, res 26 Garfield. Herman

" Eva, res 41 Etna ave

" J J, eng Erie, bds and rms 11 e Market

Dow, Chas, cond Erie, res 93 s Jefferson [Tillie] Stella. Jas

Dowell, W M, blacksmith, res 52 Mayne [Ada] Pearl, Ruby

Drabenstot, Frank, emp Erie shops, res 108 Elm

Dragoo, Margaret (wid) res 42 w Market

Drake, W T, cond Erie, res 29 Superior st [Lizzie] Hazel, Mary, Nellie

Draper & Worling (Henry Draper, Julius Worling) contractors
over 7 s Jefferson

*Draper, Henry (Draper & Worling) res near water wrks

*Draper, Royal, lab res near water wrks station

*Draper, Alvin, lab res near water works station

*Draper, W A, lab res s Etna ave

    "   Clara, domestic 45 w Matilda

Dress, Peter, res 47 w Tipton.

Drover, Herman H, photographer over 17 s Jefferson, res 38
Etna ave [Hattie E] Walter H, Carl L

Drover, Fredericka (wid Henry) res 38 Etna ave

    "   Herman W, amanuensis France & Dungan, res 8 William

    "   Theresa (wid Henry F) res 8 William.   Anna

    "   Wm H, res 64 William [Emma] Arthur, Evaline

    "   Laura, cashier J Strodel, res 64 William

    "   Simon H, foreman carpenters Erie, res 14 William st
[Mary] Katie

    "   Minnie, emp Hoosier laundry, res 14 William

    "   Henry J, fireman Erie, res 14 William

    "   George, machinist Erie, res 14 William

    "   Lena, teacher music, res 14 William

Drummond, P E (wid E M) res 166 Byron.   Alice

    "   Q J, r s 46 Whitelock   [Mary B]

    "   E Q. city clerk, res 79 Marshall   [Grace A]

Dubbs, M. teamster, res 151 First   [Delfina]

Duley, Angustus, res 21 e Tipton

Dumbauld, Wm H, lunch room 164 e Market, res 11 South

    "   James W, clk res 11 South

    "   R R (wid Uriah) res 11 South

    "   Warren (Heaston & Dumbauld) res 66 Front street
[Mary] Ida

    "   John, clk Heaston & Dumbauld, res 66 Front

*   "   Melangton, teamster, res Stringtown, e fair grnd
[Tessie] Lynden, Eldon, Ruth

Dunathan, E P, carpenter, res 146 Oak   [Nancy J]   Minnie
    L, Gaylard M, Robert B
Dunfee & Goble (Louis Dunfee, Chas Goble) books, stationery,
    etc, 9 e Market
Dunfee, Louis (Dunfee & Goble) res 11 e Market
Dungan, Zachariah T (France & Dungan) res 29 Milligan st
    [Lina C]   Harry M
    "   Carl O, agent "Up to Date" res 29 Milligan
    "   Maggie M, res 117 Guilford
    "   Isaac L, emp Erie round house, res 62 Superior street
    [Mary A]   Aurelius M, Dallas, Clyde, Elvin
Dunn, Chas E, switchman Erie, res 146 e Franklin   [Belle]
    Blanche
Dunning, Charles, emp Briant, res 84 Court   [Ella A]   Belle,
    Lillie E, William
Dyer, W D, cond Erie, res 39 Canfield   [Emma]   Francis,
    Agnes, Oscar

E

Eaken, J H, lab, res 24 Superior
    "   Thos A, res 24 Superior
Earhart, R M, fireman Erie, res 41 e Sabine   [Alpha]   Mar-
    tha, Archie
Earlywine, James L, emp Griffith & Son, res over 152 e Market
    [Florence]   Eddie
Earlywine, Mary C (wid W H) res 57 Superior, Maude, Eva,
    Ernest, Wm H jr
Eberhart, Joseph, tailor over 63 n Jefferson, res 67 Oak st
    [Tillie]   Lizzie, Herman

Eberhart, John, stock dlr, res 14 Iva [Mary] Effie, Ervin B

Ebersole, W H, carpenter, res 18 Grayston ave [Clara] Ervin, Rosa, Joseph

"   J M, carpenter Erie, res 129 e Franklin st [Anna] Jessie

"   Jennie, housekeeper 17 Erie

Eby, J S, photographer, res 87 Poplar

Eckenbarger, Conrad W, emp Erie shops, res 46 Leopold st [Alice J] Mabel, Chas W

Eckenbarger, Frank, emp lime kilns, res 13 Erie [Clara]

*Eckenbarger, Eli, section hand Erie, res n Guilford [Mary]

Eckenroad, Henry J, machinist, res 51 High

"   J A, eng Erie, res 51 High [Julia] Paul J

Edgington, W R, barber Trixler, res 17 Bingham. [Jennie] Carl, Buella, Fred

Edgington, Jennie, modeste, 3d floor First National Bank blk

*Edgington, James, emp Sutton brick yd, res e fair ground [Lillie] Chas

Edlar, Gertrude, res 10 Bingham

Edson, Thos, asst eng water works, res 27 South [Mary] Willie

Edwards, Sarah (wid John) res 147 e Market. Eda

"   Frank, painter Erie, res 130 First [Ida M]

Edwards, Chas A, prop Globe Clothing store 33 n Jefferson, res over same [Ella] Ruth

Eger, William F, eng City Mills, res 199 Cherry [Ida] Ervin

Eggleston, H H, carpenter Erie, res 105 First

"   W O, master carpenter Erie, res 105 First [Barbara]

Ehellers, Anna, domestic 110 Guilford

Ehinger, Frank, section foreman Wabash Ry, res 123 e Sabine [Cecelia] Isabella, Leonard, Sylvester, Joseph

"   Conrad, lab res 4 Second [Mary] Nora

"   Alois, emp Briant, res 4 Second

"   Ollie, emp Briant, res 4 Second

"   Engleman, emp Erie shops, res 4 Second

Ehinger, Julius, emp Briant, res 4 Second
" Eugene, emp Erie shops, res 4 Second
Eisele, Franz, stone mason, res 113 Poplar st [Katharine]
    Maggie, Rose, George
" Frank, lab res 113 Poplar
" John (Yerman & Eisele) res 113 Poplar
Eisenhauer, Andrew J. jeweler 87 n Jefferson, res 110 Poplar
Eisenhauer, Bals, banker, res 110 Poplar. (Daughter)
    " John M, bookpr First National Bank, res 40 w
        Tipton [Anna M] Magdalena, Theresa A,
        Eulalia H
    " Anna, res 10 Simon st
Elliat, Simon, res 23 London [Elzina]
Ellerman, C J, stone mason, res 9 Gay [Dessie] Fred
Elliott, Frank, carpenter Erie, res 103 Lincoln ave [Sarah]
    " Earl, machinist Erie, res 21 Wilkerson
Ellis, G, res 70 Marshall
Ellis, Ed, drayman, res 67 Wilkerson [Uria] Flora, John,
    Elizabeth, Uria
Elser, George (Day & Elser) bds 11 e Market
Elvin, T L, foreman machine shops Erie, res 72 Guilford st
    [Alice] Gertrude, Eathel, Dessie
    " R F, boiler maker Erie, res 6 Third [Maude S]
    " Harry L, foreman boiler shops Erie, res 216 e Market
        [Jessie] Claude, Chas, Mary
    " William, boiler maker Erie, res 232 e Market [Eliza-
        beth]
Emberlin, George, hostler S P Stults, res over 65 e Market
    [Hattie] May, Dolphus, Dessie
Emerick, Geo W, carpenter, res 14 Taylor [Mahala]
    " John W, emp Singer Sewing Machine Co, res 47
        William
    " Ida L, emp Hoosier laundry, res 47 William
    " Wm L, feather renovator, res 47 William [Mahala]
Emery, James, res 36 Poplar [Susan W]
    " Will R, traveling agt, res 36 Poplar

Emery, Sarah (wid John) res 53 w Matilda
  "   H E, teacher, res 69 Elm [Mary] Marie
  "   Mary (wid Peter) res over 127 n Jefferson

Emley, J R, bookpr Huntington Co Bank, res 9 Canal street
          [Lucie] Ruth
  "   H L, cashier Huntington Co Bank, res 48 Whitelock
          [Cassie] Neil, Dow, Paul
  "   D A, watchman Perrine & Bartlett, res 53 Superior
          [Nannie] Chas, Harry, Clarence
† "   Frank P, carpenter, res 32 Catharine [Kate]
  "   A C, carpenter, res 9 William [Cora]
  "   Julia A (wid Sexton) res 58 Wilkerson
  "   Jesse A, carpenter, res 154 e Tipton
  "   Byron H, carpenter, res 154 e Tipton
  "   James B, lab, res 90 e Washington [Sarah] Leon-
          ard, Flora, J D
  "   Chas, carpenter, res 154 e Tipton [Delilah] Guy
  "   Roscoe, emp Hoosier laundry, bds 287 n Jefferson

Emmons, Joseph, emp Perrine & Bartlett, res 16 Edwin street
          [Maggie]

Endres, Geo, car inspector Erie, res 20 Buchanan
  "   Edelburgh, res 20 Buchanan

Engel, Andrew, saloon 94 n Jefferson, res 120 Poplar [Maria]
          Herman, John, Josephine, Andrew jr, Marie.

Engleman, Geo, res 98 Poplar [Philipena]

Engleman, Chris, saloon 85 n Jefferson, res 119 Cherry street
          [Clara]
*   " ,   Michael, lab res s Etna ave [Arabella] Pearl,
          Emma, Walter

*Enoch, T R (Hedge Fence Co) res s Etna ave [Flora]

*Enyard, Sherman, res Jos Davies farm 156 Broadway [Mary]
          Thos, Wm

Erb, J L, meat market 94 First, res 12 Gay [Elizabeth] Ed-
          ward, Rosella, Joseph. Marie

Erlenbach, Frank, emp C Lang, res 64 Marshall [Kate]
    Francis
"   Jacob, bartender A Wyss, res 158 Byron
"   Philip, lab res 158 Byron
"   Will, emp C Lang, res 158 Byron
"   Julia, res 158 Byron
"   Arky, res 158 Byron
"   Adam, emp J Kindler, res 158 Byron [Mary]
"   John, machinist Erie, res 13 Wilkerson [Jeane]
"   Philip sr, lab res 117 Esther [Sophia]
"   Philip jr, lab res 117 Esther
"   Ignatius, lab res 117 Esther
"   Lizzie, res 117 Esther
"   Henry, fireman Erie, res 51 Oak st [Caroline]
    Marie

†Ernst, John, lab bds 7 Catharine

Ernst, J M, carpenter Erie, res 7 Grayston ave [Ida S] Jennie, Merlin

Erpelding, Geo, cooper Western Lime Assn, res 107 Oak st
    [Anna]
"   Frank, bottling works 120 w Matilda, res same
    [Matilda] Lizzie, Ferdinand, Harmon, Lawrence, Joseph, Vincent
"   Peter, cooper, res 116 w Matilda [Theresa]
"   Jacob, cooper, res 116 w Matilda
"   John V, cooper Western Lime Assn, res 62 Esther
    [Pauline] Gertrude, George, Bertha, Josephine

Ertle, Martin M, carpenter, res 137 n Lafontaine st [Mary]
    William, Marcellus, Cecelia, Estella, Josephine

Ertzinger, W L, fireman Erie, res 115 e Market [Alma]

Ertzinger, Levi A, meat market 25 e Market, res over same
    [Lavoka]

Ervin, Wm, lab, res 35 Green [Jessie]

Erwin, Wm, teamster, res 107 Elm [Millie] Grace

Eschbach, Israel M, confectionery 7 n Jefferson, res 39 Etna ave [Elizabeth] Elizabeth B, Earl E, Ray E
" Ola, clk I Eschbach, res 39 Etna ave
" Bina, clk J Frash, res 39 Etna ave
" Ella M, compositor Democrat, res 39 Etna ave
" Isadora, clk C R Smith & Co, res 67 Frederick
" Thos, carpenter, res 67 Frederick [Lavina]
" John, lab res 2 Hannah
" Mary, dressmaker, res 2 Hannah
Esson, Richard, eng Erie, res 77 Oak [Mary] Mamie, Lizzie
Esson, Richard E, bookpr E Buffalo, res 77 Oak
Etzold, Henry, emp G W Shearer, res 6 Arthur [Dilla] Hazel
" W A, tender Mt Hope cemetery, res 64 Buck [Henrietta] Mary, Emma
" Chas F, emp A Altstadter, res 112 w Matilda [Pauline] Hannah
" John C, canvasser, res 112 w Matilda
Evans, David, expressman, res 87 Frederick [Almira] Bertha, Elva, Ota
Everding, Geo, res 124 e Market
" Mattie, res 27 Walnut
" Philip, lab res 27 Walnut st [Mary] Jacob H, Lewis
Ewing, Thos, clk E Hewitt, res 177 n Jefferson st. [Pearl] Dorothy
" Ann (wid Thos) res 165 n Jefferson
" Wm (Ewing Bros) res 165 n Jefferson
" Chas F, clk, res 165 n Jefferson
" James H (Ewing Bros) res 167 n Jefferson [Margaret] J Fred
Ewing Bros (William, James H) dry goods, 81 n Jefferson
Exchange Hotel (J F J Siegmund, prop) adj Wabash depot

A Question of Facilities

When it comes to doing first-class printing it is merely a question of facilities. These are good presses, latest type faces, good material and good printers. ∴ ∴ ∴

We Have Them All.

We print catalogues, circulars, letter and note heads, bill and statement heads, cards, programs, envelopes, or anything that any Huntington shop can print. ∴

We Do Better Work.

Our office and shop is on Jefferson street, on the south side of the creek. Call and see us or invite us to see you. This is a sample of our work. ∴ ∴ ∴ ∴

...The Guide Publishing Co.,
...Huntington, Indiana.

F

Faber, Minnie, res 41 Mayne. Jenetta, Lenoe

Faber, Louisa (wid Louis) res 110 Lincoln ave

Fahrnow, Fred sr, emp Griffith & Son, res 67 German [Mary]
    Sophia, Eda, Carl

Fahrnow, Fred jr, clk D Yingling, res 67 German

Fahrnow, Harmon, hostler Griffith & Son, res 67 German

Fair, John H, emp Huntington Light & Fuel Co, res 57 Fred-
    erick [Addie] Myrtle

"   Hezekiah, blacksmith, res 24 Hasty [Rosa]   Paul

†Falk, J E, res 26 Swan [Ruby M]   Flossie T, Wm, Jacob

Falck, John, clk H H Arnold & Son, res 38 Webster st [Etta]
    Marie A

"   Geo, carpenter Erie, res 93 Dimond [Mary]   George,
    Otto, Louisa

Fallon, T F, night yardmaster Erie, res 109 e Franklin street
    [Katie] Eddie, May

Fanning, George, carpenter, res 154 Court [Effie]   Dwight

Farling, John, timber buyer Griffith & Son, res 67 Briant st
    [Anna] Dora, Edith, Arthur

"   Louis, emp Griffith & Son, res 67 Briant

"   A C, carpenter, res 288 e State st [Aldie]   Myrle,
    Addie, Ada, Ray

Farmers Guide (The Guide Pub Co, publishers) 14 s Jefferson

Farrar, Charles, janitor Central school, res 32 Whitelock st
    [Lotta] Robert

Fasnaugh, Noah, lab res 190 Byron [Adda] Wilson, Nan-
    nie, Nora, Buell, Helen

Faurot, G W, brakeman Erie, res 24 Canfield st [Elizabeth]
    Nina, Urban, Ivan, Norval

Faust, Rev F P, asst pastor SS Peter and Paul Catholic
    church, res 93 Cherry

Feighner, Wm, emp lime kilns, res 321 e State [Clara] Lucy,
    Blanche, William

Feighner, George, barber, res 51 Webster [Maude] Edna, Winnie

Felter, Mary R (wid Jacob) res 58 William
" Frank, clk F Dick & Sons, res 58 William [Edna B]

Ferguson, Geo W, laundryman Pearl Steam laundry, res 49 Frederick [Marinda] Harvey L
" Donald, physician, res 4 First [Anna] Elizabeth
" C W, emp Kolatona factory, res 25 Second [Ella] Nellie, Daisy

Fernandez, Anna (wid Joachim F) res 48 William

Ferner, Rose C, teacher city school, res 39 e Tipton

Ferrill, Patrick, baggage master Wab, res 96 Court [Hannah] James, Mary, Nellie

Fetters, Sophronia (wid) res 244 e State
" Elwood, painter Erie, res 50 Jackson. Robert, Cora
" Samuel, painter Erie, res 50 Jackson
" William, fireman Erie, res 74 Webster [Margaret] Harry, Edna, Willis, Ora, Roy

Fields, Walter T, eng Erie, res 98 Byron [Etta E] Wallace W, Bessie M

Filbert, A J, lab res 274 Etna ave [Ida E] Loran, Herbert

Fink, Daniel, emp lime kilns, res 130 e Sabine [Eliza] Geo W

Finley, Harry, barber shop 9½ n Jefferson, res 10 Elm street [Minnie] Harold

Finley, Nathan, teamster res 36 Mayne [Sarah] Newell W, J P
" Ora, teamster res 37 Briant [Allie] Edward, Fay, May

Finn, Michael, saloon 162 e Market, bds 130 e Market

Finney, W T, cond Erie, res 165 e Franklin

Firman, C J, cond Erie, res 85 e Market

First, Aaron, emp Briant bending fac, res 38 Indiana [Ida] Emery, Emma

First, D E, meat market 106 Etna ave, res 120 Clark [Anna L] J E

Fist, Chas E, carpenter Erie, res 30 Mayne [Della] Frank

First National Bank (Wm McGrew, pres; B Eisenhauer, vice
pres; Sarah F Dick, cashier) s w cor Jefferson and
Market sts

Fisher & Bailey (Leona Fisher, Maude Bailey) milliners 7 e
Market

Fisher, Keefer & Bailey (S C Fisher, Henry Keefer, J B
Bailey) contractors

Fisher, Lemuel, brakeman Erie, res 87 e Market [Lizzie]
" A C, car repairer Erie, res 137 e Market [Sarah]
Dessie, Mamie, Merrill
George, blacksmith Erie, res 36 Harris st [Melvie]
Willie, Elmer, Charles, Ray
" W M, lab Erie, res 43 e Sabine [Elizabeth] Lee
" Fisher, Lonnie, emp Perrine & Bartlet, res 43 e Sabine
" Noah, res 52 Guilford [Hannah]
" H O, janitor Allen st school, res 65 Henry st [V O]
Marie
Harry, stone mason, res 133 n Lafontaine
Samuel, teamster, res 143 Walnut [Laura] Isaac,
Charles
" Clarence, blacksmith Erie, res 9 Erie [Minnie] Wm
" S C (Fisher, Keefer & Bailey) res 28 Front [Rebecca
J]
" Leona (Fisher & Bailey) res 28 Front
" Jane (wid Daniel) res 19 Division
" John, lab res 31 Green [Mary]
" Simon, res 36 Green
" Molliston, lab res 20 London. Anna
" Harvey, lab res 73 Elm [Susan] Clara A

Fisher & Snider (I E Fisher, O N Snider) groceries 3 s Jefferson

Fisher, I E (Fisher & Snider) res 15 Olinger st [Elizabeth]
Charles A
" Maria (wid) res 15 Olinger
" Nicholas, res 123 Oak [Elizabeth]

Fisher, N W, gunsmith 20 e Market, bds 22 e Market

†Flannagan, John, emp Briant, res 71 Lindley st [Charlotte]
    Everet G

Flannagan, J D, brakeman Erie, res 43 Marshall [Sarah E]
    Libby B, John H

Fleck, A, carpenter Erie, res 202 e Market [Mattie] Sarah,
    Thurman, Clarence

Fleck, Charles, machinist Erie, res 202 e Market

Flemming, J A, agt Metropolitan Life Insurance Co, room 5
    Citizens Bank block, res 71 w Matilda [Arminda]
    Hazel C, Mary E

Flemming, John, bill clk Erie frt office, res 110 e Market

Flora, Frank (Flora & Griffith) res 208 Guilford [Della]
    "   Edith, res 35 w Market
    "   Asa, clk Ewing Bros, res 152 Guilford [Ida]

Flora & Griffith (Frank Flora, Frank Griffith) druggists 88 n
    Jefferson

Flowers, George, res 85 Whitelock

Flynn, Hannah (wid John) res 281 n Jefferson, Marie, Ag-
    nes, Irene, John, David

Folk, Howard, cond Erie, bds 11 e Market
    "   Eli, carpenter, res 120 Front [Emma] Cleo Clem
    "   Jesse, res 126 Front [Lavina]

Folk, W E, agt Standard Oil Co, res 102 First [Ella] Ber-
    nice

Fooshee, J D, barber J Berkfield, res 90 w Matilda [Lena]
    Irene, Lulu

Foote. Mrs Florence E, teacher public schools, res 39 e Tipton
    Helen, Athol

Ford, Jeff, clk Erie M M office, res 62 e Market
    "   Anthony, clk Erie R M office, res 62 e Market
    "   Alice (wid) res 130 Guilford

Ford, J W, pres Huntington Co Bank, res 225 n Jefferson st
    Georgiana

Fordyce, Alice, teacher public schools, res 68 e State

Forest, I B, res 27 Kintz [Margaret] Anna, Carl, Earl
    "   Emmet, stone mason, res 123 George [Lizzie]

Forest, Emma, domestic 151 n Jefferson
"   Arletta, domestic 92 Frederick
Foreman, Morris, junk dlr, res 75 w Tipton
"   Rose H, teacher public schools, res 39 e Tipton
Forster, Nicholas, bartender P Forster, res 112 Oak [Margaret] Catharine, Herman
"   Peter, saloon 12 e Washington, res 86 Poplar [Elizabeth]
"   Peter, stone mason, res 99 Poplar st [Katharine] Clarence, Frank, Peter, Mamie
"   Peter, lab res 120 Oak
"   John, clk P Scheiber, res 120 Oak
"   Jacob, stone mason, res 120 Oak [Catharine] Maggie, Katie, Mary, Lizzie
"   John jr, stone mason, res 99 Poplar
"   Jacob E, barber L Trixler, res 99 Poplar
"   John, stone mason, res 92 Poplar [Joanah] Katie Lulu, Joseph, Edith
Forsythe, Elias, res 146 Condit
"   James, carpenter, res 29 e Matilda
Foster, Charles, painter res Grand View hotel
"   G W, prop Marchaniel Restaurant, res 28 Guilford st [Florence] Iona, Howard
"   Deville, timber buyer, res 9 s Briant [Jennie] Addie B, Wilda
"   Michael, emp lime kilns, res 107 Grayston ave [Lizzie] Eddie, Julia, Lulu
"   C Helene, stenographer Erie Supt office, res 66 Cherry
"   George F, contractor and brk mason, res 66 Cherry
"   Chas, contractor, res 66 Cherry [Margaret] Mary, Chas jr, Freddie
†Fotteral, Barker & Brown Co, mfgs of boots and shoes, factory s Salamonie ave
Foust, William G, res 74 w Matilda [Lydia]
Fowerbaugh & Zahm (Lewis Fowerbaugh, L V Zahm) groceries 148 e Market

Fowerbaugh, William, res 13 Glenn [Barbara A] Albert

Fowerbaugh, Lewis (Fowerbaugh & Zahm) res 41 South street [Mary] Grace

Fox, Patrick, master car builder Erie, res 118 e Market [Mrs P]

Frame, J H, foreman Withington factory, res 24 Briant street [Della] John, Harry, Edna, Roy

France, William, res 115 e Market

" Charles, res 115 e Market

France, O R, prop Star Restaurant, 11 e Market, res over same [Maranda J]

France, J Fred (France & Dungan) res 83 e Market [Jackie L] Jessie

France & Dungan (J Fred France, Z T Dungan) attorneys and commercial lawyers over 35 n Jefferson

France, Henry, truckman Erie, res 11 Edwin [Grace]

" Pearl, domestic 11 Edwin

" Hiram, teamster, res 15 s Lafontaine

" Anna, teacher, res 15 s Lafontaine

† " James A, emp Perrine & Bartlett, res 20 Swan [Lavina M] Bessie A, Goldie I

" George, emp Perrine & Bartlett, res 93 e Sabine street [Nellie] Carl

" John, lab res 3 Grayston ave [Sarah] Edward, Laura, Mabel

*Francis, Wm, emp Erie round hs, res e fair ground [Kate] Viola M, Everet W

Franklin, Mary (wid John) res 38 Milligan. Rosetta, James, Wiley, Arnold, Mollie

" Samuel, traveling salesman, res 53 Buchanan street [Belle] Simon, Minnie, Mollie. Pearl

" Moses, junk dlr, res 128 George st [Sarah] Cecil, Mary, Anna, Mollie

" Meyer, junk dlr, res 128 George

Franks, Wm, emp Huntington Light & Fuel Co, res 19 Fruit [Eliza] Minnie

Frary, Henry, bookpr C E Briant bending works, res 42 Frederick [Malissa F] Edna, Ralph, Frank

Frary, Addie, stenographer Erie M M office, res 42 Frederick

Frash, John, prop Frash dry goods emporium 53 n Jefferson, res 110 Guilford [Esther]

Frash, George A, treas Congress Bicycle Co, res 110 Guilford

Frash, Eugene, mgr Frash dry goods emporium, res 110 Guilford street

Frazee, Dock, brickmaker, res 1 s Lafontaine [Laura] Maud, May, Chester, Ralph, Fred, Otis

Frazee, Mrs Mary, res 134 Elm. Chas, Earl, Effie

Frazier, Dr E, specialist over 52 n Jefferson, rms same

Frech, C Albert, drugs and sundries 16 e Market, res 65 Etna ave [Savilla] Mabel, Ernest, Eugene, Hortense, Charles

Frederick, H B, prop Windsor Hotel 151 e Market, res same [Anna] May, Albert, Frank

" A W, emp Erie car shops, res 25 Erie [Hannah E] Eddie

Freed, George, brakeman Erie, res 85 e Market

Freehafer, Elizabeth, res 24 Superior

Freehafer, J J, castrator, res 95 Lindley [Sarah] Franklin E, Howard E

Freel, John, emp fire dept, res same

" Wm, machinist Erie, res 229 e State

" Edward, lab res 229 e State

" Roscoe, butcher W H Tillman, res 44 Cline

" David R, carpenter Erie, res 15 Garfield [Martha E]

" Louis, lab res 40 Whitelock. Ella, Child

" Chas, clk Whitelock & Son, res 40 Whitelock

" Wes, lab res 40 Whitelock

*' " Mrs Hugh (wid Hugh) res e Front

* " Amanda (wid Patrick) res e Front

* " R C, machinist Erie, res e Front

* " Samuel, lab Erie, res e fair ground [Sarah] Bert

* " C F, res e Front

Freeman, William, brakeman Erie, res Windsor hotel

Freinstein, Mrs Elizabeth, carpet weaver, res 129 Oak.   Jos, John, Katie, Clara
" Nicholas, clk S Lippman, res 129 Oak
" Jacob, cow herder, res 129 Oak

French, Bessie (wid Presley B) res 69 Court.   Child

French, Geo, lab res 95 e Tipton [Mary E]   Paul

Frisner, Wm S, fireman Erie, res 65 Canfield [Belle]

Friar, John, student, res 21 Front

Friedman, Miss Thersa, res 98 Byron

Fries, Frank, emp Briant saw mill, res 5 Harris st [Emma]   Leo, Emma

Frost, R F, physician I O O F block, res 84 e State [Margaret] George, Bertha, Fred

Frost, Harry, messenger Western Union Telegraph Co, res 84 e State

Fruit, Miss Louisa, res 89 Guilford

Frutig, Adele, teacher of French, res 113 Guilford

Fry, J C, emp Briant, res 26 Kocher [Malinda M]   Viola B, Elsie

Fry, Jacob, res 109 s Jefferson [Sarah]   Ola

Fryn, Mary, res 179 n Jefferson   .

Fuller, Maurice, emp Erie, res 22 Iowa   [Ellen]
" Clara, domestic 50 Front

Fullerton, Henry H, teamster, res 35 Briant [Macy]   Harry O, Rosa M

Fulton, Jennie (wid Wm) res 77 w State
" Chas R (Fulton & Fulton) res 77 w State

Fulton & Fulton (John F, Chas R) well drillers

Fulton, Sarah (wid James) res 22 Olinger.   Mary, Harry, Carl

Fulton, Robert B, groceries 127 e State, res 125 e State [Mary E] Clara E, Tamson R, Mayme, Willis C

Fulton, John F, postmaster, res 40 w Market [Esther] Herman F
" Mary (wid Geo) res 96 Webster.   Tamson, Sarah

Fulton, Sarah, domestic, res bet Wab tracks and Webster
" Chas, emp lime kilns, res 129 e Sabine [Mary]
" Daniel, emp lime kilns, res 135 e Sabine [Sophrona] George, Jesse
" Arthur, emp Martin lime kilns, res 135 e Sabine
" Clarence, emp Martin lime kilns, res 135 e Sabine
" James, emp Martin lime kilns, res 135 e Sabine
" Miss Louisa, res 40 Frederick
" Miss Catharine S, res 40 Frederick
Furstenberger, Wm, brakeman Erie, res 42 High [Kate] Edward, Arthur, Barnard
Furstenberger, J F, bds 164 e Market
Fussleman, Mary (wid) res 5 Jacob. James, Charles,
" Jerry, fruit tree agent, res 10 Canal st [Jennie] Minnie
B F, lab res 8 Church [Agnes] Don A, Hattie

School Books, Tablets and Pencils at the Opera House Drug Store. A. Frech.

G

Gagen, John, porter Exchange hotel res same
† " Michael, emp lime kilns, res 335 e State [Mary] Jno E, Katie J
† " Martha (wid John) res 24 Brawley. Patrick
* " Thomas, lab res 337 n Jefferson st [Lucy] Frank, Anna, Edward, Simon, Lizzie, Lewis
Gaines, H F, postal clk Wab, res 55 s Jefferson [L M] Walter O
Gallogy, John, agent, res 103 s Jefferson [Mary] John G
Gamble, Shedrick, emp lime kilns, res 23 South. Emma
" Enos, emp Erie coal dock, res 91 Superior st [Florence] Emma
† " Theodore, teamster, res 18 Swan [Maggie] Oliver

Garden, Harry, inspector Erie, res 209 e Market   [Jennie]

Gardner, George, emp Griffith & Son, res 10 Everett

" Chas, emp Newcomb & Co, res 10 Everet

" Hannah (wid John F) res 10 Everett.   John,   Clarence

" Chas L, brakeman Erie, res 172 First   [Jennie] Edward,   Oleva,   Della,   Glenn

" Simon, teamster, res 61 Division   [Flora]   Mildred

* " O A, teamster, res s end Briant   [Eva]   Oliver C

" Richard, city street commissioner, res 23 Purviance [Ida]   Flora,   Mary M,   Walter H

" M C, minister of the gospel, res 24 Purviance street [Mary R]   John M,   Jesse R

Garner, Chas W, brakeman Erie, res 42 Kintz st   [Cora B] Hattie,   Cecil

Garouthe, Sarah E, teacher public schools, res 44 s Jefferson

Garr, Scott, cond Erie, res 195 e State   [Sarah]

Garrett, Marion, compositor Herald, res 165 Guilford

" Ida M (wid Chas) res 165 Guilford.   Anthony,   Florence,   Ruth,   Ben

Garretson, Harry, student, res 54 First

Garretson, W F, traveling salesman, res 18 Henry   [Jennie] Earl F,   Carl A,   Adeline

Gasper, Anthony, emp Erie shops, res 115 Broadway

Gasper, Peter, emp stone quarry, res 115 Broadway   [Catharine]

Gass, H A, clk Lipinski, res 62 Etna ave   [Pearl]

Gates, Henry, emp Erie, res 30 Canfield   [Lillie]   Zella

" Alta, res 23 London

" Wm, lab res 30 Olinger   [Ellen]

Gawne, Willis, butcher, res 30 e Matilda

" Ambrose, butcher L C Strodel, res 30 e Matilda

" George, butcher, res 30 e Matilda

" Mrs (wid Wm) res 30 e Matilda

Gaynor, Margaret (wid Michael) res 154 n Lafontaine

Geedy, Ora, clk Reichenbach & Wickenhiser, res 109 Esther
"   Geo, lab res 109 Esther   [Caroline]
Geerdink, John, emp Erie shops, res 44 n Lafontaine [Lizzie]
Geeting, Oscar, lather res Joe st
"   Joseph M, lather res Joe street   [Mary E]   Flora B.
Della M, Susan L. Owen
† "   Oliver P M, lather res s end Henry   [Rachael]
"   Austin, lather res 15 Everett   [Abbie]
Gehring, Joseph, emp Erie round hs, res 15 Leopold   [Sarah]
Bessie
Geisler, Chas, emp Perrine & Bartlett, bds 31 Mayne
Geller, George, baker, res cor Third and e Market   [Carrie]
Willie
Gelzleichter, Peter, shoemaker, res 143 Poplar
"   John, emp Griffith & Son, res 123 George
Gemmer, Joseph, furniture and undertaking 90 n Jefferson,
res 151 Dimond [Amelia] Amelia
Gemmer, Fred G, emp J Gemmer, res 80 Oak [Carrie] Her-
bert. Gertrude
"   Wm C, eng Erie, res 87 First [Wilhelmina]
"   Henry, emp city, res 112 n Lafontaine st [Louisa]
Hilda, Rudolph
†Gephart, Robert, emp lime kilns, res 339 e State [Mary]
Lewis, Blanche, Myrtle, Dolly
*   "   George, emp lime kilns, res e fair ground [Alice]
Willie, George J, Earl
†   "   Sarah (wid) res 10 Brawley
"   Wm, emp lime kilns, res 137 e State
"   Chas, teamster, res 17 Nile [Mary] Edith B. Ar-
thur, Chas jr, Emma, Clara
†   "   Lewis, lab res 14 Brawley
Gerard, Frank, boiler-mkr Erie, res 54 Whitelock st [Susan]
Eliza, Gertrude, Grace, Anna, Herbert, Eldon
"   Samuel J, boiler-mkr Erie, res 98 Whitelock [Arloa]
"   Richard F, boiler-mkr Erie, res 54 Whitelock
Gerkin, Gesina (wid Harmon) res 35 Canal

Gerlach, Gottleib, emp lime kilns, res 148 e Sabine [Catharine] Amelia, Peter, Barbara, Mary, Maggie
Gerona, Peter, emp S Buchanan, res 71 Division
    "   Leonard, lab res 71 Division [Mary] Lizzie, Tena
Gerstenschlager, John, machinist Erie, res 21 Wilkerson
Gesaman, E Frank, fireman Erie, res 42 s Briant [Nora B] Howard F
Gibbs, Mrs Mary, res 119 e Market
Gibler, John [Huntington Co Bnk) res 183 n Jefferson [Sarah]
    "   Roy, stenographer Erie M M office, res 183 n Jefferson [Cecelia]
    "   Elias, res 248 e State   [D A]
Gibson, Chas S, emp Erie oil hs, res 92 Condit [Abbie]
Gilbert, Jonas H, carpenter, res 39 Fredericka [Mary] Bessie
    "   Joseph E, brakeman Erie, res 87 e State [Lillie]
[Gilchrist, C F, truckman Erie shops, res 7 Swan [Anna M] Helen B, Robert E
†Gilchrist, Fred, res 11 Swan   [Christina]
Gilkey, Minnie, res 121 e State
Gilkey, H D, fireman Erie, res 27 High [Minnie]
Gill, Howard S, emp shoe factory, res 55 Henry
Gill, John S, watchman bicycle factory, res 55 Henry st [Lucinda B] Cora B, Dolly, Laura, Clyde
Gill, Almeda, emp Hoosier laundry, res 55 Henry
Gillispie, Alletta L (wid Wm) res 165 e Market
    "   Ernest A, brakeman Erie, res 165 e Market [Carrie]
    "   William, brakeman Erie, res 165 e Market
Gillis, Wm, emp Erie yds, res 94 Court [Hattie] Pearl, Lee
Giltner, Mattie I, teacher public schools, res 8 Guilford
*Givens, Erastus, emp Perrine & Bartlett, res e Front
Glanton, Herbert O, bill poster, res 96 w Matilda [Laura] Melba
    "   F M B, emp Griffith & Son, res 94 w Matilda [Mary] Harry, Eva
    "   Linnie (wid Hartwell) res 43 e State. Earl, Carl
Glass, Maggie (wid) res 55 Division. Willis, Ruth

LONGDON'S ART GALLERY.

(SUCCESSOR TO RADABAUGH.)

57 North Jefferson Street.

The only Strictly First-Class Studio in Huntington County, Up-To-Date in Every Respect. We have all the Late Novelties, as well as every thing made and known to the picture business. Here is a list of a few kinds and styles we make.

Corbonette Photos in all sizes, Crystaltypes. Platinotypes, Carbon Photos on Celluloid. Porcelain, Ivory or anything else that a Picture can be made on. Button Photos and Pins, Medalions, Combination Groups, Family Groups, Views, Photos on Silk or Linen, Flashlight Photos, Enlarged Portraits in Crayon. Ink, Sepia, Water Colors, Pastel, Aquarelles, Porcelain, etc.

We have not room to name all, but come and see for yourself.

✳ PRICES VERY REASONABLE. ✳

Gleich, Albert, res 75 Polk
"   Lorenna, res 75 Polk
"   Carl, res 75 Polk
"   Ernest, clk A Altstadter, res 73 Polk st [Delia] Gertrude, Eva, Clarence, Etta, Henry
Glenn, John S, secy-treas Herald & News-Express Co, res 122 Guilford [Laura] Robert R, Anna
Glennon, Thos, mgr McCaffrey & Co, res 105 e Franklin
Glick, Edna, res 161 e State
Glick, Alfred J, teamster, res 298 e State   [Mary A]   Edna E, Mary J, May, James
Goble, Chas W, (successor Dunfee & Goble) books, stationery, etc 9 e Market, res 11 e Market [Ella]
Goble, Kelso, artist, res 11 e Market
Golden, T F, loans and insurance over 37 n Jefferson, res 50 Canfield [Anna] Hugh
Goldsmith, Chas, lab res 46 n Lafontaine   [Mary]   Walter
Goodboy, Mary, domestic 51 w Market
Goodyear, Erastus, emp A Crites, res 59 Elm [Mary] Bertha, Lyman, Ora
Gooley, Geo, emp O Hasty, res 73 Clark
"   Henry, lab res 73 Clark
"   Frank, lab res 73 Clark [Louisa W]
"   John, lab res 73 Clark
"   Wm, lab res 67 Elm [Florence] Chas
"   Matt, lab res 117 William [Mary] Hazel, Howard, Henry
Goss, Edward, emp Democrat, res 56 Oak   [Florence]
Gordon, John E, teamster, res 13 Olinger [Caroline]
Gordon, Geo, painter Erie, res 146 e Franklin [Anna] Carl
Goring, John, Wab frt and ticket agt, res 82 w Matilda [Lizzie] Gertrude, John jr
Gorman, Patrick, res 182 n Jefferson
Gould, Chas A, traveling salesman, res 37 superior [Rosamond E]
Gourley, Troy, bridge inspector Erie, res 156 First [Allie] Clemmie

Graeley, Carl, lab res 153 n Lafontaine
- " Maggie, res 51 Oak
- " Mary, housekeeper 124 Oak
- " Frank, emp F Lashing, res 124 Oak
- " Wm, musician, res 124 Oak
- " Frank jr, emp brick yard, res 124 Oak
- " Peter, emp P Holtz, res 124 Oak
- " John, lab res 124 Oak
- " Louis, emp D S Leyman, res 124 Oak

Grafton, Olney, jewelry 47 n Jefferson, res 54 e Washington [Cora L] Edna

Graham, Simon, emp E A Collins, res 59 Henry [Clara M] Florence

Grappy, Fred, brakeman Erie, res 134 e Market

Grass, Chas, machinist Erie, res 144 First
- " Frank, yard clk Erie, res 144 First
- " Joseph B, eng Erie, res 144 First [Susan] Mabel
- " Wm, machinist Erie, res 176 First [Margaret] Earl
- " Geo, fireman Erie, res 178 First [Grace] Arthur

Gray, Harry, eng Erie, res 85 e Market [Sophia] Harvey

Gray, Howard H (Stell & Gray) res 85 Henry [Clara B]

Grayless, F W, fireman Erie, res 34 First [Rozella] Wm A

Grayston, Chas E, eye and ear specialist over 8 e Market, res 36 w Tipton [Jennie] Florence L, Jesse T, Anna L

Grayston, B H B (Drs Grayston) res 139 n Jefferson [Mary] Wallace, Hayden, Mary, Isabella
- " Fred W (Drs Grayston) res 141 n Jefferson
- " F S C (Drs Grayston) res 141 n Jefferson [Isabella]

Grayston, Drs (F S C, B H B, Fred W) over 49 n Jefferson

Greek, Wm, emp Erie shops, res nw cor Matilda and Guilford

Griffith, D M, fireman Erie, res 90 e Market [F Edna]
- " John J, barber S V Kintz, res 110 s Jefferson [Maggie] Ruth H
- " Elmer, emp Newcomb & Co, res 20 Everet [Nancy] Carrie, Carl

Griffith, Chas, lab res 101 Court
  "   Ed L (G V Griffith & Son) res 198 n Jefferson [Ella]
              Randolph, Lyle
  "   G V (G V Griffith & Son) res 161 n Jefferson [Evaline]
Griffith, G V & Son (G V, Ed L) plow handle mfgs, 79 Webster
* "   Joseph, baker, res 297 n Jefferson
*. "   Sarah A (wid John) res 297 n Jefferson. Lota
* "   Frank (Flora & Griffith) res 297 n Jefferson
  "   Chas, clk W H Griffith, res 28 Whitelock st [Rancy]
              Cameron
  "   Clark C, asst city civil eng, res 73 s Jefferson
Griffith, Wm H, groceries 18 s Jefferson, res 73 s Jefferson st
              [Sarahfina M]

Griggs, Frank D, emp shoe factory, res 14 Salamonic [May
              E] Edna A, Helen

Grim, Rose, domestic 83 Poplar
  "   John, emp S Buchanan, res 132 Poplar
  "   Wm L, clk L Levy, res 84 s Jefferson [Grace]
  "   J S, operator Erie, res 77 Etna ave
  "   Roland, clk res 77 Etna ave
  "   Eli P, clk Allman & Bash, res 77 Etna ave [Harriet]
              Mary

Griswold, Adeline, teacher public schools

Gross, Myrtle, domestic 5 Oak
Gross, W E, machinist Erie, res 31 Superior

Grupe, John H, compositor Democrat, res 33 William [Jose-
              phine]
  "   Henry, res 57 Guilford [Mary]
  "   William, printer, res 57 Guilford
  "   Chris, boiler-mkr Erie, res 57 Guilford
  "   Henry L, retail oil dlr 55 Guilford, res 42 w Matilda st
              [Mazie]
Guenther, Fred, clk res 57 Buchanan [Louisa] Carl, Har-
              mon
Guethler, Michael, emp city, res 112 n Lafontaine

Guethler, Geo, confectionery 117 n Jefferson, res 113 n Lafontaine [Anna]

Guhl, Julius sr, emp Griffith & Son, res 105 Bartlett [Fredericka] Anna, Freda, Eva

"   Fred, lab res 105 Bartlett

"   Helmuth, emp Griffith & Son, res 105 Bartlett

"   Chas, painter, res 105 Bartlett

"   Julius jr, emp Griffith & Son, res 105 Bartlett

Guthier, Edward, fireman Erie, res 145 Byron [Kate] Frank, Henry, Clarence, Carl, Walter

Guthrie, Frank, city civil eng, bds Exchange hotel

Guest, Lyman, eng Erie, res 76 Front [Emma] Lulu, Geo, Freeham

Guest, Stanton, machinist Erie, res 76 Front

Gusman, Joseph H, plumber and gas fitter 20 e Market, res 72 s Jefferson [Dora] Gertrude, Maude, Clair

Gusman, Ed, fireman Erie, res 106 First [Anna]

H

†Haag, Henry, night operator Wab, res 15 Catharine st [Isadore] Harold F

Haas, Anna, emp Exchange hotel, res same

*Haas, Joseph, lab res 114 Thomas [Pauline]

Hacker, Chas, emp Erie, res 86 n Lafontaine

Hackett, J H, traveling freight agt Erie, res 160 Guilford st [Nellie] Helen M

Hackney, Josephine (wid Lewis) res 240 n Jefferson

"   Chas A, clk Frash, res 108 Guilford

Hadley, Wm R, res 43 w State st [Mary E] Ora P, Elihu, Chauncey, Cybell, Clarence

Haerly, Henry M, traveling salesman, res 57 s Jefferson street [Ada M]

Haerly, Elizabeth (wid Henry) res 96 Poplar

Hage, Elizabeth (wid) res 94 Frederick

Hagey, Elnora (wid) res 25 Buchanan

Hagois, Edward, lab res 132 Condit [Mary]

Hague, Thomas H, dentist over 95 n Jefferson, res 121 Guilford [Emma] Elizabeth

Haines, L J, eng, res 226 w Matilda st [Francis] Oscar W, Clara B, Chas W, Sadie E, Geo F, Effie D, Leander I,

Hale, Frank, machinist Erie, res 124 First [Nettie] Cora, Leona, Winnie, Ruth
" Mary E (wid S T) res 99 Lincoln ave
" James, eng Erie, res 124 George [Lizzie]

Haley, Edward, blacksmith Erie, res 3 Simon [Sarah] Dorman

Haley, James, "the fisherman" res 158 Guilford [Virginia]

Hall, James, carriage mkr Sid Hall, res 109 Lincoln avenue [Elizabeth]

*Hall, Claude, machinist Erie, res e of fair ground [Dora]

Hall, Sid G, carriage mfg 38-40 Guilford, res 66 Henry [L B]

Halsey, Warren E, carpenter, res 57 Buck [Rosa] Louisa
" Wm, emp Erie shops, res 10 Bechtol [Francis]
" Henry F, emp D First, res 24 Monroe [Ella]

Ham, Alonzo, lab res 30 Front [Francis] Nettie, Allie

Ham, Joseph, lab res 84 Whitelock, Wilbur J

Ham, John (Bailey & Ham) res 84 Whitelock [Belle] Gertrude, Ilo, Gorman

Hamer, W D (Hamer & Wasmuth) res 57 Poplar [Hannah] Mark E, Darwin, Dayton, Russel

Hamer & Wasmuth (W D Hamer, A D Wasmuth) attorneys over 37 n Jefferson

Hamilton, Robert I, Supt public schools, res 53 Poplar street [Kathleen C] Claude McD, Mary E, Robert S, Ralph R

Hamilton, James, cond Erie, res 149 e Market

Hamm, Miss Mae, res 18 Guilford

Hammel, Charles, teamster, res 173 n Jefferson

"   Edward, emp lime kilns, res 8 Grayston ave

"   Jacob, emp lime kilns, res 8 Grayston ave

Hammond, Frank, brakeman Erie, res 149 e Market

"   C W, eng Erie, res 116 e Market [Lou] Wilbur

Hamrick, Davis, drayman, res 72 Frederick [Elvie] Pearl, Eva M

"   Miss Callie (Hamrick & Briant) res 98 Lincoln ave

Hamrick & Briant (Miss Callie Hamrick, Mrs Adelia Briant) dressmakers 98 Lincoln ave

Handwork, Adam, fireman Erie, bds 186 e Market

Harbert, Mrs. Alice S (Harbert & Smith) res 22 Warren

Harbert & Smith (Alice S Harbert, Columbia Smith) dressmakers 22 Warren st

Hardin, Martin, res 124 e State [Sarah]

Hare, Thomas, butcher, res 105 Oak

Hare, Matilda (wid Thos) res 105 Oak

Hare, Frank, lab res 49 Briant [Belle] Chester, Kenneth, Margaret, Marshall

*Harger, Henry H, lab res s end Buck st [Jennie] Katie M, Emmet W, Clarence D, Rudolph F

Hargrove, John, res 97 e Franklin

Hargrove, Kittie, res 97 e Franklin

Harlan, Miles, car repairer Erie, res 137 e Market

"   H S, carpenter, res 80 Grayston ave

Harley, George, caller Erie, res 24 Nile [Mary W] Jennie M

Harlow, Seth, cond Erie, res 34 Wilkerson [Agnes L] Sethcrea, Effie, Mary, Maude

Harlow, Albert, plumber, res 34 Wilkerson

Harn, A C, barber, res 89 n Lafontaine [Maggie] Paul, Ruth

Harring, Ellen (wid Geo W) tailoress, res 210 e Market street. Robert, Ida

Harrigan, John, stone cutter, res 154 n Lafontaine [Lydia] Mary, John, Willie

Harris, Cyrus W, rms over 53 Guilford

Harris, Samuel M (Harris Clothing Co) res 97 e Market

Harris Clothing Co (Samuel Harris, Albert Lowenberg) clothiers 80 n Jefferson

†Harris, Jesse, emp Briant, res 268 e State [Florence]
" Mollie, emp C & E Eating hs, res same
" W G, carpenter, res 43 w State
" Albert, emp Perrine & Bartlett, res 19 Garfield

Hart, Wealthy, res 18 Etna ave

Hart, Wm H (Hart & Hart) res 69 Henry [Etta]

Hart, Elizabeth, teacher, res 69 Henry

Hart, John J (Hart & Hart) res 36 Front [Ted]

Hart & Hart (Wm H, John J) attorneys over 57 n Jefferson

Hart, Milton, carpenter, res 48 High [Maria] Frank, Sam, Aria, Paul

Harter, Edwin, Exchange livery and feed stable 21 w State, res over 19 w State [Lucie M] Helen

Harter, Heber, res over 19 w State
" Jean, music teacher, res over 19 w State
" Lyle, sub teacher public schools, res over 19 w State
" Mrs C W (wid) res over 19 w State
" E G, insurance agent, res 116 Etna ave [Martha J] Augustus, Millie
* " George, res n Guilford [Emma]

Hartman, Kate (wid) res 11 Olinger
" Jacob L, lab res 11 Olinger [Mahala] John
" Belle (wid John) res 11 Gay
" August, emp F W Dorn, res 10 London st [Rosa] (Dessie and Jean Helton)
" J D, emp Wab section, res 57 Division st [Lizzie] Mary, Anna, Herman, Amelia, Amanda, George
" Henrietta, res 105 Poplar
" Mary E, teacher public schools, res 27 Henry

Hartman, Jacob, merchant tailor over 50 n Jefferson, res 27
          Henry [Ellen] Lee R, Ida L, Hattie, Katie,
          Clydie

Hartman, Charles, emp J Hartman, res 27 Henry
     "   Nicholas, lab res 19 London   [Matilda]   Charles,
          Cora, Herbert
     "   Elizabeth, res 101 Cherry

Hartwick, Hattie, domestic 40 w Market

Harvey, Mrs Matilda C, res 100 Etna ave

Haskins, John, emp shoe factory, bds 60 Whitelock

Hasting, Mrs Emma, res 41 Grayston ave. John, Jacob

Hasty, Sarah J, dressmaker, res 223 William
     "   Della W, teacher, res 223 William
     "   Willard, butcher O Hasty, res 223 William

Hasty, Oliver C, meat market 3 Etna ave, res 223 William
          [Anna] Maggie V, Hazel E

Hatfield, James M, attorney over 8 w Market, res 39 Henry st
          [Thursy J]

Hatfield, H D, insurance agt over 8 w Market, res 57 Henry st
          [Effie B]

Hatfield, Albert, caller Erie, res 55 Wilkerson   [Maggie]

Hauenstine, Gottleib, res 79 Oak

Hawker, Thomas, machinist Erie, res 157 First st   [Abbie]
          Lawrence

Hawkins, O E, Huntington Business University, res 46 w Ma-
          tilda st. Edwin

Hawley, D M, (Lime Assn) res 73 e State   [Louisa J] Edgar,
          Mary, Mabel
     "   Miss Mary W, stenographer, res 74 e Market
     "   Hannah (wid) res 50 Jackson
     "   Meribah (wid Samuel) res 74 e Market
     "   Anna, clk J Frash, res 41 s Jefferson
     "   W W (Western Lime Assn) res 213 n Jefferson   [An-
          na] Edith, Frank W

Hawn, Nancy (wid Benj) res 108 Elm

Hawthorne, John, master mechanic Erie, res 112 Guilford st [Francis L]

Hayes, P, carpenter, res 7 Wilkerson [Mary] Flora
" Geo, brakeman Erie, res 24 McFarland [Maggie]
" Christian, res 265 n Jefferson [Katharine] C D
" John, emp G W Shearer, res 265 n Jefferson

Hayes & Helm (Mary E Hayes, Grace T Helm) milliners 13 e Market

Haynes, Mrs Glenn, res 7 Eric

Haynes, Mrs D D (wid Daniel H) res 139 e Market. Maria

Hazzard, Mrs Mary E, res 66 e Washington. Oliver P
" Wm C, emp C W Goble, res 66 e Washington
" Lee R, clk Erie Supt office, res 66 e Washington

Heaston, I H, real estate agt, res 25 William street [Phoebe] Myrtle, Winifred

Heaston, Jacob H (Heaston & Dumbauld) res 233 Etna ave [Emma] Ethel, Edna

Heaston & Dumbauld (Jacob H Heaston, Warren Dumbauld) druggists and book dlrs 47 n Jefferson

Heath, H H, engine inspector Erie, res 54 Briant [Sarah P] Allen F

Heavey, J J, cond Erie, res 73 First [Rosetta] Earl, Ruth

Heckman, Reuben, emp Perrine & Bartlett, bds 84 Sabine

Heeter, Miss Viona, domestic 139 n Jefferson
" Lizzie (wid John) res 78 Esther

Hegner, Joseph H, confectionery and cigars 79 n Jefferson, res 19 Oak [Emma]

Heiney, Enos B, principal central school, res 98 s Jefferson st [Della] Hildreth, Ruth
" B F, res 69 First

Heiss, Simon, carpenter, res 9 Nile [Lou] Wilson, Edna

Helm, W W, stock dlr, res 23 Mayne [Louise]
" Harvey, carpenter, res 28 Warren
" C E, brakeman Erie, res 5 Simon [Louise] Keith
" Floyd, eng Erie, res 9 Wilkerson [Grace] Harry

Helm, Constantine, lab res 79 Elm   [Sarah A]   Etta G,   So-
       phrona L,   Clinton L,   Charles M,   Opal M
   "   Wm I, clk T VanAntwerp, res 79 Elm
   "   John, lab res 17 e Tipton

Helser, Mary, res 58 E Market

Helser, D H, bicycle repair shop 15 e Washington, res 95 Oak
       [Caroline]   Anna,   Fred

*Helton, Edith, res n Guilford

Henderson, Howard, traveling salesman shoe factory, res 72
       Henry   [Clara L]   Lottie M,   LeRoy S,   Don W,
       Guy C

Hendricks, Augustus, traveling salesman, res 93 n Lafontaine
   "   Chas, printer, res 93 Lafontaine
   "   George, cigar mkr, res 93 n Lafontaine
   "   Christian, wagon-mkr w Washington, res 93 n La-
       fontaine   [Anna M]   Lizzie,   Laura,   Clara
† "   Levi, carpenter Erie, res e Catharine st   [Rebecca]
       Milo

Henley, Almeda, res 46 e Washington

*Henline, John, emp W A Berry, res n Guilford

Henline, Geo, emp Hoag livery, res 95 Railroad st   [Susan]
       Pearl,   Zella

Henline, Jacob, lab Erie, res 21 Edwin st   [Sidney E]   Della,
       Stella

Henry, John, res 3 Foust   [Elizabeth J]
   "   Mrs Ida M, res 3 Foust   (Pearl Stults)
   "   Frank, asst foreman car dept Erie, res 222 e Market st
       [Sallie]   Ray,   Clarence
   "   Samuel, bds cor e Market and Byron
   "   Daniel, fireman Erie, res 162 e Franklin
   "   John R (Turner & Henry) res 29 London   [Elizabeth]

Henshaw, Effie, res 14 w Matilda

Hentzell, Wm, emp Erie, res 37 Poplar   [Mary]   James W,
       Mary E

Herald & News-Express Co (C E Briant, pres; John S Glenn, secy-treas; Thad Butler, managing editor) publishers Herald, daily, weekly and mid-weekly, 23 w State street

Herberg, Emily, res 93 Cherry
" Geo, prop City Bottling wrks, res 2 Harrison ave
" Frank, emp City Bottling wrks, res 5 Marshall
" Amelia, res 5 Marshall
" Joseph, driver City Bottling wrks, res 5 Marshall
" Adam, emp City Bottling wrks, res 5 Marshall st [Anna E]

Herndon, Anthony, res 32 Wagoner. Selma, Curtis, Otis, Hazel, Beauna

Herneise, James B (Koch & Herneise) res 74 Whitelock [Elizabeth] Bertha, William, Retta, Arthur, Hugh

Herr, Patrick, cond Erie, res 50 Second [Addie] Mamie

Herran, Levi, carpenter Erie, res cor Erie and Sabine [Elizabeth] Earl, Kenneth
" Chas A, emp Erie shops, res 16 Taylor [Elizabeth] Arthur, Darel

Herzog, Andrew, well driller, res 49 Buck st [Tracey] Otto, Noah, Jacob, Anna, Christena, Tracey, Mary, Herman
" Wm, carpenter, res 128 Elm [E] Chas, Daniel
" Mary, domestic 193 n Jefferson
" John, lab res e Everett [Samantha]

Hessin, J H, mgr United Telephone Co, res 65 Cherry [Agnes] Nellie
" Henry, res 63 Poplar [Sarah]
" Effie, music teacher, res 157 n Jefferson
" Wm H, bookpr B F Nichols, res 157 n Jefferson street [Rebecca H]

Hesting, Nicholas, lab res 31 w Matilda [Mary] Rosa

Heubner, Frank, lab res 59 German
" Fred, emp Griffith & Son, res 59 German [Mollie] Minnie, Clara
" Wm, baker A Crites, res 59 German

Heubner, Fred jr, emp Griffith & Son, res 59 German

Heuser, Rev J H, D D, pastor SS Peter and Paul Catholic church, res 93 Cherry

Hewitt, E G, hardware 91 n Jefferson, res 93 Guilford [Josephine]

Hewitt, Grace G, teacher public schools

Hiatt, Carrie, res 57 s Jefferson

Hibbard, Elinor, res 11 e Market

Hibbert, William, hostler S P Stults, res 65 e Washington st [Leeta] Fern, Vaughn

Hicks, J M, physician over 62 n Jefferson, res 54 Guilford st [Zella]

Hicks, Amelia (wid) res 56 Frederick

Hier, Mat, emp C & E Eating house, res same

Hier, Wm, emp Griffith & Son, res 11 Grayston ave [Olivia] Lester, Jessie

Hier, Frank D, emp Briant, res 255 e State [Addie] Zelma, Ruby

Highland, Geo, res 19 s Briant. Hazel

Highlands, Matthew, blacksmith 26 Cherry, res over same. Ida, Belle, Eva

Highlands, Chas, blacksmith M Highland, res over 26 Cherry.

Hildebrand, John, clk J Frash, res 19 Purviance st [Nancy] Dottie, Grace

"   I N, lab res 171 Etna ave [Lyndia] Leland, Algernon, Robert, Ruth

* "   Martin, emp Erie shops, res 2 mile n of city [L]

* "   G W, huckster, res s end Etna ave [Clara] Winifred, Mabel, Everet, Mildred, Howard

* "   W W, mail carrier, res 2 mile n of city [Nannie] Helen, Clellah

*Hildrath, Ed L, emp Withington fac, res e Front

Hilgenberg, Henry, merchant tailor 19 w Market, res 81 w Tipton st [Anna] May

Hilgenberg, Elizabeth, tailoress, res 81 Tipton

"   Mollie, stenographer City Clerk's office, res 81 w Tipton

Hill, G Wesley, hostler Brown livery, res over 32 Cherry

Hill, Edward, machinist Erie, res 118 e Market

Hill, Maude, res 118 e Market

Hilling, Mrs Ada, music teacher, res 7 Elm. Hayden

Hilyard, Frank, brakeman Erie, res 9 Mayne [Alice]

Hine, Mary (wid Geo) res 13 Wilkerson st. Calla, Edward, Zetta, Marie

Hines, James, ex-cond Erie, res 149 e Market

Hippensteel, John, lab res 147 Byron [Ollie] Ernest

*Hire, L Frank, lab res s end Briant st [Mary J] Jacob E, Jonas O, Charles S

Hitzfield, Mrs Cordelia, res 210 w Matilda

    " George, farmer, res 210 w Matilda [Tillie] Bertha

    " David, carpenter, res 19 Simon Rosa Tillie Geo Louis Etta

Hively, Albert, lab Erie, res 53 e Sabine [Dora] John, Wilson

Hoag, A L, livery barn 16 Warren, res 91 e State [Lochey] Augustus

Hoban, A T, brakeman Erie, res 45 Grayston Ave [Louise P] Lena, Loella

Hockensmith, Henry, lab, res 19 McFarland [Anna] (Percy Sheer)

Hockman, Rev M H, pastor English Lutheran Church, res 19 Foust [Henrietta]

Hofman, Henry, emp shoe factory, res 35 Elm [Edna] Geo Edward, Earl

Hoffman, Anna M, (wid Charles,) res 86 e Franklin Minnie, Lulu

    " Chas, fireman Erie, res 73 Webster [Mary] Albert, Howard

    " James, eng Erie, res 115 Lincoln Ave [Angeline]

Hohe, Jacob, tailor, res 47 Oak

    " Rosena, res 47 Oak

    " Lizzie, (wid John) res 35 German John Louise

Hoke, Lincoln, carpenter, res 151 Byron [Harty L] Chloe
        G, Homer D, Carl, Burl
"   Quinter, contractor, res 133 First [Mrs Q]
Holbrook, Charles, pattern maker Erie shops, res 62 w Tipton
        [Elizabeth] Carl, Frank, Henrietta, Magdalena
Holden, J G, cond Erie, res 165 E Franklin [Clara] Clair E
Holland, Richard, foreman interlocking switch, res Windsor
        Hotel
"   George H, fireman Erie, res 16 Salamonic Ave [Lil-
        lie] Arthur, Nettie
*Hollett, John A., fruit tree agent, res so end Etna [Elma]
        J Bert, Orpha D, Cora E, Opal H, Oliver P,
        Child not named
"   J H, fruit tree agent, res 92 Frederick [Celia A]
        Samuel, Rudolph Fay
*Holley, Jacob, carpenter, res n Guilford [Mary] Mary
* " Clifford, res n Guilford
"   Marion, emp Briant, res 17 Kocher [Emma] Ora,
        Goldie, Floyd
"   William, res 49 South
Hollinger, B W, emp Erie, res 170 First [Ella] Rex
Holm, D D, clk Kitch & Daniels, res 114 n Lafontaine [Sarah]
        Edwin
" Otis, res 114 n Lafontaine
" Frank, painter, res 114 n Lafontaine
Holmes, F C, attorney, res 8 w Matilda [Lelia]
"   Mary, stenographer roadmaster's office, res 43 Leo-
        pold
"   Mrs S, (wid Robert,) res 132 e Market Cora
"   John C, eng Erie, res 43 Leopold [L R] Martha,
        Cora E
Holloway, Viola B, clerk master mechanic's office Erie, res 117
        e Franklin
Holloway, A R, time keeper Erie, res 117 e Franklin
Holloway, Cephas, res 117 e Franklin [Ethelinda R]

Holtz, Jacob R, teamster, res 14 Wilkerson [Catharine] Frederick, Anna, Clara, Edward
" Peter, teamster, res 88 Cherry [Mollie C] Carl J, Albert A
Hook, Jennie, (wid Benj F,) res 37 Polk Everet E
Hooker, Chas E, carpenter Erie, res 90 s Jefferson [Catharine] Maude, Edith, Laura, Leslie
Hoon, C A, fireman Erie, res 39 Superior
* " M W, blacksmith, res east of fair ground [Lou] Von E, Everet
*Hoone, Ernest L, res n Guilford
Hoover, A J, boiler helper Erie, res 13 e Sabine [Cora E]
" Samuel, res 13 e Sabine [Emma]
" Charles, carpenter, res 11 Allen
" David, carpenter, res 11 Allen [Lydia] Bertha, Melvin
" Hannah, (wid David) res 30 Whitelock Berta E, Gertrude
" George, house mover, res 26 Purviance [Alice] Frank, Mattie, Minnie, Lloyd, Edward, Georgie
" James, butcher, res 55 Elm [Sarah] Ora, Brotha
" G W, brakeman, Erie, res 52 First
" John, res 99 Oak
" Eph, blacksmith, res 99 Oak
" R L, clk John Clayton, res 125 Etna ave [Laura] Fordyce
" Mary A, (wid) res 44 Indiana Ora
Hopwood, Thomas, machinist, Erie, res 5 Sabine [Anna]
Horn, John, fireman, Erie, res 139 Court [Amanda] Lawrence, Jessie
" Emma Miss, res 124 e Market
" George, carpenter, res 124 e Market [Anna]
Horrel, Amanda, (wid John) res 24 Fruit Esther
Horrell, J L, deputy co recorder, res 39 Marshall [Mary E] Chas H, Mamie G, Maude, John, Robert
Horseman, Frank, lab, res 127 Elm [Lucinda] Blanche, Pearl

Hosler, James, barber, res 112 First　[Daisy]　Kenneth

Hosler, Frank, emp Erie, res 39 Grayston ave [Ada]　Lovetta

"　　Aaron, carpenter Erie, res 49 Grayston ave　[Ida]
　　　Mearl,　Roy,　Eldon

†　"　　J, emp Erie shops, res 35 Swan　　[Mary A]　Emery,
　　　Willie

"　　Simon, blacksmith Erie, res 143 Court [Mary]　Alfred

"　　Miss Rella, res 46 e Market

Houck, C F, fireman Erie, res 142 e Franklin　[Emma]　Helen

Hough, Mary, res 43 Leopold

Houghton, Anna Z, teacher public schools, res 36 Henry

Householder, Geo, tower tender Erie, res 16 e Sabine [Agnes]

*　　"　　James E, lab res e of s Etna ave　[Caroline]
　　　Bertha A

*　　"　　John J, lab res e of s Etna ave

"　　John W, fish dlr, res 182 Etna ave [Jennie] Iva,
　　　May

*Housman, Cora E, dressmaker, res s Etna ave

*　　"　　Minnie W, emp shoe factory, res s Etna ave

*　　"　　Maggie F, res s Etna ave

*　　"　　C L, gardener, res s Etna ave　[Sarah J]

Houser, Caroline D (wid) res cor First and Sabine.　Mary,
　　　Celia,　Anna,　John

"　　Mrs Adda, res 107 s Jefferson,　Glenn

"　　D S, plasterer, res 61 Division　[Hattie]　Merl,　De-
　　　Loss,　Marie

Hover, B G, ticket and frt agt Erie, res 71 Poplar　[Naomi]

Howard, John, switchman Erie, res 86 Wilkerson　[Ollie]
　　　Olive

Howell, Enos, emp Erie, res 187 William

Howell, Sarah (wid Wm) res 187 William

Howett, John, medicine merchant, res 39 Briant　[Jane]

Howett, Chas W, lab res 39 Briant

Howrand, Wm, emp C Lang, res 174 Cherry

Hubbell, Rosamond (wid A A) res 19 Frederick

Hubbell, Alida, prop P O news stand, res 19 Frederick

Hoosier Steam Laundry (John Wisner, prop) 13 Frederick

Hubric, John, emp lime kilns, res 143 e Sabine [Mary]

Hudnall, W C, mgr Board of Trade, res 61 Henry [Corrine] Willie

Huffman, Fred, shoemaker Neuer & Eisenhauer. res 61 e Market

" Martha (wid John W) res 17 Fredericka

Hughes, John, lab res 94 Byron st [Mary] Clara, Bessie, Bertha, Howard, Cyrus, Roy, Donald

" Mrs Minnie, res 4 Whitestine

" Ora, cooper, res 137 e Sabine

Hull, Miss Martha, domestic 137 Guilford

Hullinger, J C, brakeman Erie, res 22 Canfield [Jennie] Wilbur, Violet

Humbert, Geo W, res 62 e Market [Martha]

" Geo sr, res 62 e Market

" Geo jr, res 62 e Market

" Robert, res 62 e Market

" Edward, clk Erie M M office, res 235 e State

" Chas, car repairer Erie, res 50 Leopold st [Alice] Bertha, Lena, Emanuel, Paul

Hummell, Chas, teamster, res 108 e Washington st [Anna] Ethel, Claude

Humphrey, John, merchant police, res 64 w Matilda

Hunt, Col Cornelius (col'd) res over 26 Front

Huntington Business University (O E Hawkins, pres) Roche block, over 116-118-120 n Jefferson st

Huntington County Bank (J W Ford, pres; E B Ayres, vice-pres; H L Emley, cashier) 61 n Jefferson

Huntington Light and Fuel Co (Geo J Bippus, pres; Frank B Townsend, supt) 10-12 w Franklin

Huntington Mill Co (I N Arnold, pres) 2 s Jefferson

Huntington Opera House (H E Rosebrough, mgr) e Market st

Hurd & Smith (Arthur Hurd, K Smith) clothiers 35 n Jefferson

Hurd, Arthur (Hurd & Smith) res 61 e Franklin [Nettie]

Hurdle, J W, lab res 164 n Lafontaine [Dora]

Hurley, R E, jeweler, res 148 Court
Hurley, Mrs Anna, res 148 Court
Huselman, Flora, domestic 140 Etna ave
Hutchison, Jesse, brakeman Erie, res 37 Elizabeth [Cora]
          Harry, Lee, Mabel
Hutsell, Francis E, teacher public schools, res 167 n Jefferson
Huyette, Arthur R, teacher, res 121 Byron
Huyette, Juniata, teacher public schools, res 121 Byron
Hyde, A W, carpenter Erie, res 52 Harris st   [Jennie]   Eliza,
          Edna, Burl, Maude

I

Immell, Chas H, bookpr Democrat, res 22 Salamonie avenue
          [Mary]
Immell, Harmon P, pressman Democrat, res 22 Salamonie ave
Immell, Mrs C H, millinery over 54 n Jefferson
*Ingham, Inez, res s end Henry
Inskip, Fred, brakeman Erie, bds 139 e Market
Ireland, Thomas, carpenter Erie, res 101 e Franklin [Martha]
Ireland, Almond D, driver Wells Fargo Express Co, res 44
          Marshall [Ella] Ray, Stanley, Leslie
Ireland, Tessie, emp Hoosier laundry, res 16 Allen
Isenberg, W M, emp Briant, res 11 Kintz   [Della]
†Isenberg, Joshua, lab res 16 w Catharine   [Mrs J]   Harvey,
          Emma
Isenberg, Clifford, emp Briant, res cor Elm and London sts
          [Cora] Grace, Gladys, Carl
Irick, Archie R, lab res 164 n Guilford

J

Jackman, Lyman H (Jackman & Son) res 7 w Market [Sarah]

Jackman, Clifford (Jackman & Son) res 7 w Market

Jackman, L H & Son (L H, Clifford) restaurant 7 w Market

Jackson, S W, architect, res 34 Byron [Florence J] Lawrence M

" W A, boiler-mkr Erie, res 90 e Washington [Nina]

" James, retired, res 207 William [Louisa]

" Frank, fireman Erie, res 68 Superior st [Sarah L] Bertha, Anna, Ira, Lulu

" C R, blacksmith Erie, res 61 Etna ave [Daisy] Donald

" Frank M, blacksmith Erie, res 61 Etna ave [Sarah] Bessie, Beatrice, Hazel

" Anna, emp C & E eating house, res same

Jacobs, Miss Sarah, domestic county jail, res same

* " M V B, drayman, res e Front [Charlotte]

" John A, lab res 36 Halstead [Anna] Clarence, Donnalulu

* " Mary, domestic, res w of Buck st

* " Samuel, lab res w of Buck

* " Charles, lab res w of Buck

* " George, lab res w of Buck

* " Peter, lab res w of Buck

* " Henry, lab res w of Buck [Louisa] Harmon

" Amos, butcher N Windemuth, res 71 William [Ida] Albert, Wilbur, Eva

Jacobs, W T, saloon 26 n Jefferson, res 78 Clark st [Matilda] Fay, Ora, Iva

James, Chas, machinist Erie, res 3 Wilkerson [Lillie M] Walter S, Lucie I

" Georgiana (wid Harry H) dressmaker, res 48 w Market. Claude M

† " Daniel, emp Perrine & Bartlett, res 22 Swan [Kate]

Jamison, Wm, brakeman Erie, res 70 Superior [Ella] Le-
    Roy, Stella, Dean, Virgil

Janesmith, Mrs A (wid A) res 251 e State

Jarvis, John, lab res 26 Nebraska [Elsie] Mabel, Rose,
    Ethel, Earl

  " ·   Wm, emp Perrine & Bartlett, res 77 s Jefferson [Ruth]
    Ethel

* "   Welmuth, teamster, res s Jefferson

* "   Emery, teamster, res s Jefferson [Mary] Myrtle A,
    Hazel G, Mary A, Elsie

Jeffrey, R O, lab res 69 Court [Amanda]

  "   Mary, housekeeper over 20 s Jefferson. Lizzie

John, Adna, clk co treasurer's office, res 60 Etna ave

  "   Frank, dpty co treasurer, res 60 Etna ave

  "   Jacob W, co treasurer, res 60 Etna ave [Ruhannah]
    (Fay Richards)

  "   J B (Wm John & Son) res 7 Monroe [Leona] Donald,
    Marie

  "   William (Wm John & Son) justice of the peace, res 81
    William [Sally]

John, Wm & Son (Wm, J B) pianos, organs, musical instru-
    ments, bicycles, sewing machines, etc, 17 w State

Johnson, W W, ex-cond Erie, res 161 First [Sadie] Vernie,
    Carrie

Johnson, John F, insurance agent over 58 n Jefferson, res 54
    Marshall [Emily] LeRoy

Johnson, James E, lab res 26 Randolph [Catharine]

* "   Wm, emp Perrine & Bartlett, res e Front [Rena]
    Meryl, Clara, Mamie

  "   Margaret, res 123 Oak

  "   Ervin, brakeman Erie, res 5 Grayston ave [Julia]
    Carrie, Virgie

  "   J H, cond Erie, res 96 Lincoln ave [Desta] Ray

  "   F C, emp Wab transfer hs, res 10 Wilkerson [Anna]
    Clifford

Johnson, Gustave F, emp Briant, res 102 Grayston ave [Eulalie] Lemhurst W

" John E, meat market 15 e Market, res Edna st [Carrie] Lillian

" Elmer J, lab res Edna st [Christena] Ethel M, Frank, Ferd

" A G, contractor, res 36 Bingham [Emma] Walter, Floyd

" S T, cond Erie, res 25 Faust [Rena] Earl, Dale

" Augustus, clk O C Morgan, res 3 High [Minerva]

" J H, emp Standard Oil Co, res 39 Whitelock [S A] Chloa M, Amanda, Virgil F

" Henry C, saloon 12 Front, res 3 Edna st [Sarah A] Emma J, Albert F, Mabel R

Robert, saloon 12 Front, res 30 Milligan [Kate] Bessie

" Mary A (wid Robt H) grocery 177 Etna ave, res 175 Etna ave, Edward M, Francis

" F M, lab res 5 n Briant [Sarah]

Jones, G F, lab res 54 First

" J H, fireman Erie, res 60 Front [Barbara G]

" Harry, lab, res 133 n Lafontaine

" Caroline M (wid G W) res 133 n Lafontaine. Clyde

" D I, train despatcher Erie, res 42 e Franklin [M] Marie

" W A, traveling salesman, res 44 Briant [Mary F] Fred L, Richard, Bessie L, Pearl H, Grover C, Isabella F, Paul E

" W R, clk C C Nave, res 37 Milligan [Margaret S]

* " Robert, lab res s Etna ave [Nettie] Willie

" S J, brakeman Erie, res 40 Webster [Ella] Harry, Roy

" Edith L, authoress, res over 5 Etna ave

" Rev Allen A, res over 5 Etna ave [Lydia A] A Olive, Matthew M, Allen A jr, Paul F

Jones, Wm A, emp Erie, res 12 Taylor
"   Chas F, teamster, res 12 Taylor
"   Samuel W, lab res 12 Taylor [Minerva]
Jordan, Chas, brakeman Erie, res 116 e Franklin [Mary] Marie A
Jordan, W E, operator Erie, res 116 e Franklin
Jordan, Mary (wid Martin) res 116 e Franklin

K

Kacy, William, cond Erie, res 143 First [Augusta] Paul D, Roy J, Nellie, Kathleen
Kaiser, Rev W J, pastor St Peter's German Evangelical Lutheran Church, res 79 Lafontaine [Minerva E] Marichen S, William F, John C, Paul M, Magdalena, Hugo
"   Sebastian, carpenter Erie, res 14 Canal
Kalb, Samuel, gas inspector H L & F Co, res 52 First [Laura] Pearl, Blanche, Grace, May, Jean
"   Miss Ida, waitress Star restaurant, res same
Kalenbeck, Gertie, res 99 Dimond
"   John, lab, res 99 Dimond
"   Fred, farmer, res 99 Dimond
"   Charles, res 99 Dimond
Karns, James F, cond Erie, res 144 Court [Mary E]
Kassinger, Charles, emp Erie shops, res 80 e Sabine [Rosa]
Kase, Henry Sr, emp Erie shops, res 48 Buchanan [Minnie] Paul, Minnie, Sophia, Anna, Marie
"   Henry, stationary engineer, res 48 Buchanan
"   Charles, clerk Reichenbach & Wickenhiser, res 48 Buchanan

Kase, William J, painter Erie, res 48 Buchanan
" George H, student. res 48 Buchanan
" Peter, machinist Erie, res 63 Dimond [Myrtle] Herbert
" William, blacksmith Erie, res 43 Polk [Fredericka]
    Edward W, Martha Lydia A
" William Sr, carpenter, res 30 Buchanan
" John, barber, emp Bonebrake & Bonbrake, res 106 w
    Matilda [Mrs J] Bessie
" Wilhelmina (wid John) res 4 Church Mary, Anna
" Leonhart, clerk, res 4 Church
Kastner, Joseph, galvanizer Erie, res 101 Broadway [Cath-]
    arine] Loretta
Kaufman, R A, attorney over 24 e Market, res 239 n Jefferson
    [Anna] Marie (Mamie and Eldridge Kinkade)
Kaylor, Milo, druggist opera house drug store, res 52 Marshall
    [Harriett]
" C P, switchman Erie, res 60 e State [Louise]
" Israel, carpenter, res 106 Lincoln ave, [Margaret]
    Jennie
Keating, Lydia M, (wid J B,) res 36 Henry
" Truman M, res 36 Henry
Keefe, Daniel, brick and stone mason, res 80 Grayston ave,
    [Mary] Mamie, Otto, Iva, Maude, Henry
" William, emp Griffith & Son, res 80 Grayston ave
" Michael, line rep Erie, res 6 Leopold [Ellen] Mary
    E, Thos, Francis, Geo W
Keefer, John H, eng Griffith & Son, res 20 London Earl
" Hattie, (wid) res 19 Salamonie ave Louis
" Sarah, domestic 22 Salamonie ave
" Boyd, lab res 121 e Franklin
" Henry, (Fisher, Keefer & Bailey,) res 58 Whitelock
    Mary, Lizzie, Ida
" Frank, emp Fisher, Keefer & Bailey, res 58 Whitelock
" Andrew, emp Fisher, Keefer & Bailey, res 58 Whitelock
* " W F, stationary eng, res e Front
* " J W, farmer, res e Front, [Lowina]

Keefer, Emma, (wid Perry) res 4 Whitestine
" E E, insurance agent, res 37 Marshall [Martha E] Ilo B
" Hannah, (wid George K) res 121 e Franklin
" Charles F, teamster, res 121 e Franklin [Rosa]
" Anna, domestic, 63 Cherry
*Kessler, Harry, car repairer Erie, res e of fair ground [Sarah J] Mervin, Irene, Anna, Lucy R
Kehler, Geo W, eng Erie, res 4 Jacob [Alferetta] Hadassa, Cary, Anna, Frank, Dow, Georgie
Kehler, Guy, machinist Erie, res 4 Jacob
Keiser, Chas, teamster, res 22 Randolph
" John F, watchman Fist National Bank, res 22 Randolph [Mrs J F] Gertrude, Blanche, Fred, Bessie
† " Oscar L, lab res Salamonie ave [Alfaretta] Earl L, Orvilla, Freda
" Ruth, student, res 65 Division
Kelley, W S, eng Erie, res 35 Poplar [Mattie] (Inez Bodiker)
Keller, Samuel, lab res 112 Grayston ave [Dorothy] Pearl, Vernie
Keller, Cash, eng Erie, res 111 Lincoln ave [Catharine] Lloyd
†Keller, Henry, stone mason, res Wright st [Rosa E]
Kelsey, Edgar E, attorney and insurance agt over 33 n Jefferson, res 8 Salamonie ave [Francis] Alice B, Knowlton H
Kelso, Noble, brick mason, res 119 e State [Lizzie] Glenn
Kells, Ross, machinist Erie, res 58 e Franklin
Kendrick, Rev H C, pastor First Christian church, res 137 e Franklin [Carrie] Harold H, Lewis E
Kennedy, John A, carpenter, res 215 e Market [Maranda J] Dessie L
" Benjamin, boiler-mkr Erie, res 215 e Market
" James, watchman Briant, bds 136 Briant
" Samuel, teamster Collins Ice Cream Co, res 118 Clark [Ella] Mabel

Kennedy, James, foreman round house, res 39 Leopold [Sarah A,] Guy R, Homer D
" Charles, emp Briant, res 29 e Tipton

Kenner, James B, (Kenner & Lesh,) res 29 Henry [Minerva C,] Sumner, Bertha, Mabel

Kenner & Lesh, (J B Kenner, U S Lesh,) attorneys over First National Bank

Kenner, Prudence, stenographer Kenner & Lesh, res 29 Henry
" George W, res 83 Whitelock [Hattie] Gresham W, Edith M, Emerson
" W H, stock buyer, res 9 High [Anna]

Kenner & Calvert, (M A Kenner, O W Calvert,) feed store, 26 Warren

Kenner, M A, (Kenner & Calvert,) res 9 High

Kenower, A Q, undertaker and furniture dealer, 93 n Jefferson, res 19 w Matilda [Anna] Sarah A

Kenower, Willis E, bookpr A Q Kenower, res 75 w Matilda [Belle,] Jean
" Sanford K, machinist Erie, res 19 w Matilda
" Herbert, clerk A Q Kenower, res 19 w Matilda
" Charles Edgar, clerk A Q Kenower, res 19 w Matilda
" J W, clerk A Q Kenower, res 29 n Lafontaine Nora, Sadie

Kenower, John & Sons, (John, John P, Wm W,) planing mill and lumber yard, 41 Cherry

Kenower, John, (Kenower & Sons,) res 26 w Matilda [Sarah E,] Clara I
" William W, (Kenower & Sons,) res 26 w Matilda
" John P, (Kenower & Sons,) res 45 w Matilda [Letitia B] Mary L, Josephine

Kenyon, M G, machinist Erie, res 53 Marshall [May] Fern, Harley

Kirchoff, Anna, res 18 Bingham
" Edward, lab res 18 Bingham

Kern, Dora, res 66 w Tipton

Kerns, Michael, lab res 47 Walnut

Kessler, Herman, blacksmith Erie, res 24 Superior

Kettering, Wm, lab res 154 n Lafontaine [Clara] Frank
      "   Adam, res 18 Bingham [Elizabeth]

Keyes, J E, tonsorial parlor cor Market and Third, res 12 Railroad [Celestia]

Kilander, Lulu, clk Economy, res 63 William
      "   Cora, clk Purviance & Provines, res 63 William
      "   Hezekiah, res 63 William [Mary A] Dessie
      "   George, mail carrier, res 87 Clark
      "   Samuel, res 87 Clark

Killerman, George, barber, res 37 Condit [Taney]

Kindig, J H, bicycle repair shop 40 e Market, res 19 Charles st
      [Ella M] Laura F

Kindler, Andrew, boots and shoes 57 n Jefferson, res 153 Cherry [Lou] Chas, Henry

Kindler, Frank, clk A Kindler, res 123 Cherry [Mary] Therisa, Frank, Jacob

Kindler, John, harness and carriage dlr 89 n Jefferson, res
      105 Poplar [Elizabeth] Herman, Lizzie, Chas

Kindler, Geo, clk A Kindler, res 105 Poplar
      "   Andrew, clk John Kindler, res 105 Poplar
      "   Nicholas, clk, res 105 Poplar
      "   Joseph, contractor, res 79 Poplar [Maggie] Cecelia, Mary
      "   George, barber, res 79 Poplar
      "   John W, lab res 79 Poplar
      "   George, saddler J Kindler, res 86 Poplar [Barbara]
      Eddie, Kate, Julius, Albert, Leo

King, E M, cond Erie, res 174 First [Martha L] Neil F, Arthur M, Theron G

King, George W, cigars and confectionery 29 s Jefferson, res
      108 s Jefferson [Margaret M] Loretta J, Mary M, Frank L, Leo G, Lucy E

King, Anna R, clk G W King, res 108 s Jefferson

King, **Frank M**, meat market 15 s Jefferson, res 54 Elm street
[Xantha]

King, Emmett, clk F M King, res 54 Elm

" Loy, car inspector Erie, res 65 Mayne [Sarah] Orlan,
Blanche

King, **Otto**, dentist over 22 s Jefferson, res 54 Elm

Kintz, Thos J, horse trainer, res 74 Frederick [Jane]

" John A W, real estate, res 20 w Matilda [Margaret]

" S V, barber shop 5 Frederick, res over 15 s Jefferson
[Martha]

*Kiracofe, C H, prof U B college, res Stults Pike [Anvilla]
Charles H, Alvin R

Kirk, **C C**, prop C & E Eating House, res same [Phoebe]
Calvert, Jean

Kiser, Ira, emp Erie, res 249 e State [Minnie] Ray

" James, janitor library building, res 128 n Lafontaine
[Tillie] Earl, Hazel, Ralph, Arthur

" Jacob, lab res 118 George [Lou] Lizzie

Kissinger, Chas, emp Briant, res 67 e Sabine

" John, bridge gang Erie, res 67 e Sabine [Malissa]
Ola, Emma, Milton, Hattie, Iva, Gustie,
Rolla, Ambrose, Netha

*Kitch, Daniel, farmer, res n Guilford [Nancy]

Kitch, John G (Kitch & Daniels) res 123 Guilford [Maggie]
Jessie, Chester

Kitch & **Daniels** (J G Kitch, T E Daniels) groceries 95 n Jefferson

†Kitch, Anna, emp shoe factory, res s Salamonie ave

*Kitt, J M, lab res s Etna ave

Kitt, Sylvanus, drayman, res 60 Whitelock [Francis]

Kitt, J Milton, mail carrier, res 30 Whitelock

Kitt, Obediah, carpenter, res 50 Frederick [Saloma] Thur-
low M, Homer L, Amy B

Klein, James H, chief train despatcher Erie, res 134 Guilford
[Francis] Bessie, Lucile

Klein, Lou, operator Erie, res 134 Guilford
"   Herman, train despatcher Erie, res 134 Guilford
Klemm, Wendell, shoemaker 115 n Jefferson, res 153 n Lafon-
            taine
"   Lizzie (wid Wendell) res 153 n Lafontaine
"   Geo, lab res 81 Grayston ave   [Susan E]   Earl W
†Kline, Amos, emp Perrine & Bartlett, res s Salamonie ave
            [Mary A]   Grace, Marie
"   Thomas, emp Erie round hs, res Canfield st   [Melissa
            J]   Edith, Chester, Edna
"   John, foreman Nichols fac, res 155 Guilford   [Aman-
            da]   Dora, Henry, Fred, Ethel
"   Wm, emp Griffith & Son, res 3 Lee   Russell,   Earl
"   Henry, res 3 Briant
"   Henry, lab res 47 Buchanan [Mary]   Anna,   Isa-
            bella,   John,   Estella M
"   Hattie, teacher public schools, res 225 n Jefferson
"   Peter, res 28 Madison   [Elizabeth]
Kloth, Almira (wid C) res 46 Mayne
Klumpp, John, lab res 100 Dimond   [Emma]   Viola
"   Chas, emp Erie shops, res 123 w Tipton   [Anna]
"   Mary (wid Joseph) res 102 w Matilda
"   Albert, machinist Erie, res 102 w Matilda
"   August, storekeeper Erie, res 54 German   [Mary]
            Blanche, August, George
"   Joseph, painter, res 32 German   [Carrie]   Marie
Knapp, L J, machinist Erie, res 163 Guilford   [Edith A]
Knight, Chas, tinner Erie, res 85 n Lafontaine   [Cecelia]
            Anna E,   Mary A,   Gertrude,   Wallace M,   Gor-
            don Y
"   Chas E jr, tinner Erie, res 85 n Lafontaine
"   John, res 85 n Lafontaine
Knipple, Henry, res 17 e Tipton
Knoke, Henry, emp lime kilns, res 26 McFarland [Catharine]
            Elizabeth, Mamie

Koch, W E, carpenter Erie, res 63 Elm [Maggie] William
    A, Sarah B, Celestia P

Koch, Martin (Koch & Herneise) res 102 Cline [Martha] Carl,
    Henry, Arthur, Hilda, Meriam

Koch & Herneise (Martin Koch, James B Herneise) stone dlrs
    and cutters e State st

Kocher, Mary A (wid Wm C) res 60 s Jefferson Louisa M

Kocher, Christian, carpenter Erie, res 25 Elm [Mary] Law-
    rence, Jesse, Iva, Vernice

Kocher, Emma, res 146 William

Kohl, Wm, jeweler, res 110 Cherry

Kohl, John, harness maker cor Washington and Warren, res
    110 Cherry [Magdalena] Clara B

Kohlenberg, Henry, lab Wabash Ry, res 37 Dimond [Mary]
    Henry jr, Anna

Koontz, Leander, brakeman Erie, res 257 e State [Mary A]
    Dessie B, Ervin P

†Koontz, Blanche, res s Henry

Koontz, Lafayette, lab res 32 Salamonie ave

Koontz, Mary (wid) res 32 Salamonie ave

Kopp, Aurelius, clk M B Stults, res 48 e Market

Krall, W M, emp Erie yards, res 53 South [Ellen] Lorel,
    Etna, Clara

Kramer, Henry W, sawyer Briant, res 25 Kocher [Lenora]
    Mary M, Edward, Henry, Nina

"   Samuel, emp Briant, res 13 Second [Catharine] Al-
    fred C, George

"   Frank, emp Erie yards, res 31 Briant

"   Susan (wid Simon) res 31 Erie

"   Al, spoke polisher Briant, res 40 Grayston ave

"   Clarence, cigar mkr, res 225 n Lafontaine

"   Ed, lab res 40 Grayston ave [Sarah]

"   Ed jr, emp Briant, res 40 Grayston ave [Mary]

"   Mary J (wid Adam L) res 225 n Lafontaine. Chas,
    Almond, Dessie

"   Chester A, emp Briant, res 25 Kocher

Kreamer, J W, postal clk Erie, res 48 Second [Belle] Ethel
Kreig, Gus, emp H L & F Co, res 73 Guilford
"   Wm, carpenter Erie, res 58 First [Emma] Lloyd
"   Pius, drayman, res 101 Court [Caroline] Marshall H,
            Ellat, Mary E, Paul V
"   Kate (wid) res 11 Olinger
Kreiger, Chas, lab res 21 Kocher [Bridget] Mary, Anna,
            William, Emma, George
"   Henry, emp Briant, res 21 Kocher
"   John, emp Briant, res 21 Kocher
Krider, D L, machinist Erie, res 17 Salamonie ave [Rosa]
Kriegbaum Bros (John, George) agricultural implements 50
            Warren
†Kriegbaum, John (Kriegbaum Bros) res w Catharine [Anna]
            James, Albert, Baby
"   Mary (wid Philip) res 44 London. Bertha
"   Albert, sub mail carrier, res 44 London
"   Edward, emp Kriegbaum Bros, res 44 London
"   George (Kriegbaum Bros) res 44 London
Kronck, August, eng Erie, res 17 Foust [Lizzie]
"   Wm, lab, res 26 Garfield [Estella]
"   Harmon, bartender Newlove, res 24 Garfield [Amy]
Kronmiller, Gottleib sr, lab res 43 Buchanan [Katharine]
            Katie, Henry, Clara
"   Louis, cigar mkr, res 43 Buchanan
Kronmiller, Gottleib jr, emp Griffith & Son, res 43 Buchanan
Kuhlman, Elizabeth, dressmaker, res 27 Byron
"   Jesse, emp shoe factory, res 46 William
"   N H, drayman, res 46 William [Mattie]
"   Albert, mail carrier, res 28 Bingham [Lizzie]
            Helene
"   Matilda, clk J Frash, res 146 Guilford
"   Joseph, plasterer, res 146 Guilford
"   Elizabeth, clk New York Cash Store, res 146 Guil-
            ford

RUBBERS All Kinds and Styles. **ZELLER.**

Kuhlman, Fred, plasterer, res 146 Guilford [Varena] Anna, Maude

†Kuester, Henry W, switchman Erie, res 337 e State [Mollie] Benjamin O

Kunce, Thomas J, res 165 William [Eliza]

Kunce, Oren, lab res 165 William [Mary]

Kunce, A W, blacksmith Erie, res 44 Byron [Mary E] John, Harvey

Kunce, Clara, res 154 e Tipton

Kunce, T J, hack driver S P Stults, res 13 Fout [Julia]

Kunkel, J A, eng Erie, res 62 High [Margaret] Chas E, Earl E, Edna E, Louis E, Paul E

Kunze, William, drayman, res 52 Webster [Amanda]

Kussard, Alonzo, lab res 41 Grayston ave [Mary] Sherman, Nina

Kussmaul, Godfried, res 16 Polk [Susanna]

Kussmaul, J J, emp Briant, res 19 Gay [H A] Martha

Kussmer, J R, fireman Briant fac, res 42 Superior [Libby] Hazel

---

L

LaBar, Elizabeth (wid Amos) res 153 e Franklin

" W H C, fireman Erie, res 153 e Franklin [Jennie] Mary E, Everett H

Lacey, Anna, bookpr shoe factory, res 22 Mayne

" Sarah (wid Chas) dressmaker, res 22 Mayne

Laflamb, W D, fireman Erie, res 52 Superior [Laura] Carl, Floyd

---

Lahr, John, fireman Erie, res 40 Sabine [Emma]
  "   Fred, shoemaker A Kindler, res 151 Guilford [Mary]
         Edward
  "   Frank, emp shoe factory, res 151 Guilford
* "   John, lab, res e fair ground [Sarah]
  "   Albert, clk C Mader, res 48 Frederick
Lamarble, Lewis, emp shoe factory, res 50 n Lafontaine st
         [Minnie] Arcade, Adrian, Ellen
  "   Ernest, emp shoe factory, res 50 n Lafontaine
  "   Miss Georgia, res 9 Wilkerson
Lambert, S, second hand dlr 108 n Jefferson, res 25 e Tipton st
         [Hattie E]
Lamboley, J A, bill clk Wab frt office, res 5 Wilkerson [Dora]
LaMont, Jacob, contractor, res 27 Madison [Jennie] Myrtle,
         Gertrude, Marmie, Edith
* "   John, res n Guilford
* "   A L, carpenter, res n Guilford [Ella] Vanemin,
         Winfield
  "   Robt, carpenter, res 91 First
  "   Miss Lionel, res 5 Sabine
  "   Heber, res 5 Sabine
  "   James A, carpenter, res 20 Madison [Nina B]
  "   William J, carpenter, res 287 n Jefferson [Emma]
         Laura, Eva
Landen, James, emp Briant, res 268 e State [Martha]
Landgrave, Ida, domestic 166 e Franklin
Landis, Manassah, traveling saw filer, res 29 South [Effie]
         Clyde, Gordon, Roy
  "   Ephriam, foreman Briant, res 88 Webster [Adaline]
         Marmie, Eva
  "   Aaron, emp Perrine & Bartlett, res 161 e Franklin
         [Ida] Melvin, Bertha
  "   Jessie, traveling saw hammerer, res 8 Grayston ave
         [Mrs J] Oscar, Goldie M
Landis, Ira, meat market 154 e Market, res 64 Superior [Cy-
         rene] George, Boyd

Landis, A G, emp I Landis, res 38 Jackson [Julian]

Lane, J L, cond Erie, res 86 e State [Laura] Alvah W, J M, Lottie H

Lane, Q X Z, optician over 50 n Jefferson, res over 11 w Market [Jennie] Robert

Lang, Carl, prop Huntington Brewery 147-157 e Tipton, res same [Catharine] Clara, Josephine

Langston, Ambrose, teamster, bds 15 Olinger

Lans, Mary E (wid H D) res 84 s Jefferson, Alice

Lantis, Malinda, domestic 83 e State

LaPointe, E, blacksmith Erie, res 1 Wilkerson [Lucie] Gertrude

" Will, boiler-mkr Erie, res 1 Wilkerson

" Frank P, machinist Erie, res 2 Leopold [Laura] Elmer

Larkins, Chas H, expressman, res 64 Guilford [Julia]

Larkins, Silas, stone cutter, res 58 Superior

Lashing, Fred, ashery 2 Herman, res rear same

*Laudig, E W, machinist Erie, res e fair ground [Lydia] May, Edith, Lulu, Fred

*Laudig, Chas, carpenter Erie, res e fair ground [Maggie] Harmon, Emmett

Laughlin, Michael, brakeman Erie, res Windsor Hotel

Lautzenhiser, Jos, mgr Beyer Bros, res 100 Cherry [Ella] Blanche, Bernice, Edith

Lavine, Louis, emp Briant, res 164 e Franklin [Ida]

" Boston, machinist Erie, res 23 Iowa

" Lewis blacksmith Erie, res 23 Iowa [Amelia] Winnie

Lawler, John, laborer, res w city near dock

" James, laborer, res w city near dock

Lawrence, Mary, emp Osborne Hotel, res same

* " Amos, tinner Erie, res 309 n Jefferson [Susannah] Alton, Emmett V, Nettie, James, Harold

" W F, foreman Briant spoke factory, res 68 Grayston ave [Carrie] Briant

Lawrence, Mary (wid Jno) res 8 North. Cora, Gertrude, Ethel
"   Wm R. invalid, res 10 William
Lawver, J W, (Smith & Lawver.) res 37 Scott [Emma] William E, Dwight A, Eldon, Virgil
Leach, Mrs L, (wid S S,) res e State
Ledger, Geo, cond Erie, res 37 Sabine [Mary] George, Robt, Earl, Donald
Ledman, Abbie, clk Fisher & Bailey, res 91 Railroad
"   Daniel, brakeman Erie, res 91 Railroad [Alice M] Grace
"   Edward, machinist Erie, res 91 Railroad
Lee, Ezra T, res 96 e State [Amanda A]
"   Elijah, carpenter, res 51 Wilkerson [Sarah E] Fairy, Herbert E
Lee, H F, cond Erie, res 14 Jackson [Mary E] Lloyd L, Gilbert D, Erie V
Lee, Frank, eng Erie, res 89 s Jefferson [Nannie] Herbert, Jesse, Nina
Lee, Earl, machinist Erie, res 52 Whitelock
Lee, M J, eng Erie, res 52 Whitelock [Mary A]
Lehman, William, emp E W Stover, res 37 Poplar. Charles, Everett
Lehmeyer, Wm H (Lehmeyer & MacGhan) res 135 William [Caroline] Fred A, Amelia B, Fredia E, Nettie W
Lehmeyer & MacGhan (Wm Lehmeyer, J C MacGhan) blacksmiths 44 Cherry
Leiben, Harry, emp Singer Sewing Mac. Co., bds 11 e Market
Leicht, Chas, lab res 54 Buchanan [Henrietta]
Leon, Chas, emp lime kilns, res 111 Dimond [Francis] Julia
Leonard, Michael, machinist Erie, res 220 e Market [Anna] Mary, Kathleen, Helen, Charles, Lenera
"   M L, (wid S,) res 46 w Matilda
"   Edward, teamster, res 35 Kocher [Ionis] Ella, Mary, Myrtle, Merriam, Harry
Lesh, Mrs Martha, trimmer H S Wells, res 286 n Jefferson Pearl

Lesh, Frank, machinist Erie, res 280 n Jefferson
" U S, (Kenner & Lesh) res 6 Elm [Winnie] John W
Leverton, James A, sheriff Huntington county, res county
      jail, 28 w State [Lydia J] Iva M, Elinor R,
      J Eddie, Ralph O
Leverton, George G, barber 243 e State, res 260 e State
" Edward S, dept co clk, res 107 Clark [Elnora B]
      Garrett H
Levi, Henry (col'd) cook Exchange hotel, res 38 First [Maria]
      Jeannette, Eldon D
Levy, Jesse, clk Leopold Levy, res 15 e Market
Levy, Leopold, clothing, etc, cor Jefferson and Franklin, res
      15 e Market [Theresa] Daisy
Lew, Bert, tinner, res 11 High
Lew, Chas E, car repairer Erie, res 11 High
Lew, Jacob C, tinner Reichenbach & Wickenhiser, res 11 High
      [Henrietta] Will, Mamie, Ethel, Darmie
Lewis, H M, fireman Erie, res cor First and Wilkerson [Lil-
      lie] Benj L, Fred
" Evangeline E, teacher public schools, res 168 n Jefferson
" Anna (wid W H D) res 33 e Tipton
" Francis, domestic 7 s Lafontaine
" Hester, (wid) res 47 Frederick Effie A, Izetta, Mary
      L, Frank E, Bertha N, Gertrude
Lewis, Chas H, prop Koh-I-Noor billiard hall, cigars, etc, cor
      Market and Jefferson, res 64 w Matilda
" Bettie, (wid Oscar A,) res 64 w Matilda
Leyman, Dr E H, physician, res Exchange Hotel
" Edward, dancing instructor, res 235 n Jefferson
" Dr D S, physician Opera House blk, res 235 n Jeffer-
      son [Amanda] Lawrence
" Mordecai W, constable, res 37 Walnut Wilbur
Lieber, Harry, cook Circle restaurant, res 39 w State st [Cor-
      delia] Geo A F
Lindsey, W C, cook Marchancil, res 55 Grayston ave [Gertie]
      Mabel, Edith Raymond

Linsey, A E, emp section Erie, res 172 Byron [Mary E]
James H, William O

Line, W H, abstractor, res 116 Byron [Margaret A] Grace
L, Paul L, Arthur M

† "   Clarence, lab res rear Brawley

† "   Gertrude, res rear Brawley

† "   Estella, res rear Brawley

Linerode, Theo, emp Erie boiler shops, res 17 Iowa [Mary]
William, Berne, Mary, Frank

Lingquvist, Andrew, gardener, res 41 Hartman [Elizabeth]

Lininger, Peter, res 132 Byron [Mary J]

"   Joseph, lab res 21 n Lafountaine [Marticia] Chloe

† "   Emily, res s Salamonie ave

† "   Ida, clk Willis bakery, res s Salamonie ave

"   Albert, confectioner cor Market and Jefferson, res
20 Wesley [Catharine]

"   Jacob D (Lininger & Mentzer) res 23 Bingham
[Sarah W] Ethel M, Ray T

Lininger & Mentzer (J D Lininger, Geo A Mentzer) bakery 7
s Jefferson

Linn, Mary, domestic 2 Leopold

Linville, Harry, res 106 e State

Lipinski, Simon H, cigars, tobaccos, whiskies, retail and
wholesale cor Market and Jefferson, res 38 s Jefferson [Rebecca A] Lester H, Harold A

Lippman, Stuart, groceries and bakery 11 e Franklin, res 81 e
Franklin [Belle] J Beryle

Lippman, Orville S, student, res 81 e Franklin

Little, Sampson, cond Erie, res 20 Arthur Lorena, Anna

"   Chas B, real estate and abstractor, res 75 William
[Alice D] Russell

Little, M W, insurance and real estate Citizens Bank block,res
75 William [Lavina] Grace W

Loftin, Fred T, pub Trader's Journal over 11 w Washington,
res 42 Byron ·[Elizabeth K] Edith F

Logan, Trellah B, teacher public schools, res 111 Guilford

Long, Mary (wid Lewis) res 27 e Market
" Emmett, machinist Erie, res 74 w Matilda
" Thos J, clk Adam Mader, res 16 Randolph [Alice] Ralph, Mamie
" F M, lab res 83 Broadway [Sarah] Blanche, Floyd, Ethel, Iva, Stella
" Chas M, teamster, res 124 Elm [Phoebe]
" Rev Ernest, res 8 Elm
" C M, emp Sid Hall, res 8 Elm [Ida] Bessie M
* " Edward, plasterer, res s Etna ave [Josephine E] M G, Theo M
" R M, plasterer, res 4 Everett [Hannah] Myra, Grace
Longdon, C W, photographer over 57 n Jefferson, rms same
Longfellow, Chas, brakeman Erie, res 81 Whitelock [Nora]
Longwell, C L, cond Erie, res 103 First [Eliza] Robt S
Loomis, Lydia W (wid) res 21 Olinger
Lowenberg, Albert (Harris Clothing Co) res 97 e Market [Minnie] Ruth
Lowry, J W, carpenter Erie, res 123 Lincoln ave [Ida M]
Lowry, Della, emp C & E Eating hs, res same
Lowman, P L, ice dlr, res 13 Bingham [Mary] Marvin A, Emery R, Clark L, Hazel R, Mabel C
Lowmaster, W T, brakeman Erie, res 16 Grayston ave [Laura] Pearl, Archie, Frank
Loville, G C, cond Erie, res 107 First [Jennie] Clarence
Lovett, Justin R, pharmacist C R Smith, res 68 Henry [Daisy]
Luber, Matthias, wholesale and retail dlr in tobaccos 19 e Franklin, res 17 e Market [Elizabeth] Minnie, Rose, Katie
Lucas, Jesse, res 235 e Market
Lucas, Chas K, attorney, res 235 e Market [Pearl] Edith, Jenera
Luckey, C M, brakeman Erie, res 20 Superior
†Luckey, Nathan, painter, res Wright st [Maria] Vernie, Anorma
Lukins, B C, clk Bradley Bros, res 42 w Market [Dell] Boyd

Lantz, Harry, peddler, res 75 Tipton [Lena] Martha, Rose

Lusch, John, lab res 80 Superior [Belle] Raymond

Lusch, Barbara (wid Jacob) res 104 w Matilda

Lutz, Caroline (wid John) res 41 Byron. Lawrence, Martha, Howard

Lyons, W B, physician, res 29 e Franklin [Isabella]

Lyons, Etta, res 10 William

Lyons, Ira E, physician, res 73 e Market. Kate M, Ella

Mc

McAdam, Terry, lab res 82 Henry

McArthur, D, lumber buyer, res 111 Guilford [C Margaret] Priscilla, John A

McArthur, Fred, brakeman Erie, res 80 e Market [Alice] Mildred, Neil

McCabe, John, clk Pacific and Wells Fargo Express Co, res 3 n Lafontaine [Emma] Gordon, Donald

McCaffrey & Co (H McCaffrey, Jas McGourty, John Sullivan) wholesale and retail grocers 84 n Jefferson

McCahill, Chas, operator Erie, res 131 Guilford street [Edna] Nellie

McCammack, Ola, res 70 w Matilda

McCammack, Clona, res 70 w Matilda

McCartney, George (McCartney & Son) res 21 Garfield [Ada] Ray

McCartney & Son (P McCartney, Geo McCartney) stoves and tinware 96 n Jefferson

McCartney, Patrick (McCartney & Son) res 101 e State [Mrs P]
"   Maggie, night operator United Telephone Co, res 101 e State

McCarty, Richard, emp Bauer & McCarty, res 257 n Jefferson
"   J M (Bauer & McCarty) res 257 n Jefferson
"   Mary (wid John) res 257 n Jefferson. Mary
"   Patrick (Beaver & McCarty) res 257 n Jefferson st [Margaret] Patsy
"   J A, chief detective Erie, res 68 w Market [Grace] Ruth

McCauley, Frank (McCauley & Ryan) res 72 First

McCauley & Ryan (Frank McCauley, Oscar Ryan) plumbers and gas fitters 3 e Washington

McCauley, Casper, emp Erie, res 72 First
"   William, plumber, res 72 First
"   James jr, fireman Erie, res 72 First
"   James, emp Erie yards, res 72 First [Anna]
"   W E, fireman Erie, res 21 Whitestine st [Allie] Alonzo V, Frank C
     Hugh, res 238 e Market [Rose] Mary, Maggie, Rose, Sarah, John

McCaughey, Chas, lab res over 55 Guilford

*McClanahan, Frank, res s Etna ave
"   Emma (wid Geo) res 138 Byron
"   Eva, emp Exchange hotel, res 138 Byron
"   Daisy, emp Exchange hotel, res 138 Byron

McClellan, Frank P, car repairer Erie, res 11 Harris [Matilda] Lettie, May, Everett J
"   B, carpenter, res 14 Iva

McClelland, H D, trainmaster Erie, res 240 n Jefferson [Lizzie] Homer, Frank, Donald, Myra

McClure, Wm, eng Erie, res 90 Front [Mary] Ethel, Clinton, Gladys, William, Lucile

McCombs, Wm, student, res 33 e Tipton

McConkey, W E, eng Erie, res 70 Wilkerson [Kate] Ethel, Edith, Josephine, Thomas, Dorothy

McConnell, Willard, emp Withington fac, res 25 Simon street [Sarah] Anna, Virgelia, Robert

McCrum, Robt, teamster, res 2 Everett [Caroline] Jesse, Mary M, James

* "   Thos B, salesman, res s Jefferson st

* "   Chas A, salesman, res s Jefferson

* "   Robt C, traveling salesman, res s Jefferson [Harriett] Elma, Arthur, Leedy, Lela

McCutchen, Dora (wid Maywood) res 38 Jackson

McDevitt, John, emp Perrine & Bartlett, res 14 s Briant [Lucinda] Nora, Wm T, Jessie, Grace, Ruby.

" Ben, emp Perrine & Bartlett, res 25 s Briant [Minnie] Ruth

McDonald, Rev H F, pastor First Baptist church, res 70 w Market [Hattie L] Owen, Royal, Herbert, Donald

McDowell, W H, brakeman Erie, res 31 Superior [Melissa] Arthur, Samuel

McEnderfer, Alvin, marble cutter, res 67 Whitelock [Clara] Oscar, Lodema, Paul M

McEntire, Martha (wid James) res 257 e State

McFerren, Geo, emp H L & F Co, res 5 s Lafontaine [MaryE]

McFerren, Levi, lab res 124 George [Mary]

McFerren, Lou, clk, res 124 George

McFerren, Harry, lab rms over Day's livery

McGourty, James (McCaffrey & Co) res 195 n Jefferson [Kate]

McGowen, Edward, insurance agent, res 76 Etna ave [Sarah] Dollie, Mamie, Sadie, Wm, George

McIlvaine, Thos O, eng Erie, res over 14 w Market [H K] Merodith

McIlvaine, H K, physician over 14 w Market

McKee, Ora, blacksmith res 131 e State [Minnie] Child

McKee, Miss Minnie, res 131 e State

*McKee, Serioma, cook Orphans Home res same

McGhan, J C (Lehmeyer & McGhan) res over 44 Cherry

McGlinn, John, res cor Franklin and Guilford [Mrs J]

McGrew, Wm, pres First National Bank, res 151 n Jefferson Emma L, Mrs Anna E

McGrew, Chas M, bkpr First Fational Bnk, res 151 n Jefferson

McGuire, E C, machinist Erie, res 22 n Lafontaine [Ella]

McLain, Chas M, eng Erie, res 91 s Jefferson [Anna] Kirk, Ione

McLean, Neil, bridge inspector Erie, res 25 Wilkerson [Alice] Mary A Gladys W

McLin, Dr G H, office over cor Jefferson and Market, res 119 e Market [Odassa] Ileene, DeForest

McLin, Jacob, res 119 e Market [Adelia]

McLin's Kolotono Factory (G H McLin, prop) 26 Second st

McMahon, Mary, head waitress Star restaurant, res same

McMahon, Catharine (wid Stephen, res 118 e Franklin

McMahon, Edward, machinist Erie, res 118 e Franklin

McMahon, J C, brakeman Erie, res 70 e Market

McMarlan, J C, lab bds 11 e Market

McMullen, J A, contractor, res 144 Cherry [Mary]

McMullen, Wm, stone cutter, bds 104 Court

McMullen, Matthias H, res 75 Poplar

McMullen, W B, contractor, res 75 Poplar [Mary B] Ida, F Donalas, Michael, Marie E, Anna G, R Elmore

McNamee, Nellie, teacher public schools

McNulty, Frank, plumber J Gusman, res 45 e Matilda [Mary V] John, Edward, Mary, Francis, Joseph, Magdalena, Anna

---

M

Mace, Geo A, cond Erie, res 72 w Market [Sarah M]   Mary,
          Carrie, Etta, Georgiana, Armina
"   John, machinist Erie, res 72 w Market
"   Emma, res 68 Marshall

Mader, Adam, grocery 27 e Market, res over same. [Nora]
          Charles

Mader, Lewis, clk C Mader, res 48 Frederick [Maggie] Bertha
"   Jacob, res 19 e Market
"   Minnie, cashier C Mader, res 19 e Market

Mader, Chas, grocery 14 e Market, res 19 e Market

Mahoney, Jerry, operator Erie, res 58 e Franklin
"   Marion, lab res 31 Mayne [Anna] Ruth, Mitch-
          ell, Helen, Luther, Inez
"   George, deputy co sheriff, res 5 Olinger [Jennie]
          Eva S, Tinia F, Paul

Malcolm, L J, machinist Erie, res 151 Court [Florence]

Malins, A H, merchant tailor 14 w Market, res 32 w Market st
          [Adeline]

Maloney, Ed, switchman Erie, res Windsor hotel

*Mankin, B W, cond Erie, res e fair ground [Celia]   Grace,
          Gertrude

*Mankin, Harry, painter Erie, res e fair ground

Mann, Harvey, boiler mkr Erie, res 79 Court
"   John H, timber buyer, res 79 Court [Maggie] Lura B
"   Harry, barber E Nix, res 79 Court

†Manning, W J, lab res s Salamonie ave [Josie] Frank
*   "   Mrs Lizzie, res s Etna ave

Maplethorp, Joseph, emp Erie shops, res 43 Superior
"   Walter, emp Erie shops, res 43 Superior

Maranda, J B, foreman Griffith & Son, res 68 s Briant [Mary
          F] Lucy L, Jorge M, Paul E, John W
"   Otis, emp shoe factory, res 85 Whitelock
"   Fred, barber J E Keyes, res 85 Whitelock

Maranda, Joseph, barber L Trixler, res 85 Whitelock
" Peter, emp Griffith & Son, res 85 Whitelock [Elizabeth]
March, Geo, emp Wab section, res 15 Harris [Metta] Earl
Mardinis, W R, groceries and provisions cor State and Condit res rear same [Mary E]
Marchaneil Restaurant (G W Foster, prop) 22 e Market
Maring, Ellen (wid) res 28 Briant
Mark, L C, carriage mkr 58 Guilford, res 13 Canal [Mary] Lola C, Melvin
" James, painter, res 13 Canal
Marker, Winfield, res 116 Front [Flora] Leonard, Hugh
Marks, James, picture vender, res 146 Court [Lottie] Emma
Marshall, S R, brakeman Erie, res 6 Iva [Gladys] Verna
" John, brakeman Erie, res 13 Third [Rose] Wilbur
Marston, Wm H, eng Erie, res 16 Briant [Jennie]
" Geo H, eng Erie, res 16 Briant
Martin, Peter (Western Lime Assn) res 110 Cherry [Elizabeth] Lena, Adelena, Julia, Edward, Herman
Martin, Lillie (col'd) cook Grand View, res 38 First
" Jacob (Western Lime Co) res 131 Cherry [Amelia] Clara, Frank, Martin, Joseph, Mary, Tricy
Marx, Adolph, clk D Marx, res 51 w Matilda
Marx, Isadore, clk D Marx, res 51 w Matilda
Marx, David, clothier 54 n Jefferson, res 51 w Matilda street [Amelia] Louie, Henrietta
Mason, Ben, clk Grand View, res same
" Michael, cond Erie, res Windsor hotel
*Mast, Michael, traveling engineer Erie, res e end Tipton
Mattern, Andrew, res 72 Poplar [Sophia]
Matthews, Wm, emp shoe factory, res 60 Whitelock
Matson, Inez, teacher public schools
May, Wm F, teamster, res 99 Broadway [Mary A] Emma
Mayne, Robert, res 56 s Jefferson, Anna, Dolly
Mayne, John W, teamster, res 15 Mayne [Minnie] Lizzie, Claude, Cyril

Mayne, Monroe, stationary engineer, res 183 Etna ave |Catharine| Nellie, Maude, Guy, Howard

Mayne, J C, lab res 30 Hasty [Clara] Lillian F, Esther M, Bessie A

Meade, Chas, foreman shoe factory, res 54 Henry [Josephine] Ralph C

Meadlowen, Mable, waitress Grand View, res same

Mealey, Cyrus, hostler M Luber, res over 19 e Franklin

Meech, Chas L, res 33 e Tipton

Meeker, H N, lab res 93 Oak [Mary L] George

Mehre, Henry F, eng Erie, bds Star restaurant

Meier, Veronika (wid Wm) res 30 Buchanan. Willie, Adolph, Fred, Anna

Meisch, Geo, emp lime kilns, res 105 Broadway

Menefee, A J, supt water works Erie, res 20 Garfield [Anna]

*Menner, Mrs (wid) res 131 Thomas
  "   Jacob, clk res 95 n Lafontaine

Mentzer, G A (Lininger & Mentzer) res 41 High [Amelia] Una, Clarence, Mamie

Merrill, Fred, machinist Erie, rms 115 e Franklin

Merriman, Curtis, emp Erie shops, res 31 Harris [Anna] Etta, Ervin
  "   Basil, compositor News-Democrat, res 21 Herman. [Elsie]
  "   A B, emp Erie yards, res 11 Bechtol [Laura] Harley, Elvie

Merritt, Jas S, emp Erie car shops, res 111 Warren
  "   Lou (wid Henry) dressmaker res 111 Warren
  "   Jessie, clk Princess store, res 111 Warren
  "   L E, brakeman Erie, res 83 e Market [L E]

Merl, Peter, emp Erie section, res 78 Esther [Caroline] (Lizzie and Jacob Heeter)

Metsker, Robert, res 42 Front [Sarah]
  "   Geo D, photographer, res 42 Front

Mettert, H C, hostler W C Chafee, res 98 Oak [Rebecca] Edith, Anna, Orval, Hazel

Metz, Estella, student, res 96 w State
" Conrad, boiler mkr Erie, bds 41 Hartman
Metzler, Max, brakeman Erie, res 109 Railroad [Rice] Eva E
Meyer, Adam, painter, res over 5 e Market
" Chas, auctioneer, res 29 Lehmeyer
" J R, painter, res 67 Henry [Mary M] Lulu M, Clarence L, Florence S, Hazel L
" Millie, housekeeper, res 38 Everet. Ollie, Ruth, Grace
" Cora, res 170 William. Coto, Lulu
" John, painter, bds 113 Lincoln ave
" Louis, res 14 William
" Lewis, lab res 71 w Tipton [Christena] Rosa, Eliza, Lewis jr, Chas
" Jacob, mgr Pottlitzer Bros, bds Exchange hotel
Michaels, Maggie, milliner, res 122 Lincoln ave
" Lewis H, plasterer, res 30 Elm [Mary E] Lulu B, Grace A
Millenbaugh, Helen (wid John) res 172 e Franklin. Maggie
Millen, Wm, dpty city marshal, res 147 Cherry [Amanda]
Miller, Barbara (wid John) res 33 Green. Mary B
" H H, tailor room 4 Citizens Bnk blk, res 43 w Tipton [Kate R] Jennie M, Eva B
" Will, machinist Erie, res 80 Frederick
" Geo C, cigar mkr, res 67 Clark [Hattie] Cora P
" Frank, emp Erie round hs, res 12 Nile [Ella] Russell, Marie, Ray
" Rufus, lab, res 52 s Briant
" Lewis, clk Wabash freight office, res 60 Guilford [Stella] Delbert, Mona
" Frederick, carpenter, res 52 s Briant [Caroline] Milton I
" Clark, fireman Erie, res 17 Mayne [Florence] Earl, Ora
" C W, clk city treasurer's office, res 43 w Tipton
" Charles, painter, res 39 Everet

†Miller, Anna, domestic, res Catharine bet Briant and s Jeff's'n

"   Miner, bartender, res 10 William [Josie] Blanche, Floyd

* "   Adam, brakeman Erie, res e Front [Alice] Flossie

"   Harry, emp Erie shops, res 49 e Sabine [Cora] Jesse Lyle

      Nicholas, section hand Erie, res 83 Grayston avenue [Rose] Bernard, Julius

"   Joseph, lab res 25 First [Lucy] Jennie G, Cora

"   John, teamster C Lang, res 92 Oak [Louisa] Agnes, Virgelia, Harmon

      J M, carpenter, res 74 Oak [Flora E] Ethel, Coign

      John shoemaker, res 80 Frederick [Catharine] Loretta, Agnes, Celia

      John A, carpenter Erie, res 110 e Market [Amanda] Fred

"   E E, brakeman Erie, res 120 Byron [Della]

"   Geo F, fireman Erie, res 127 Byron [Tena] Paul, Mable

"   John, lab, res 154 Guilford

"   Jacob, machinist Erie, res 154 Guilford

"   Maria, (wid) res 154 Guilford. Elizabeth

"   Cora, waitress Osborne, res same

"   John, clk, res 53 e Washington

* "   Wm H, lab, res s Etna ave

* "   Eli, lab, s Etna ave [Nancy] Mary A, Emma M, Chas H, John F

* "   Franklin, lab, s Etna ave [Screpta] Willis A

* "   Roscoe E, lab, s Etna ave

"   Christian, Hewitt hardware, res 71 Frederick [Matilda L] Carl V, Waldo H, Cleo C

"   William S, stationary eng, res 22 Hasty [Eva]

"   Jane, (wid Andrew) res 35 Walnut. Ellen, Cleveland, Charles

"   Elmer, emp N Windemuth, res 35 Walnut

†Miller, Charles, teamster, s Henry [Florence] Raymond, Leota
"   J C, emp Briant factory, res 77 Briant [Johannah] Weema M
* "   David B, brakeman Erie, e Front [Moni C] Inez M, Olive, Grace, Goldie, Flob
"   Jacob, lab, res 33 Green
"   Frank, lab, res 33 Green
* "   H J, stone mason, res 4 Swan [M E]
"   James, lab, res 290 e State [Della] Melvin, Searles
"   Geo, car inspector Erie, res 290 e State
"   Esther, domestic, 116 Guilford
Miles, Benjamin, emp Briant factory, res 8 Everet [Emma] Julia, Chas
"   William, lab, res 8 Everet
Miles Wall Paper Co, (Will C Miles) wall paper, decorations, etc, 90 n Jefferson
Miles, Will C, (Miles Wall Paper Co) res 78 Oak [Anna] Wilbur, Lesh, Houston
     Spencer B, paper hanger, res 66 w Market
     L C, postal clerk Erie, res 66 w Market [Lelia] Edith
"   Darwin P, paper hanger, res 66 w Market
Milligan, Moses, prop Silver Moon saloon 27 n Jefferson, res over same [Mary C]
Milligan, Whitelock & Cook, (Col L P Milligan, O W Whitelock, S E Cook) over 25 n Jefferson
Milligan, Lew P, lab, res w city near dock
"   Col L P, (Milligan, Whitelock & Cook) res over 23 n Jefferson, summer res 1 mile w city [Maria L]
     Chas M, emp Briant, res Hotel Eastern [Emma]
     Sarah, (wid James) res 60 Front James, Katherine, Margaret, Winifred
"   Emma, (wid William S) res 18 Guilford
Mills, Valentine, cooper, bds 137 e Sabine
"   William, lab, res 8 Everet

Miltenberger, W A, carpenter Erie, res 25 Everet [Susanna] Belle, Geo W

Mindnich, Martin, lime and stone dlr, res 107 Poplar [Mary] Theresa, Amelia, Jacob

Mingus, Cyrus, lightning rod dlr, res 5 William [Olive] Maud

Minnich, John, prop City Mills 15 w Washington, res 89 Guilford [Elizabeth] Lillie

"   Frank H, emp City Mills, res 58 Henry [Adorah J] Clara E, Harry G

Mire, Mary, domestic 63 Etna ave

Mishler, Jacob, res 83 Poplar

"   Sarah (John H) res 47 e Tipton. James, Myrtle

Mitchell, James C, res 21 Glenn [Matilda J]

"   Robt G, clk J Frash, res 21 Glenn

Mitchell Sisters (Margaret and Charlotte) dressmakers over 16 s Jefferson

Mitchell, Margaret E (Mitchell Sisters) res 21 Glenn

"   Charlotte (Mitchell Sisters) res 21 Glenn

"   Cassius, lab res 22 Elm [Amanda] Mark D

"   Bert, emp J Kindig, res 40 e Market

"   W E, insurance agent, res 40 e Market [May] Ralph

"   Walter, emp H V Peden, res 40 e Market

Mitten, Daniel S, carpenter, res 75 Buck [Elizabeth]

"   Lewis F, butcher D First, res 39 Walnut. Laura, Harry

"   L C, contractor, res 11 s Lafontaine [Sarah J] Carr A, Ethel L, Nina M. Ralph E

"   Bessie, res 235 n Jefferson

"   Sarah (wid James) res 29 e Tipton

"   Ladocia, res 29 e Tipton

"   Flora, res 72 Polk. Fred S, Jas R

"   W H, clk res 72 Polk

"   Charles, elevator boy Arnold & Son, res 72 Polk

"   D D, emp H Weis, res 121 Buck [Louisa] Clara, Anna, Emma R, Lulu, Geo

"   Clarence, emp H Weis, res 121 Buck

Moak, Henry, brakeman Erie, res 20 Superior [Carrie] Harry S, Pearl O

Moffitt, W P, co clk, res 99 s Jefferson [Mary C] Dora, Goldie
" Harl, emp Withington fac, res 5 Kitt [Letitia] Bernice
" J W, dpty co clk, res 99 s Jefferson

Mohler, A D, architect over Koh-I-Noor, res 141 Guilford [Sarah A] Ruth, Viola
" Lizzie, teacher public schools, res 94 e State
" Amos, carpenter, res 94 e State. Mary, Harold

Mohn, Alice, res 95 Lindley

Monroe, Angeline (wid John) res 79 Court

Montz, A I, carpenter Erie, res 102 Poplar [Mary I] Cleo C, Hazel
" Jesse, huckster, res 102 Poplar
" W Hurshel, huckster, res 102 Poplar

Moon, Fred, res 138 Byron [Alice]
" S S, machinist Erie, res 12 Leopold [Emma] Ervin, Helen

Moore, Eva, tailoress, res 289 n Jefferson
" Sarah (wid Geo W) res 289 n Jefferson. Albert G, Warren M
" F F, cond Erie, res over 18 w Market
" M W, ins agt over Citizen's Bank, res 108 Byron [Louisa F] Stacy, Ella J, William C, Ethel R
" C W, emp car shops Erie, res 95 Lincoln ave [Mary A]
" Charles, soliciting agt, res 6 Simon [Mary A]
" Edwin F, clk Clayton Household Furnishing Co, res 6 Simon
" Miss Dessie, organist M E church, res 19 Etna ave
" L B, capt Soldiers' Home, Marion, Ind, city address 54 First

Moore, Belle (wife of L B) res 54 First. Thos, Ed, Frank
" Mary, res 53 e Washington
" Lydia (wid Geo W) prop Princess store, res 72 w Matilda. Lulu

Moore, Claude, clk Princess, res 72 w Matilda
"   Joseph E, farmer, res 62 w Matilda. Mary W, Lizzie
Moran, Wm, emp Erie section, res 23 Simon [Mary] Jennie,
            Willie, Mary, Julia, Daniel, Paul
"   J B, brakeman Erie, res 93 Franklin [Margaret] Alva
Morford, Thursa, domestic 33 Frederick
"   Ella, res 125 Guilford
Morgan, O C, agricultural implements 19 s Jefferson, res 64 s
            Jefferson [Ella] Herbert
Morgan, James, car repairer Erie, res 160 First [Anna]
            Mary, Grace, Stella, Harold, Catharine
"   Aldon R, machinist Erie, res 38 Marshall
"   Wm R, boiler-maker Erie, res 38 Marshall [Alice C]
            Wm, Ethel, Imo
"   Frank, cook Osborne hotel, res same
"   Edward, asst cook Osborne hotel, res same
"   Frank, cook and baker, res 244 e State [Ida]
"   J Carl, compositor Farmer's Guide, res 32 Etna ave
"   Fred, clk O C Morgan, res 32 Etna ave
"   Wm J, lab res 32 Etna ave
"   John, res 32 Etna ave. Daisy T
"   John V, bookpr Farmer's Guide, res 85 William st
            [Nellie] Mabel, Ralph, Bernice
Morris, J W, roadmaster Erie, res 140 Guilford [J P]
"   Clarence, emp Briant fac, res 26 Jackson
"   Clement, emp Briant fac, res 26 Jackson
"   Winfield, emp Briant, res 26 Jackson [Ida]
Morrison, W S, traveling passenger agt Erie, bds Osborne
Morse, W A, emp Briant, res 199 e State [Amanda]
"   C L, switchman Erie, res 247 e State [Linnie] Pearl,
            Lester, Arthur
Morton, J M, brakeman Erie, res 125 First [Jennie] Blanch
            M, Joseph A, Alma I
Moses, W F, machinist Erie, res 208 e Market [Allie] Edna,
            Charles, Goldie

Mosher, W H, painter and paper hanger, res 49 Division
[Harriett D] Ralph L, Bessie P, Mamie B,
Blanche J, Myron E

Mosier, Val, molder F W Dorn, res 41 Byron
" Linda, stenographer, res 181 Grayston ave

Moyer, Jesse, traveling salesman, rms over 51 n Jefferson

Mozier, M L, train despatcher Erie, res 7 Roche [Agnes]

Muckley Bros (O P, O K) dentists over 8 e Market

Muckley, O P (Muckley Bros) bds Star restaurant
" O K (Muckley Bros) bds Star restaurant

Munson, Rush, horse trainer, res 80 e Franklin [Minnie]

Murray, Elizabeth (wid John) res 82 Henry. James, Alice,
Agnes, Chas, Clara, Herbert
" Nora, waitress Star restaurant, res same
" M O (wid Byron) res 101 Guilford

Murray, L E, physician Bippus blk, res 28 Frederick [Mary
E] Ralph V, Dudley E

Murphy, Artemus, emp A G Johnson, res 82 Elm [Martha J]
| " Frances J, lab res 35 Swan
" Elsie, emp Briant, res 82 Elm
" Edward, eng inspector Erie, res 132 e Sabine [Julia]
Bartholomew, Joseph
" Richard, res 74 Frederick [Kate]
" A C, fruit tree agent, res 6 Lehmeyer [Nettie] Ada
M, Fay I, Ida F, Laura B
" Michael, lab res 130 e Market [Catharine] Katie

Myers, Frank P, train despatcher Erie, res 88 e Market [Ly-
dia] Ruby, Irene
" Angeline, res 91 First. Cora
" B P, machinist Erie, res 134 e Market [Jessie] Lura
" Deitrich, res 129 w State [Fredericka] Fred, Mary
" Henry, machinist Erie, res 129 e State

Mygrants, S C (wid) res 54 Mayne. Lloyd
" J F, painter, res 39 Everett [Anna] Floyd, Fred,
Virgil
" Allen, carpenter, res 78 Front [Mary]

Mygrants, Elmer, saloon Grand View, res 30 Front
"   Jessie, waitress Osborne hotel, res same
"   D C, painter, res 30 Salamonie ave   [Francis]
          Earl, Glenn, Virgil, Marie
Myres, Bert, eng Erie, res 121 First   [Anna]
Myres, N A, marb'e and stone dlr 14 n Jefferson, res 113 First
          [Lucinda]

N

Nagel, Mary (wid Peter) res 118 Grayston ave
†Nave, F, fish dlr 16 n Jefferson, res 96 Henry   [Elizabeth]
Nave, Samuel F, prop Brunswick Billiard Hall 18 e Market,
          res 8 Bingham
Nave, Edward (C C Nave & Son) res 8 Bingham
Nave, C C & Son (Charlotte, Edward) hardware, stoves, etc, 9
          s Jefferson
Nave, Charlotte (wid C C) res 8 Bingham.   Cora,   Laura
Nave, Rev H L, pastor First Presbyterian church, res 33 w
          Tipton [Florence]   Mark D,   Karl,   Grace
Neagle, James, flagman Erie, res 138 e Market   [Mary A]
"   Frank, lab res 138 e Market
Neiswinter, Henry, lab res 48 Halstead
Nethercutt, Hattie, res 25 Salamonie ave.   Glo
Neuer, Jacob, lab res 66 e Market   [Catharine]
"   Chas, lab res 61 e Market   [Elizabeth]   Elizabeth
"   Alex, emp Erie round hs, res 21 Erie   [Maggie]
"   Daniel, lab res 4 n Lafontaine   [Louise]

Neuer, John jr (Neuer & Eisenhauer) res 122 Poplar [Theresa M] Theresa E
" Chas, coppersmith Erie, res 141 Oak
" Nicholas, machinist Erie, res 141 Oak
" John sr, lab res 141 Oak [Magdalena] Ruth, Anna, Eddie, Katie
Neuer & Eisenhauer (John Neuer, A J Eisenhauer) boots and shoes 87 n Jefferson
Nevius, Bert B, timber cutter, res 26 Monroe [Dora] Andrew
Newcomb, Frank, barber Trixler, res over 12 e Washington [Elizabeth] Dessie, Blanche, Ethel
Newcomb, G L, produce, flour and feed 7-11 w Franklin, res 27 Fredericka [E R] Almeda, Wm D
Newcomb, G Otis, clk G L Newcomb, res 40 Fredericka [Anna] Nellie
Newcomb, C E, machine shop 16 e Washington, res 113 w State [Carrie M] Dean B
Newell, Rose E, teacher public schools, res 152 Court
" Mary E, teacher public schools, res 152 Court
" Chas, foreman painters Erie, res 152 Court [Elizabeth] Clarence
† " Henry, brick setter Martin, res Brawley st [Clara] Bertha, Maude, Irene, Linden
Newhart, N L, truckman, res 79 w State [Mary] Effie, Kittie
Newlove, Otto, saloon 25 s Jefferson, res 9 Etna ave [Anna] Earl
Newman, Catharine (wid Peter) res 37 Polk
New York Cash Store (M G Norton, prop) notions 25 n Jefferson street
Nichols, Henry, foreman bridge gang Erie, res 187 e Market [Emma] Pearl
" Fred, res 187 e Market [Mary] Baby
Nichols, B F, lumber, lath and shingles 50-58 e State, res 111 n Lafontaine [Lauretta H] Samuel
Nichols, Lucy, teacher public schools, res 111 n Lafontaine

118 DIRECTORY OF HUNTINGTON.

Nicholson, John, painter, res 105 Esther [Lena] Edward,
    Marie, George
Nifer, Edward, lab res 71 Superior [Mary] Cora, Homer
Nifer, Chas, apprentice Erie shops, res 71 Superior
Niles, John, brakeman Erie, res 128 e Franklin [Gustie]
    Hattie, Harold, Adda
Nille, Emma A, clk Western Lime Assn, res 83 w State
Nix, John, carpenter, res 36 w Market [Katharine]
Nix, Edward, barber 18 e Market, res 36 w Market. George
Nix, Emma, clk J Strodel, res 36 w Market
Nix, Nicholas, carpenter, res 101 w State [Eva] Cecelia,
    Lena, Joseph, Ada, Harmon, Fred, Agnes,
    Clarence
Noggle, Martha E, teacher public schools, res 71 Elm
Nolan, Enos, fireman Erie, res 10 Arthur [Cora] Esther
Nook, Joseph, carpenter and contractor, res 45 e Tipton
    [Mary J] Lena, Edith, Cary, Chas, John,
    Lauretta, Joseph
Norman, Chas, interlocker Erie, bds Windsor hotel
Norris, Dora, tailoress J W Van Arsdol, res over 14 w Market
Norton, Maxwell G, prop New York Cash store, res 97 Warren
Norton, Claude, clk New York Cash store, res 97 Warren
Null, Hugh S, blacksmith Erie, res 99 Oak [Kate]
Nunemaker, Isaac, car repairer Erie, res 165 e Tipton [Anna]
Nunemaker, Joseph, emp lime kilns, res 15 Iowa [Sarah]
    Grace, Ethel B, Wm H, John F

O

{Oatis, John C, meat market, 32 e Market, res s Jefferson [Dora]

Oats, Wesley, emp lime kiln, res 57 e Sabine [Sarah]
" Chas, yard man Erie, res 159 First [Ella] Harry
* " Joseph, lab, res s Etna ave [Margaret] Laura
" William, res 61 e Franklin [Adelaide]
" Ceph, emp Briant, res 91 Henry [Anna] Blanche, Maude, Beulah, Curtis
" Lillie, emp shoe factory, res 91 Henry
" Henry, emp Griffith & Son, res 56 Salamonie ave [Rebecca]
" Harvey, hosler Briant, res 78 Webster [Mary A]
" Michael, butcher, res 78 Webster

Obermeyer, John, emp lime kiln, res 51 McFarland [Nellie] Harvey, Emma, Carrie

O'Brien, Luke, eng Erie, res 145 First [Mary] Harry, Cleo
" Wm, switchman Erie, res Windsor House
" Pat, civil eng, res 138 Poplar
" Mary, res 138 Poplar

O'Connor, Bryan, eng Erie, res 9 Faust [Anna] May, Willis, Blanche, Anna, Elendor, Hildegard
" Miss Emma, emp Longdon, res 60 e Franklin
" John, eng Erie, res 80 First

Oglesbee, Esther, teacher public schools, res 47 Henry

O'Hara, James, shoemaker, res 9 Kitt [Catharine] James, Emma, Florence, Elias, Esther
" Anna, emp shoe factory, res 9 Kitt
" Geo, emp shoe factory, res 9 Kitt

O'Herron, Timothy, emp Erie, res 50 Wilkerson [Elizabeth]

Olmstead, Elizabeth (wid G W) emp Pearl Steam laundry, bds 96 w State

O'Laughlin, John, roadmaster T A A & N M Ry, res 11 Marshall [Kate] Mamie, Paschaline, Bridget

O'Laughlin, Michael, yard foreman Erie, res 85 e Tipton
        [Francis] Mary
     "   William, fireman Erie, res 11 Marshall
O'Leary, G M, veterinary surgeon, res 119 e Market
Orchard, Harry, machinist Erie, res 57 Court [Jessie] Paul
Osborne Hotel (J F J Siegmund, prop) 22-26 w Market
Ostertag, William, lab, res 64 Buck
Oswalt, Francis, res 122 e Market
    "   C G, watchman Briant, res 109 e State [Ellen] Mary
    "   Samuel, fireman Erie, res 109 e State
    "   John, fireman Erie, res 109 e State
    "   Edward, fireman Erie, res 109 e State
*Ott, Wm, emp Perrine & Bartlett, res Stringtown e fair
        ground [Mollie] Barbara
*Overholt, Thomas, res n Guilford [Dessie] Stella
    "   Philip, carpenter, res 190 Guilford   [Rhoda]
    "   Dessie V, domestic, 10 Randolph
    "   Daniel J, agt sewing machines, res 24 Whitelock
        Ethel
    "   Theresa, (wid John) res 24 Whitelock
    "   Levi, lab, res 154 e Franklin [Abbie J]
Overmyer, J R, carpenter Erie res 60 Whitelock [Mary] Roy,
        Clarence, Susie
    "   S C, carpenter Erie, res 80 Whitelock [Flora]
        Fred, Dessie, Hobart
Owen, C B, jeweler with Grafton, res 5 Elm

A man may guy,
And a man may lie,
    And a man may sweat and blow;
But he can't get trade
Setting in the shade,
    Waiting for business to grow.

H. COUCH,

THE TAILOR,

HUNTINGTON, INDIANA.

P

Pabst Brewing Co, (J L Brown, mgr) cor 3rd and Faust

Pacific Express Co (Geo Reynolds, agt) 26 n Jefferson

†Pagls, Henry, emp shoe factory, res Catharine st [Mary]
Hattie, Clara

Palmer, Henry, fireman Erie, res 68 Whitelock [Clara]
Jessie

† " Geo T, carpenter, bds 32 Catharine

Parker, Eva, waitress Star restaurant, res same
" Thos J, lab, res 50 Buck [Caroline] William E,
Florence M, Elvin H, Laura

Parks, William, teacher, res 80 Elm [Edith]
" Sam, barber, res 28 Warren

Parry, Carl, clk M M office Erie, res 110 e Market

Parnin, L C, res 48 Mayne [Lucinda]

Paschong, Frank, bartender Allman & Boos, res 106 e Franklin [Kate]

Paschong, William, grocer 104 e Market, res 147 First [Minnie] Nevada

Passwater, Milo, boiler mkr Erie, res 136 Court [Della]
Floyd, Harry

Pastor, Chas, gardener, res 72 Cline

Pastor, Geo, prop City Green House 97 Frederick, res same
[Barbara] Emma L, Carl, Gertrude

Pastor, Ed, clk A Pastor, res 94 Frederick

Pastor, Adam, grocery and bakery 18 n Jefferson, res 94 Frederick [Emma]

Patterson, C W, fireman Erie, res 67 Cherry [Mary] Robert
" Rachael, dressmaker, res 48 Henry
" Ella, dressmaker, res 48 Henry

Patten, Joseph, emp Foster brick yard, res 167 Byron [Anna]
Gertrude, Myrtle, Sherman
" H W, carpenter Erie, res 49 Marshall [Matilda]
Bertha, Chas

Patten, John, emp Erie, res 107 Byron
"   William, teamster, res 10 Nile [Dora] Chester
*Paul, Samuel, carpenter, res s Salamonie ave [Ida M]
        Belma
Paul, W S, dls in agricultural implements, 48-50 Warren, res
        29 Lehmeyer [L V] Russell K, Grace M,
        Fordia M
Paygman, T M, emp Erie, res 35 w Market [Emma E] Geo,
        Harry
Payne, Miss Addie, res 32 w Market
"   William, emp Briant, res 45 Briant [Belle] Philip
"   Washington, emp Briant, res 32 Superior [Lydia]
        Guy, Bessie
"   Jesse, emp Briant, res 32 Superior
"   Anna, res 49 South
"   Lawrence, emp C & E eating house, res same
Payton, E C, brakeman Erie, 21 Jackson [Dessie I] Roy J
"   Chas, cond Erie, res 126 e Market [Clara] Hazel,
        Thomas
Pearl Steam Laundry (H H Wagoner, H M Sprinkle, props)
        98 w State st
Peavey, Fred L, fireman Erie, res 142 Court [Lillie] Esther
        Winifred
Peden, H V, stone and marble dlr 98 n Jefferson, res 48 e
        Washington [Mary] Mabel, Williard, Dow,
        Marie, Katharine
Penfield, James G I, jeweler O Grafton, res 46 e Washington
"   A P, eng Erie, res 46 e Washington [Emma]
"   Harry A, res 46 e Washington
Penfold, J A, traveling salesman, res 24 Superior [Laura]
Penn, E G, insurance agt, res 118 Etna ave [Ellen] Myrtle,
        Charles
Pens, H F, brakeman Erie, res 107 Lincoln ave [Alice]
Perrine & Bartlett (Z D Perrine, W P Bartlett) lumber yard
        and saw mill 141 Front
Peting, Fred, wagon maker, res 108 Hitzfield [Anna]

Peting, August, lab res 108 Hitzfield

Peters, Earl, clk H H Arnold & Son, rms 32 w Market

Peterson, Michael, lab res Windsor hotel

Petrie, Nicholas, cigar maker, res 255 n Lafontaine

"   Peter, gardener, res 255 n Lafontaine

"   Matthias, bartender Engleman, bds Star restaurant

"   J, res 71 Oak

Pfeifer, Philip, saloon, 166 e Market, res 66 e Market

"   Henry, res 149 Cherry   [Mary]

"   George, emp Lang's brewery, res 33 e Sabine   [Carolina] George J,   Rosella

Phillabaum, Lewis, teamster, res 59 Grayston ave   [Mary E]

Phillips, Myrtle, domestic, res 128 Byron

Pierce, Frank, teamster, res 27 Lehmeyer   [Sarah]   Julia, William R,   Maude L

"   Elizabeth, teacher public schools, res 47 Henry

Pike, F H, brakeman Erie, res 141 e Market

Pimlot, Harry, eng Erie, res Grand View hotel

Pinkerton, Thos, res 4 Simon

*Pinkerton, Laura, res s Etna ave

"   W S, teacher high school, res 191 n Jefferson

"   Chas, plasterer, res 4 Simon [Mrs C] Jessie, Ruth, Ida

Pipenbrink, Henry, emp shoe factory, res 286 e State

"   Andrew, emp Briant, res 286 e State

"   Ernest, shoemaker 166 e Market, res 286 e State [Lizzie]   Chas

Piper, Harry, eng Erie, res 61 e Franklin

Planck, Edward, car repairer Erie, res 45 Webster   [Kittie] Domit, Mabel

"   Geo B, brakeman Erie, res 1 High   [Laura B] Hugh A,   Edna A

"   F A, inspector Erie, res 72 Front   [Clara]   Bruce

"   John, tinner Erie, res 211 e Market   [Matilda] Ola, Mattie, Grace, Fred, Bessie, John

Plane, Herbert, res 59 Webster   [Maude]   Dorothy

Plasterer, F S, teller Citizens' Bank, res 81 William [Edna]

Pleanitz, Lydia (wid Wm) res 2 Hannah. Wm jr

Plum, C Edward, eng Erie, res 57 High [Lizzie] George, Walter

Plummer, James P, carpenter, res 130 w Matilda [Margaret A] Joseph E, Olive E, Florence M, Arthur J, Emily, Lewis W

Pohler, John H, wagon mkr, res 26 Olinger [Mary C] Elizabeth, George C, Wm H, Laura

" Fred, clk Whitelock & Son, res 26 Olinger

Pomeroy, Mrs E A (Pomeroy & Blackburn) res 67 w Matilda

Pomeroy & Blackburn (A E Pomeroy, M Blackburn) milliners 83 n Jefferson

Poorman, Frank, emp Collins Ice Cream Co, res 17 Everett [Ella] Everet, Carl

Poorman, Theo, new and second hand goods 9 n Jefferson, res 276 Etna ave [Julia] Chas A, Aurelius, Etta, Clara

Pope, F H, night engine despatcher Erie, res 64 e Market [Alice] Lena, Howard

Porter, Blanche, res 54 Grayston ave

" Helene, res 54 Grayston ave

† " Calvin, book agt, res 23 Catharine

† " Chas, salesman, res 23 Catharine

† " Harriett, res 23 Catharine

Pottlitzer Bros (Jacob Meyer, mgr) commission merchants 112 n Jefferson

Powers, Edward, hostler Harter livery, res 11 Canal [Kate] Nona, Robert, Jessie, Sadie

" Will, hostler, res 11 Canal

Powell, W A, barber 29 n Jefferson, res 62 s Jefferson [Effie] Bertha, Philip, Muzetta

Powell, A P, carpenter, res 97 Warren [Auginina] L G A

" Nettie G, clk New York Cash store, res 97 Warren

" W C, meat market cor Mayne and Indiana, res 42 Indiana [Nina] Henry W, Frank A, Lucinda

Prices Always Correct, at MALIN'S

Prescott, Anna, emp shoe factory, res 36 Salamonie ave
Pressell, Ervin, machinist Erie, res 29 e Tipton [Barbara]
" Elmer, emp Erie shops, res 103 Railroad [Eva]
Agnes, Hermie, Willie
Pressler, Joseph, emp Briant, res 64 Mayne [Lillie] Myrtle,
Edna, Winfield
Price, Scott, switchman Erie, res 141 e Market [Maude] Thos
" Mollie, seamstress, res 140 Court
" Bridget (wid Wm) res 140 Court
" Wm, carpenter, res 50 Swan [Lydia] Lulu, Emma,
Fay, Pearl, Imo, Donald
J G (Price & Rosebrough) res 69 Poplar [Mary H]
Boyd, Bert A, Harry C, Hattie C, Henry H

Price & Rosebrough (J G Price, H E Rosebrough) insurance
and loans over 74 n Jefferson

Priddy, Will, emp Thompson & Co, res 28 Warren
*Priddy, Phoebe (wid) res s Etna ave. Bertha, LeRoy
Pride, Col Geo G, civil engineer, res 32 w Market
Prill, Wm, sawyer Griffith & Son, res 44 Buchanan [Caroline]
Edith, Elmer, Laura
Prince, Chas M, teamster Perrine & Bartlett, res 86 Garfield
[Lena] Edith, Floyd, Dwight, Mildred, Hobart
Princes, The (Lydia Moore, prop) department store 24 e Market
Provines, John W (Purviance & Provines) res cor Elm and
Sophia [Amelia]
Pumphrey, F M, carpenter Erie, res 25 South [Alice M] Ray
Purdue, Cora, res 14 William
Purviance, Mary A, res cor Byron and Franklin
" W R, emp Singer Sewing Machine Co, res 235
William [Mary L]
James A, clk Dickover & Altman, res 60 Mayne
[Ella] Maude, Madge, Geo, Helen, Paul

Purviance & Provines (Marshall J Purviance, J W Provines)
dry goods and notions 11 s Jefferson
Purviance, Marshall J (Purviance & Provines) res 41 s Jeff's'n

Abstracts prepared with care, at BLACK'S ABSTRACT OFFICE.

Purviance, Emma, stenographer Western Lime Assn, res 41 s
    Jefferson
"   Henrietta (wid Jos W) res 128 Etna ave. Lucy
"   Flora, student, res 156 n Jefferson
"   D A, loan agent, res 156 n Jefferson [Elizabeth]
    Mabel, Donald

Q

Quick, Edward, cond Erie, res 97 e State [Anna] Myrtle,
    Charles
Quigley, Rhoda (wid John) milliner over 60 n Jefferson, res
    44 w Matilda
Quigley, Ethel, clk R Quigley, res 44 w Matilda
Quinlan, Rev Father, pastor St Mary's Catholic church, res
    182 n Jefferson

R

Rader, A W, traveling salesman, res 9 Charles [Jennie]
    Wilbur K, Lucile, Allen
Rae, G W, brakeman Erie, res 129 Court [Jeff]
Rahn, Edwin, foreman Farmer's Guide, res 147 William street
    [Mary] Emma, Elmer
[Rains, R W, res Wright st, w of s Jefferson

Rall, W C, cond Erie, res 23 Salamonie [Laura] Pearl F

Randolph, Wm, res 105 e State

Raney, Chas, carpenter, res 55 Whitelock [Alice] D M Freda

Raper, Wm, emp lime kilns, res 110 Hitzfield [Dora] Minnie, Sophia

" Wm jr, emp Erie, res 110 Hitzfield

" Dora, emp Exchange hotel, res 110 Hitzfield

Rathgaber, Jacob, plasterer, res 55 e Tipton

Rausch, Catharine (wid Andrew) res 88 Cherry

" Frank, lab res 88 Cherry

" John, emp Erie shops, res 94 Cherry [Matilda] Lucas, Clara

" Henry, clk Erie M M office, res 94 Cherry

" Peter, bookpr, res 94 Cherry

Raver, Park, clk Reichenbach & Wickenhiser, res 5 High [Eva] Lura, Clydie

Ray, Pearl (wid Wm) res 103 Lincoln ave

Raymer, Patrick, teamster, res 25 Canfield [Neva] Francis, Robert, Ralph

Raymond, Charles, make-up Democrat, res 15 s Lafontaine st [Emma]

" John P, blacksmith C E Newcomb, res 64 Frederick [Rose] John jr

Reagan, Charles, brakeman Erie, res 101 Court [Amelia] Wilbur

Ream, A J, emp city fire dept, res 7 Oak [Lizzie] Edith B, Cecil M, Geo W

" Al, emp Erie, res 38 Sabine [Minnie] Grace

" Henry, eng Erie, res 34 Canfield [Anna] Orin, Lulu, Clara, Nona

Rease, Ella, domestic 29 Frederick

Recklau, Henry, tailor, res over 94 n Jefferson

Recklau, Chris, merchant tailor over 94 n Jefferson, res 98 n Lafontaine [Mary] Elizabeth, (Adolph Ackerman)

Redding, John, emp Lang brewery, res 55 e Tipton [Mary]
        Clarence, Harmon
Redman, Joseph, flagman Wabash, res over 16 n Jefferson
    "   Amos, boiler mkr Erie, res 27 South [Jennie] El-
        ma, Walter, Estella, Dale
Reed, A, switchman Erie, res 122 e Market
    "   John, lab, res 173 n Jefferson
    "   W E baker Star restaurant, res 119 e State [Hattie]
Reed, Isaac D, real estate agt over 29 n Jefferson, res 34
        Bingham [Ida V] Jessie B, Edna, Fred
Reed, Verda, clk sheriff's office, res 22 Monroe
    "   Laura P (wid Levi) dressmaker, res 22 Monroe
Rehling, Richard, emp Fred Lashing, res 29 e Matilda
Rehm, Nora C, teacher public schools, res 8 Guilford
Reichard, Henry, cigar mfg, res 36 William [Hallie] Kenneth
    "   Mary (wid John P) res 76 Cherry
    "   G Fred, cigar mkr, res 76 Cherry
    "   Ferdinand, cigar m'f'g 78 Cherry, res 76 Cherry
        [Flora E]
  | Ellsworth, lab, res e State near Brawley [Ella]
        Mary E, Hazel N
Reichenbach, A (Reichenbach & Wickenhiser) res 113 Guilford
        [Ida] Lucie
Reichenbach & Wickenhiser (A Reichenbach, F E Wicken-
        hiser) hardware 51 n Jefferson
Reifert, Otto, blacksmith Wm Dimond, res 244 e State
Reiley, W R, policeman, res 43 Matilda [Martha] Katie,
        Edson, Anna, Frank
Reilley, Frank, eng Erie, res 30 Webster [Mary]
Renbarger, John H, driver fire dept, res 100 w State [Sarah]
        Pearl, Etta
    "   James, res 53 Etna ave
    "   John M, res 53 Etna ave [Charity] Eliza
Renn, John, principal Lutheran school, res 42 Polk
Repp, David, clk Wells Fargo express, res 202 Guilford
    "   Leonard, emp Wm McGrew, res 202 Guilford

Repp, J W, teamster, res 202 Guilford [Lucy]

†Ressler, Henry S, miller, res s Salamonie ave [Mattie E]
Effie

Reub, John, lab res 75 Bartlett [Augusta] Flora, Dora,
Chris

Reust, Anna (wid John) res 61 w Matilda

Reynolds, Geo, agt Pacific and Wells Fargo express, res 22
William [Kate E]

"   C C, supt Erie, res 130 Guilford [Agnes] Ray W,
Marie M, Charles, Lewis, Louise

Rinehart, Geo, carpenter Wabash, res 107 s Jefferson [Etta]

Rhodes, Mary, housekeeper, res 25 Mayne. Chester

Rice, George, lab bds 207 William

Rice, Joseph L, teamster, res 105 Broadway [Mary C]

*Richard, B W, emp Perrine & Bartlett, res s Etna ave [Ida]
Nellie

Richards, E T., carpenter Erie, res 9 Edwin [Emma J]
Mable C

"   B A, shoemaker 19 n Jefferson, res 28 William
[Clara] Earl R.

Richardson, J. L, prop garment cutting school 14 Henry, res
same [Ella] Hazel.

"   Aaron, emp H. L, & F. Co., res 73 Guilford
[Sarah] Harrison, James, Reiley, John.

Richwine, William E, emp Bucher & Weber, res 3 Hannah
[Lucy] Leon, Edith, Cleo, Watson.

"   Hannah (wid John) res 25 Elm.

"   George, barber, res 62 s Jefferson.

"   Walter, emp Withington factory, res 28 Briant
[Jessie] Kenneth.

Ricker, Jessie, plumber emp J H Gusman, res 58 Marshall

"   Eliza (wid David) res 58 Marshall. Iva, Sadie

Ridgley,, Allie (wid) res 228 e State. Wando.

Rife, Alva, lab, res 35 Mayne.

Rifenberick, Elizabeth (wid John M) res 40 Frederick

Riggers, William, lab, res 7 Hitzfield.
"   Maggie (wid William) res 7 Hitzfield. Madie Anna
"   Charles, lab, res 7 Hitzfield,
†Rinehart, J C, lab, res 18 Catharine [Jennie] Myrl Grace
Ritter, Andrew, lab, res 60 Hitzfield [Lena] Francis,
          Joseph, Mary, Lizzie, Edith, Pauline.
Rittenhouse, E M, emp Briant's factory, res 59 Superior
          [Mary] Austin S, Realy R, Mable R
†Robbins, L S, emp shoe factory, res s Salamonie Ave
†   "   Jennie (wid) res s Salamonie Ave. W W
"   W A, brakeman Erie, res 27 Gay
"   Chas, res 73 e Sabine
Robins, James, L, carpenter, res 27 Division [Sarah I] Gar-
          land A
          Orange, carpenter Erie, res 188 E Market [Sarah]
          Fernie
Robinson, Dottie, domestic Osborne hotel, res same
"   John, machinist Erie, res 106 First [Belle] Grace
"   Ed, tailor A H Malins, res 28 Warren
"   Michael, emp Erie, res 40 Fredericka [Ida]
"   Lee, eng Erie, res 83 First [Kate] Agnes, Alice,
          Mabel, Harry, Lillie
"   Emeline (wid Joseph R) res 83 First
"   John, fireman Erie, res 230 e State [Louisa]
          William
"   Mina, domestic, res 141 n Jefferson
*   "   Richard, traveling salesman, res s Henry [Leona]
          Ruth
"   E M, emp Perrine & Bartlett, res 29 Briant [Anna]
          Eva, Jennie, Ethel, Frank
Robertson, Charles, lab, res 12 Allen [Jennie] Ethel
Roche, Thomas, attorney, office over 81 n Jefferson, res 137
          Cherry [Hannah]
"   David, res 27 Sabine
"   Bridget, res 182 n Jefferson

Rockafeller, W H, druggist, 21 n Jefferson, res 26 n Lafontaine [Esther]
" J F, machinist Erie, res 11 Arthur [Jennie] Ruby, Lyle, Edith

Rodgers, Dr Leroy, physician, office and residence 60 Frederick [Louisa] Tressie, Don, Jessie, Tennie
" Edgar L, insurance agent, res 60 Frederick

Rogers, J Mat, barber, 29 n Jefferson, res 55 High [Vert]
" Douglas, baker, res 8 Canal [Minnie] Charles E
" James, lab. res 160 William
* " Joseph, emp Withington factory, res e Front
" George, boilermaker Erie, res 15 Faust [Nancy] Charles
* " James M, agent, res s Etna ave [Etnie] Cressie
" Ray, emp Byer Bros, res 60 Frederick

Roher, C, fireman Erie, res Windsor hotel

Rohlman, George, brakeman Erie, res 7 Iowa [Minnie] Ralph, Bert, Raymond

Roller, Miss Louisa, teacher Lutheran school, res 91 Buck
" Herman, clerk Schaefer & Schaefer, res 91 Buck
" Louise (wid Jacob) res 91 Buck. Rosa

Roof, Jacob, junk dealer, res 92 Buck [Seth] Peter, Minnie, Sam, Nier
" Myer, umbrella mender, res 165 Etna ave [Rosa] Meyer

Rose, Jacob, timber dealer, res 49 Frederick [Lucy]

Rosebrock, Henry, jeweler, 10 w Market, res 131 n Jefferson

Rosebrock, H F, jeweler 10 w Market, res over 131 n Jefferson [Lena] Carl

Rosebrough, A J, drayman, res 35 William [Sidney] Harry B, Mary C.
" Frank L, lab, res 35 William
" J, A, lab, res 35 William
" E, M, clerk F Dick & Son, res 63 Henry [Etta]
" H E (Price & Rosebrough) res 9 Roche [Mamie]

Rosebrough, A B (wid Elisha) res 28 Warren
"   Adele, res 28 Warren
"   Henry, res 19 Buchanan [Hattie] Jessie
Ross, L B, traveling salesman, res 56 Elm
"   Frank, policeman, res 7 Whitelock [Fannie] Edward
Rosswurm, Fred, emp lime kilns, res 52 Thomas [Louisa]
        Fredericka, Amelia
"   Fred jr, student, res 52 Thomas
"   Conrad, emp lime kilns, res 52 Thomas
†Roth, Herman, foreman shoe fac, res s Salamonie ave [Emma] Amy, Albert, Dale
Rothermel, Owen, emp Stults livery, res 17 Iva
"   S M, fruit tree agt, res 17 Iva [Emma] Harley
        M, Iva L, Alvah D, Floyd
Rouch, Willard, clk Globe Clothing store, res over same
Rourke, James, boiler mkr Erie, res 112 Lincoln ave [Carrie]
        Blanche, Bertha, Raymond
Royston, John W, brakeman Erie, res 145 e Market [Jennie]
        Lambert R, Olive M, Iva, Otho
Rudig, James, res 29 Briant
Ruggles, Thos J, county surveyor, res 86 n Lafontaine [Lavina] Dessie
"   Chas, cement walk builder, res 89 Whitelock
† "   Wm, fruit tree agt, res s Salamonie ave [Mahala]
        Gertrude
"   Dora, cement walk builder, res 89 Whitelock
Rupley, Daniel, res 92 Front. Miss Mary
Ryan, John, plumber and contractor, res 132 Poplar
"   Harvey, emp Midway restaurant, res 114 e Franklin
"   Daniel, attorney, res 33 Roche [Louisa] Edith
"   Henry P, attorney, res 33 Roche
"   Jacob, medical student, res 33 Roche
"   D Oscar (McCauley & Ryan) res 33 Roche

S

Saal, Andrew, clk McCaffrey & Co, res 119 Court [Frona]

Saal, O A, painter, res 92 William [Mary]

Sammetiner, Martin, carpenter, res 170 William [Josephine] Henry, John, Fred

*Saner, Perry, miller Stults & Dorsch, res s Etna ave

Savage, R F, foreman Erie yards, res 180 First [Maggie] Carl H, Lulu C, Paul, Clyde

Sayler, Sayler & Sayler (H B, S M, J M) attorneys 47 Warren

Sayler, Henry B (Sayler, Sayler & Sayler) res 18 Etna ave

" S M (Sayler, Sayler & Sayler) res 18 Etna ave [Luella C] Oliver M, Isabella, Arthur

" J M (Sayler, Sayler & Sayler) res 51 William [Jennie W] Agnes, Henry

* " Levi, plasterer, res e Front [Ella] Hazel

Salterthwaite, Wm, lab res 69 Etna ave [Jane] Martha, Chas, LeRoy, Roscoe, Harry

" Hiram W, res 56 Henry [Mrs H W]

Saul, Chas C, emp Western Lime Assn, res 22 Grayston ave [Lusodie]

Schaef, Daniel, foreman tinner Erie, res nw cor Market and First [Mrs D]

Schaefer & Schaefer (R O, M B) drugs se cor Jefferson and Market streets

Schaefer, Martin B (Schaefer & Schaefer) res 76 William [Hannah] Lucien, Waldo, Lela, Wanda, Alma

" Elizabeth (wid Carl) res 10 Bingham

" Rudolph O (Schaefer & Schaefer) res 7 s Lafontaine [Catharine] Gertrude, Carl R, Irene M, Geo L, Ruth

Schaeley, Albert, emp lime kilns, res 157 Broadway [Caroline] Amy, Ricka, Albert

Schaffer, Elizabeth (wid Lawrence) res 165 n Lafontaine

Schagel, Belle (wid Nelson) res 88 Grayston ave

Schearer, Jacob, lab res 35 Erie [Mary] Chas, Carl, Ralph
" Jacob, wagon-maker, res 99 William [Julia]
Scheer, Jos, emp lime kilns, res 26 McFarland
" John, stone mason, res 26 McFarland
" Catharine, res 26 McFarland
" Nicholas sr, res 24 McFarland
" Nicholas jr, contractor, res 28 McFarland [Minnie]
Paulus, Leo, Baby
" Jacob, fireman Erie, res 144 e Sabine [Elizabeth]
Scheerer, Jacob, car repairer Erie, res 206 e Market [Susan]
Albert, George
Scheiber, Peter, grocer 119 n Jefferson, res 64 w Tipton [Anna M] Julia, Helen, Bertha, Lauretta, Paul,
Cecelia
Scheiber, Lizzie, music teacher, res over 131 n Jefferson
" August, clk Arnold & Son, res 147 Cherry [Mary]
Agnes, Edith, Geo, Stella, Alice, Fred
" Henry, drayman E Shanks, res 49 e Matilda [Lydia] Mabel
" Kinsgunda (wid John) res 112 Oak
Scheiblin, Fred, brick mason, res 47 Wilkerson
" Geo (Scheiblin & Son) res 5 Leopold [Elizabeth]
" Jacob (Scheiblin & Son) res 11 Leopold. Amelia
" Chris, emp Thompson & Co, res 11 Leopold
" Wm, clk Scheiblin & Son, res 11 Leopold
Scheiblin & Son (Jacob, George) saloon 6 w Market
Schepper, Christian, res 113 Lincoln ave. Dora
" Lizzie (wid Christian) res. 113 Lincoln ave. Edith,
Rudolph, Amelia
" Sophia, res 94 Buck
" Lizzie, res 94 Buck
" Edward, fireman Erie, res 122 Lincoln ave. [Mary]
Schinboom, Solomon C, junk dlr, res 92 Buck [Lillie] Allo,
Frader
Schindler, John, eng Erie, res 65 e Market [Mary]

Schoenfeld, Chas, clk trainmaster's office, bds Star Restaurant
Schoolcraft, Jessie, res 133 First
" Ezra E, res 37 Whitelock
" Mariah (wid John) res 37 Whitelock
" J O, res 70 Marshall. L B, H E, Jessie M
Schooley, Samuel, lab, res 34 Front [Katharine] Bedford, Floyd
Schoonmaker, Josephine, res 90 Webster
" C V, brakeman Erie, 90 Webster [Lottie] Roy
Schoenell, Clarence, lab res 78 e State
" Helena, res 78 e State
" Henrietta, emp shoe factory, res 78 e State
" John, fireman Erie, res 66 Webster [Sadie]
Schott, Mrs Elizabeth, res 123 Dimond. Maggie, John, Baby
Schnieder, Wm, emp shoe factory, bds 60 Whitelock
Schnurr, Wendall A, prop Club saloon, res 23 German. Catharine
Schrage, William, tailor Malins' Tailor Shop, res 8 Warren [Rettie] Jessie, Ida, Harry, Alma
Schreyer, P H, carpenter, res 9 e Tipton [Katie]
" Allen C, car inspector Erie, res 9 e Tipton
Schroeder, Richard, clk Strodel's dry good, res 113 Lincoln ave
Schultz, William, clk G L Newcomb, res 99 Dimond
" Harmon, lab, res 99 Dimond
" Fred, emp Griffith & Son, res 99 Dimond [Minnie] Eddie, Martha, Lena
" Henry, lab W Linne Co., res 105 Dimond
Schuyler, Maggie (wid William) res 69 w State
Schwartz, John, lab res 74 n Lafontaine [Matilda]
" Wm, supt water works, res 57 Oak [Beana] Carl, Anna, Lizzie, John, Hannah, Walter, Paul, Gertrude
Soott, J Z, res 232 n Jefferson [Nancy J]
" Laura, res 168 n Jefferson
Scott, N W, physician, office and res 91 e Market [Pearl] Frank T

Sculley, John, lab res box car near Wab and Erie transfer

Searles, Ellis, city editor Democrat, res 59 Etna ave   [Nellie]
    Paul, Bessie

Searles, J D, physician, office and res over 17 w Market st
    [Mrs J D]

Seber, Jacob, lab res 14 Hannah [Barbara] Otto
   "   Ollie, emp Arnold & Son, res 14 Hannah
   "   Edward, emp Harter livery, res 14 Hannah
   "   Peter, lab res 171 William [Mary E]

Sees, Patrick, carpenter, res 14 Wesley [Mary]
   "   John V, teacher, res 14 Wesley

Seeley, W D, machinist Erie, res 116 Lincoln ave [Vade]

Sell, Carl, teamster, res 95 n Lafontaine [Mollie] John

Sellers, C W, eng Erie, res 30 w Matilda [Lizzie A] Chas,
    Burton, Benj, Howard

Septer, John, emp Erie shops, res 29 Grayston ave [Orpha A]
    Willis

Sessions (Norman, R N) dentists over 9 w Market

Sessions, N (Sessions) res 187 n Jefferson [M]
   "   R N (Sessions) res 187 n Jefferson

Severence, S F, boarding house, 41 e Franklin, res same [C
    E] Emma
   "   Arthur L, clk H H Arnold & Son, res 21 Front
   "   Hattie, clk H H Arnold & Son, res 21 Front
   "   H H(wid LaGrange) res 21 Front. Jessie, Henri-
    etta, Howard

Sexton, Edwin, cond Erie, res 76 e Franklin [Sarah A]

Shaffer, D A, foreman Briant bending works, res 93 First
   "   Jane (wid A W) res 93 First
   "   Louisa (wid Edward A) res 23 Wilkerson. Anna,
    Laura, Henry V

Shaffer, E W, physician over Herald office, res 115 e State
    [Ella] Herbert, Nellie, Mabel

Shaffer, Edward, blacksmith, res 56 Grayston ave [Ida]
    Frank

Shaffer, Hattie (wid Theo) res 38 Kocher
" Ella, res 19 Foust
Shaffer, Abner H, physician and surgeon over First National
Bank, res 168 n Jefferson [Elizabeth]
Shaffer, Emma J, res 74 e Market
" Jas H, eng Erie, res 122 e Franklin [C A] Augustus
" Jacob, teamster Nichols, res 235 n Lafontaine [Mary]
Anna, Joseph, Celia, Mary
Shank, Martha J (wid Daniel) res 63 w Matilda
" Emmet, drayman and storage 53-55 Guilford, res 53 e
Washington [Alice B]
" T M, res 178 Guilford [Elizabeth]
" Laura E, stenographer Farmer's Guide, res 178 Guilford
Shank, W H, blacksmith 110 n Jefferson, res 21 e Tipton
[Lucinda M]
Shank, Z B, fireman Erie, res 7 Third [Olive] Walter
Sharer, Wells, lab res 102 Cherry [Sarah E] Lorenzo D,
Jessie C, Hayden R
Shaw, Mrs Bertha, res 74 Oak
" R M, eng Erie, res 133 e Franklin [Josephine] Earl,
Frank, Genevieve, Agatha, Irene
" Chas, brakeman Erie, res 139 e Market
Shearer, Frank, painter Erie, res 5 Foust [Lizzie] Helen
" Tillie, dressmaker, res 5 Fredericka
" F M, car repairer Erie, res 51 Whitelock
" Belle, res cor Marshall and Tipton
Shearer, G W, grain dlr 109 n Jefferson, res 71 e Tipton [Mary
O] (Bessie Briant)
Shearer, Sarah (wid Sexton H) res 15 Frederick
" Edward, clk D Marx, res 95 William [Hannah]
Herman, Ernest, Arthur, Hayden, Evalyn
" Frank, emp Beyer Bros, res 2 Lehmeyer
" John, lab res 117 Elm. Gladys
" Jacob, lab res 114 Elm. Icy D, Viola
" J W, eng Erie, res 51 Grayston ave [Lizzie]
" Lucetta, res 167 e Market

Sheets, John H, carpenter Erie, res 26 Elizabeth [Eliza] Victoria, Daisy, Marion
* "   Jacob, lab res e Front
  "   John, res 33 Milligan [Lydia]
  "   Chas, teamster, res 68 Superior
  "   Geo W, teamster, res 33 Buck [Delitha] Alma, Theo, Otto, Arthur, Laura
| "   Samuel M, emp lime kilns, res 33 Swan [Emma] Cleo M
  "   Albert, emp Erie round hs, res 11 Gay [Augusta] Virginia
Shelby, Myrtle, cook Hotel Eastern, res 122 e Market
  "   James F, emp Erie, res 89 e Sabine [Rena] Frank, George, Chas, Alta, William
Shellenbarger, John (Jack the Ripper) res any convenient spot
Shepper, Daniel, res 95 w State [Catharine]
Sheridan, Elmer E (Amos & Sheridan) res 216 William street [Orange Grove] Harry A
Sherwin, Sabie (wid Herman) res 57 Henry
Shideler, H D, co supt, office Court House, res 25 Madison st [Laura] Mark H
  "   W H, fireman Erie, res 109 First [Emma] Opal
+ "   J E, baggage master Erie, res 16 Catharine [Christa] Paul, Howard
Shingle, Lewis, fruit tree agt, res 125 Byron [Sarah] Grace
Shipley, O C, brakeman Erie, res 76 e State [Elizabeth]
Shirk, W H, fireman Erie, res 12 Edwin [Louise] Mary J, Fred J
Shisler, Chas, brakeman Erie, res 16 Third [Cora] Park
Shoboy, W H, brakeman Erie, res 165 First [Cora]
  "   H L, clk res 165 First
Shock, Philip A, tubular well man, res 89 w Tipton [Lydia A] Myrtle M, Edith P, Mary C, Raymond M, Geneva
  "   Mary D (wid Adam S) res 121 e Franklin

Shock, Samuel jr, lab res 91 Broadway [Bessie] Mary
" Ed, clk C Walter, res 53 e Washington
" J W, cement walk builder, res 82 e Market [Bertie]
Fay
" Frank, brakeman Erie, res 133 Court [Carrie] Harry
Shoemaker, Anna, domestic 158 Guilford
" Henry, carpenter Erie, res 235 Etna ave [Jennie]
Tessie, Laudie, Lewis
" G W, emp Ira Landis, res 153 Court [Caroline]
Glenn, Edna
" Ora M, teacher public schools, res 8 William
" John A, emp city, res 11 Etna ave [Mary E]
Ephriam A, Bernie, Eldon, Harry
Sholl, Harry S, fruit tree agt, res 14 w Matilda [Laura]
Mayme
Shoffner, Harry, clk, res 23 Wilkerson
" Ruth, res 228 e Market
Shonnessey, John, eng J Kenower & Sons, res 38 Byron
[Clara] Florence
Shores, E A (wid) res 87 w State. Lillie, Emma
Shorker, Rosa, res 93 Cherry
Show, L C, installment agt, res 115 e Market [Ollie] Ocia
Shroyer, G W, brakeman Erie, res 34 Kintz [Adda] Pearl,
Chas, Ora, Goldie
" H V, blacksmith Erie, res 77 Superior [Lizzie] Dale
. E, Elvin B
" E W, sawyer Perrine & Bartlett, res 3 Gay [Mary]
Meda, Marie
Shultz, Wm, emp lime kilns, res 18 Kocher [Minnie] Minnie,
Martha, William
" Fred, emp lime kilns, res 22 Kocher [Fredericka]
Edith, Harmon, Sophia
Shurtleff, Chas, brakeman Erie, res 8 Iowa. Maude, Ada,
Grace, Wayne, Vivian
" W C, eng Erie, res 72 High [Amelia] Eva, Clar-
ence, Edward

Shutt, Emery, emp Bucher & Weber, rms cor Matilda and
    Warren
† " Lewis A, contractor, res s Salamonie ave [Lida] Car-
    rie, Effie, Ora, Allie
† " John, carpenter, res Wright [Kate] Jessie, Winifred
    Herman
Siegmund, J F J, prop Exchange hotel, res same [Mrs J F J]
    Bertha, Lillian, Fred
    " Rudolph, clk Exchange hotel, res same
    " Oscar L, res Exchange hotel
    " Edward, student, res Exchange hotel
Silver, Henry, grain elevator Wabash tracks, res 93 e State
    [Carrie]
Simons, Gertrude, student, res 58 William
    " Harry, res 58 William
    " Robert, lab, res 58 William
    " Nicholas, drayman, res 156 n Lafontaine [Lizzie]
    " Oliver, stone mason, res 75 Elm [Ida] Emerson,
    Dessie, Lena
    " Mary A, dressmaker, res 53 Webster
    " Lizzie, dressmaker, res 53 Webster
    " Adrain, lab res 38 Superior [Hannah]
    " W E, reporter Democrat, res 3 Kitt [Belle]
    " Nicholas sr, carpenter, res 97 Poplar [Katharine]
    Mary, Joseph, Philip, Caroline, Celia, John,
    Charlie, George
    " Joseph, merchant tailor 10 w Market, res 20 Poplar
    [Francis]
Simonton, Robert, real estate agent, res 44 Henry [Melissa J]
    " H B, res 44 Henry
Sing, Joe, Chinese laundry 35 w State, res same
    " Chas, Chinese laundry 35 w State, res same
Singer, V D, cond Erie, res 29 High [Rosa] Millie, Beatrice,
    Fred, Walter, George, Marie
Sisson, D W, res 30 w Matilda
    " Chas, brakeman, res 30 w Matilda

Sister M Raineria Superior,SS Peter and Paul school, res same
Sister M Josine, SS Peter and Paul school, res same
Sister M Quirine, SS Peter and Paul school, res same
Sister M Rhoda, SS Peter and Paul school. res same

*Sitloh, Henry, emp Erie round hs, res e Front [Rosa] Chas, John, Henry, Myrtle
Skelley, Thos, stone cutter, res 104 Court
    "   J A, stone cutter, res 104 Court
Skidmore, Henry, eng Erie, res 130 e Franklin [Emma] Sam'l
Skiles, John, clk Pottlitzer Bros, res 20 e Tipton [Sarah J]
    "   Mary M, teacher, res 53 Frederick
    "   Harmon D, expressman, res 53 Frederick [C L] J D
Skinner, Wm, switchman Erie, res 17 Edwin [Cora] Irene
Slack, Sarah A (wid Theo) res 29 Superior
    "   A P (wid Gen J R) res 94 Guilford
    "   J R, res 94 Guilford [Flora M] Belle, Lizzie, Mamie
    "   Helene, teacher public schools, res 53 w Matilda
Slagel, David S, carpenter, res 10 Grayston ave [Rebecca J] Elmer E, Carrie B
Slagel, Wm, carpenter Erie, res cor Buck and Etna ave
*   "   Thos, carpenter Erie, res s Etna ave [Celestia] Rose
Slater, Joseph, truck foreman Erie, res 229 e State [Martha]
    "   Dessie, res 26 Leopold
    "   Arthur, res 26 Leopold
Slattery, Daniel, boiler maker Erie, res 14 Third [Minnie]
Slaudruf, Henry, lab res 56 Swan [Adda] Baby
Slusser, Ira, lab res 70 South [Eldora] Harry, Loretta. Cleo, Fred, Irene, Jacob M
    "   Wm T, eng Erie, res 17 w Market [Maggie]
    "   F F, eng Erie, res 59 Webster [Josephine] Howard, Dessie
    "   Claude, fireman Erie, res 59 Webster
    "   Lemuel, plasterer, res 256 e State [Dora]
*   "   Milton, traveling salesman, res n Guilford
*   "   Samuel, gardener, res n Guilford. Matilda, Bertha

Slusser, J Q, student, res 54 First

" Chas, clk Bradley Bros, bds Star restaurant

Smetzer, Abraham, emp lime kilns, res 61 Sabine [Eva] Emma, Albert, Frank, Dora

Smith, Will, machinist Erie, res 45 Byron [Agnes] Robert

" M J, eng Erie, res 127 First [Carrie] Jewell

" W H (White & Smith) res 84 Byron [Mary C] Guy R, May I, Hazel D

" Arthur, res 55 Wilkerson

" Margaret (wid Wm G) res 93 w Tipton

" Orlistus C, drayman, res 93 w Tipton

" F D, cutter shoe factory, res cor Kitt and Salamonie ave [Edna]

* " Geo A, painter, res e fair ground [Hattie] Elizabeth

" Peter, carpenter Erie, res 15 Oak [Mary] John J, Chas M, Maggie E, Bertha E

" Mat, lab res 57 w Tipton [Theresa] Lizzie, Esther

" Michael, res 140 Oak [Catharine] Effelina, Leo, Herbert, Cornelius

* " Benj R, emp Erie, res e fair ground

" J C (Smith & Bro) res 40 Grayston ave [Maggie] Otis, Orange E, Mabel F

" Edward, lab res 173 n Jefferson

" Frank C, fireman Erie, res 21 Whitestine

" J R, res 48 w Market

" James, eng Erie, res 109 w State [Alice]

" Rosa (wid) res 169 Guilford, Wm, Anra, John, Chas

" Joseph, machinist Erie, res 169 Guilford

" Mamie, res 178 Guilford

" M D, carpenter, res n Guilford [Anna] Glenn

" Come, emp Exchange hotel, res same

Smith, T G, attorney over 29 n Jefferson, res 63 Etna ave [Josephine A]

Smith, Jos N, mail carrier, res 150 e Tipton [Jennie] Otha

Smith, Mrs J N, grocery 150 e Tipton, res same

*Smith, Wm O, emp H L & F Co, res s Etna ave [Mary C]
    Louis, Gertrude
* "   Samuel, lab res s Etna ave [Mary] Roscoe, Colum-
    bus
* "   James, lab res s Etna ave [Belle] Wilbur
  "   Melissa (wid Atchison) res 50 Frederick
  "   Ora E, painter and paper hanger, res 50 Frederick
  "   Mahlon D, teacher, res 58 Frederick [Sarah] Waldo
    A, Emery, Cleo, Hazel
  "   Chas A, emp Withington, res 24 Briant
  "   S B, res 62 e State [Lydia]
  "   Frank, brakeman Erie, res 110 e State [Dora] Fred,
    Edward
  "   A C, hand car builder Erie, res 210 e Market [Anna]
    Grace
  "   Paul, boiler mkr Erie, res 210 e Market
  "   Luther, machinist Cycle Co, res 210 e Market
* "   Samuel W, emp brick yd, res n Guilford [Lizzie] Iva
  "   K (Hurd & Smith) res 58 e Franklin
  "   Columbia (Harbert & Smith) res 22 Warren
  "   R D (Smith & Lawyer) res cor Byron and e Franklin
Smith & Lawyer (R D Smith, J W Lawyer) real estate and in-
    surance agts over 4 e Market.
Smith Bros (L A, J C) pump dlrs 54 Warren
Smith, L A (Smith Bros) res 18 Guilford [Ida Mangus]
  "   Rob't, emp Kolotona fac, res 119 e Market
  "   Ida, res Windsor hotel
  "   Andrew, res 72 e Market [Sarah A M] Ralph A
  "   Nancy (wid) res 72 e Market
Smith, C R, drugs and jewelry 60 n Jefferson, res 64 e Market
    [Matilda]
  "   Wesley, lab res 101 Grayston ave [Nancy]
  "   Frank P, emp Erie shops, res 93 Railroad [Lena]
    Marie
  "   Fred, res 93 Railroad

Smith, Otis, painter, res 93 Railroad
"　　Wm, emp Withington fac, res 84 German　[Amanda]
　　　　Maggie, Willie, Louie, Maxmilian
"　　Barbara (wid Henry) res 84 German
"　　Jacob, cooper lime kilns, res 15 Oak
"　　Lulu, res 116 Railroad. Baby
Snape, Geo, emp shoe factory, res 88 Frederick [Amelia]
　　　　Willie, Ray, Pearl
Snapp, William, lab res 43 w Market [Adda] Flora, Di-
　　　mond
Snider, Oliver N (Fisher & Snider) res 64 Etna ave　[Lydia J]
　　　Wilbur R
Snyder, John, emp Erie round house, res 115 George　[Mag-
　　　gie]
"　　Fannie, res 11 William
"　　Jos, eng Griffith & Son, res 100 Court　[Margaret]
　　　　Gertrude, Jessie
"　　Frank E, clk Boston store, res 41 c Franklin
Snyder, H C, boots and shoes 4 c Market, res 214 n Jefferson
　　　　[Ida M] Eva, Alice
"　　Ella, res 78 Clark
"　　Ella (wid Lewis) res 127 n Jefferson
*　"　Lizzie (wid F) res 131 Thomas. George
"　　Cora, res 183 n Jefferson
†　"　Henry, teamster, res cor Wall and Lindley　[Susan]
　　　　John, Chas, Eva, Goldie
Souers, Jacob, res 54 Elm
Sowle, Jeremiah, lab res 56 High. Jennie, Chloa, Ophir
Spach, Thos, switchman Erie, res 138 c Franklin　[Fannie]
Spach, A B, cond Erie, res 27 Foust [Blanche] Leo L, Ma-
　　　bel, George, Grace, Marjory
Spangler, Bert, emp Erie shops, res 13 Edwin
"　　K S, cond Erie, res 13 Edwin [Ella] Cora, Per-
　　　ry, Franklin, Emma, Earl
Spatt, Henry, res 125 Byron

Speaker, Jacob, machinist Erie, res 87 Dimond [Minnie]
    Carl, Bertha, Eda
"   Adam, barber, res 87 Dimond
"   Erhart, lab res rear of 69 Dimond   [Theresa]
    Clarence, Helen
Spencer, Herbert, student, res 11 Randolph
"   M L (Spencer & Branyan) res 11 Randolph [Blanche]
    Edith, Paul
Spencer & Branyan (M L Spencer, W A Branyan) attorneys
    over Citizens Bank
Spencer, Lee, lab res 136 w Matilda
"   Lincoln, lab res 136 w Matilda
"   J E, carpenter, res 136 w Matilda [Olive] Mary,
    Frank, Edna, Clifford, Gertrude
Spice, Geo, gardener, res 160 William [Florence M] Geo A,
    Florence, Mary
"   Arthur, lab res 160 William
Spigelmyre, Ford, emp Farmers Guide, res 7 Monroe
Spitzenberg, Nicholas, emp lime kilns, res 24 First [Bridget]
    Mary, A S, Willie
"   John, emp Briant, res 24 First
"   Joseph, emp Briant, res 24 First
Sprinkle, Sherman, emp Pearl laundry, res 144 n Lafontaine
    [Mary] Clyde, Eva, Rilla
* "   Chester, lab res s Etna ave
* "   David, emp Pearl laundry, res s Etna ave
* "   Absolom, wagon mkr, res s Etna ave [Eliza J]
"   H M, fireman Erie, res 5 Water
"   Jonathan, emp Pearl laundry, res 5 Water [Catha-
    rine]
"   J J, co recorder, res 5 Monroe [Lucinda E]
Sprowl, Jacob, emp Erie, res 37 Erie [Rebecca] Goldie E,
    Earl M, Mildred V
Stacker, M E (wid Lawrence) res 86 Etna ave
Stahl, G W, emp Griffith & Son, res 59 Polk [Katharine]
    Ernest G, Mabel L

Stahl, Fred C, painter Erie, res 59 Polk
" Henry A, emp Griffith & Son, res 59 Polk
" Gottleib sr, res 42 Buchanan
" Chris, emp city, res 42 Buchanan [Mary] Albert, Otto, Lucile, Henrietta, Baby
Fred, emp Griffith & Son, res 36 Buchanan [Mary] Elsie, Nora, Helen
" Wm, cigar mfg 73 Esther, res same [Grace] Percis
* " J H, res 317 n Jefferson [Margaret O]
* " E M, clk and school teacher, res 313 n Jefferson [Rosa] Otto
Staldter, John, brakeman Erie, res 226 e Market [Stella]
" Fred, lab res 92 Grayston ave [Rose] Amelia, Martha, Jacob, Lizzie, Anna, Rudy
" Henry, emp Erie, res 92 Grayston ave
" William, emp Erie, res 92 Grayston ave
Stalnaker, John R, bookkeeper, res 73 w State [Helen] Macy, Daniel, Kemp
Stambaugh, John, lab res 17 Broadway [Elizabeth] Frank, Ira
Stameth, Clara, res 143 e Franklin
Standard Oil Co (W E Folk, mgr) cor Third and Foust
Stanley, John, cond Erie, res 147 e Market
" Noah, emp Erie boiler shops, res 21 Iowa [Estella]
Stanton, Chauncey, fireman Erie, res 145 e Sabine [Vida]
Star, Frank, emp shoe factory, res cor Byron and Market
Star Restaurant (O R France, prop) 11 e Market
Starbuck, James, res 239 Etna ave
" Maggie, res 239 Etna ave
" Lona, res 239 Etna ave
" James F, emp E A Collins, res 9 Olinger [Clara] Nora, Ora, Pearl
Starke, Lizzie, servant, res 38 w Matilda
Stauch, Albert, clk C Mader, res 6 Herman [Tena M]
Steele, Daisy, res 77 e Market
" Elizabeth, emp Grand View hotel, res same

Steele, John, emp Theo Poorman, res 36 Whitelock [Mary] Earl
" H Wirt, reporter, res 36 Whitelock
" Carl P, clk F Dick & Sons, res 36 Whitelock
" Nancy L (wid Wm L) res 36 Whitelock
" Emma (wid James) res 69 w State

Steinbrenner, J H, tile cutter, res 75 Polk [Louisa]

Steininger, Rev Howard, pastor Evangelical church, res 84 Front [Eliza] Ervin, Forest, Gladys

Stell, Harry (Stell & Gray) res 25 Buchanan [Laura]

Stell & Gray (Harry Stell, Howard Gray) feed mill 37 e State

Stephan, Adam J, lab res 16 Nile [Catharine] Christena, Augusta

Stetler, Jack, brakeman Erie, res 110 e Washington [Emma]

Stetzel, Samuel, teamster, res 59 Whitelock [Maude] Hazel
" Chas, lab res 17 Briant [Tina] Nettie, Lona, Lillie
* " Henry, res e Front [Lulu V]
* " Daniel P, emp lime kilns, res e Front
* " Jacob D, brakeman Erie, res e of fair ground [Martha] Leah
* " D A, emp Withington, res e fair ground [Mary] Jessie, Twin Daughters
* " Perry, emp Erie shops, res e fair ground [Sarah] Harry
* " W E, emp Erie round hs, res e fair ground [Ida] Everet, Ethel

Stevens, Milo, res 13 Green
" Andrew, saddler John Kindler, res 99 Cherry [Barbara] Victor
* " Conrad, lab res s Etna ave. Stella, James, Owen
" Rebecca (wid Adam) res 122 Cherry
" Daniel, slate roofer, res 122 Cherry

Stevens, Emanuel M, slate roofer, res 132 Cherry [Lena] Robert

Stevens, Albert J, drugs and notions 158 e Market, res 137 Guilford [Lenora] Gertrude, Genevieve

Stewart, Chas C, boiler washer Erie, res 67 Superior [Cora]
    Ralph
"   Mrs W H (wid) res cor Matilda and Guilford, Ira,
        Minnie, Vera
"   Elija, lab res 118 Railroad [Ida] Ida P, James B,
        Vernie A
"   W H, policeman, res 115 Court [Alice] May, John
        H, Howard C, Grace, Homer, Cecil
Stewart, T, prop Boston Store, res 97 n Lafontaine [Mrs T]
    Margaret
Stickel, Samuel, butcher F M King, res 45 Elm [Rosella]
    Leo
Stinson, J J, butcher, res 11 Edna [L V] Lillian B, Worth-
    ington W, Harry H, Vivian
Stopher, Frank, lab emp Perrine & Bartlett, res 165 Etna ave
    [Mary]
Stoffel, John P, meat market 104 n Jefferson, res 65 e Matilda
    [Maggie] Georgia, Emma, Mamie, Willie G,
        Charles, Leo, Herman
Stoffel, Henry, driver Allman & Bash, res 65 e Matilda
"   John, butcher J P Stoffel, res 65 e Matilda
"   Jacob, butcher J P Stoffel, res 65 e Matilda
Stokesberry, Eva M, teacher public schools
Stoltz, J J, blacksmith 59 Warren, res 141 n Lafontaine [Kate]
    Katie, Joseph, Willie, Peter
"   John G, blacksmith J J Stoltz, res 141 n Lafontaine
"   Barney, blacksmith J J Stoltz, res 153 Poplar [Mary]
"   Adam, blacksmith J J Stoltz, res 276 n Jefferson
        [Mary] Herman, Gertrude
Stone, Edward, boilermaker Erie, res 64 Byron [Sarah] Ruth
"   F M, pastor M E church, cor Market and Guilford, res
        70 e Washington [Lillian] Ruth, Laura, Ray-
        mond
Stork, Emil, lab res 211 w Matilda [Mary] Anna, Amelia
Stouffer, Harry, emp Erie round house, res 42 Grayston ave
    [Lizzie] Ethel, Alonzo

Stout, W E, principal William street school, rooms 29 Milligan

Stover, E W, Eagle bakery 17 w market, res 5 Oak [Melissa] Emmet

Stover, G W, painter, res 173 n Jefferson [Mary E]
" Harry, barber, res 173 n Jefferson
" Bert, barber Bonebrake & Bonbrake, res 173 n Jeff's'n

Stratton, John, barber, res 63 w State [Ruth]

Straughn, John M, clk C Mader, res 85 Railroad [Amanda] Blanche

Strayer, James, emp J Kenower & Sons, res 64 Front [Clara] Cleo, Vivian

Streng, Henry, bartender Club saloon, res 66 w Tipton [Barbara] Elizabeth, Henry jr, Pauline

Strickland, Rev C V, music publisher and pastor Christian Chapel, res 25 Salamonie ave [Rev Mary] Chas

Strickler, C C, fireman Erie, res 45 e Washington st [Rosa] Clara

*Stickler, ——, shoemaker, res e Front [Cora] Roy, Inus, Ralph, Paul

Strodel, J C (John Strodel) res 150 n Lafontaine [Edith] Emma, Carl

John Strodel (Sophia, John C, Martin) dry goods and notions 59 n Jefferson

Strodel, Wm, clk John Strodel, res 79 Oak [Carrie] Hilda
" Anna Barbara (wid John G) res 81 Oak. Anna B

Strodel, L C, meat merchant 127 n Jefferson, res 66 Oak [Amelia] Amelia, Edward

Strodel, Sophia (wid John) res 139 Poplar
" Martin (John Strodel) res 139 Poplar

Strother, Geo B, res 49 Loudon [Emma]

Strouse, Adam, miller, res 87 Poplar [Sevilla] Myrtle, Lizzie, Winnie
" Milton, clk Harris Clothing Co, res 87 Poplar
" Wade, clk Economy, res 87 Poplar
" Frank E, emp Huntington Mill Co, res 121 Etna ave [Emma] Donald G

Strover, Lena, nurse, res 29 Frederick

Strover, Henry W, painter and decorator, res 107 n Lafontaine [Anna] Edith, Harry

Strover, May, compositor Farmers Guide, res 107 n Lafontaine

Stults, Sherman P, livery and feed stable 65 e Market, res 99 e Market [Ione] Virginia

Stults, William, real estate agt, res 15 Arthur [Rebecca F]

    "   Ernest W, clk Erie frt office, res 15 Arthur

    "   Emma J, music teacher, res 15 Arthur

    "   Cora E, milliner, res 15 Arthur

    "   Francis I, student, res 15 Arthur

    "   Austin W, res 15 Arthur

    "   Harmon W, res 48 Henry [Lucinda] Morton

    "   Ida M, dressmaker, res 48 Henry

    "   Dillie K, teacher public schools, res 48 Henry

    "   Blanche B, teacher public schools, res 48 Henry

    "   Sarah (wid Harmon) res 164 Guilford. M C

    "   Joseph, res 55 Marshall [Mrs Jos]

Stults, Geo W, attorney, res 55 Marshall

* "   Cyrus D (Stults & Dorsch) res s Etna ave [Lizzie E] Mabel A, Ralph W

    "   Jacob, real estate agt, res 125 Guilford [Hannah]

Stults, M B, furniture and undertaking 86 n Jefferson, res 84 Poplar [Lydia A] May F

Stults & Dorsch (Cyrus D Stults, Fred Dorsch) millers s Etna ave on Wabash river

Stuver, Wm, lab res fire engine house

    "   Alfred, eng Nichol's mill, res 2 Lehmeyer [Martha] Chas, Anna

    "   Wm, expressman, res 2 Lehmeyer

    "   John, emp Beyer Bros, res 2 Lehmeyer

    "   Ona, domestic 183 William

    "   Edward, emp H L & F Co, res 5 Cline [Ellen] Henry

Sullivan, Hannah, res 32 Webster

    "   T J, gen foreman Erie shops, res 32 Webster

    "   Anna, res 182 n Jefferson

Sullivan, Frank, boilermaker Erie, res 17 w Tipton
" Phoebe (wid John) res 107 First

Sult, Cora L, housekeeper, 36 Bingham
" Howard, emp shoe fac, res 32 Salamonie ave
" David D, carp res 32 Salamonie ave [Samantha] Buena
V, Mary M, Frederick P

Summers, Manda, emp shoe fac, res 39 Whitelock
" Laura, domestic, 94 s Jefferson
" Myrle, res 157 n Jefferson

Sunderman, Dietrich, res 56 n Lafontaine

Suttles, Ernest, emp Erie round house, res 68 Marshall
[Amanda] Cleo, Walter

Sutton, Barney, plasterer, res 32 Cherry

Sutton, S F, physician, office over 46 n Jefferson, res same
* " Chas, lab res s Briant

Swafford, N W, clk McCaffrey's groc res 27 William [Rebecca]
" Samuel, lab res s bank Little river near Lafontaine
[Margaret]
" Frank, lab res 21 Everett [Anna] Jennie, Bessie,
Edith
" Wesley, lab res 70 Polk [Anna E] Sadie, Howard

Swan, John, painter res 27 e Tipton [Ella] Carl

Swaim, Florence, domestic 29 Superior
" J F, caller Erie, res 73 Superior [Nora] Earl D
Ray L
" Fred E, Deputy Co Auditor, res 19 Mayne [Amelia]
Edith M
" James, painter Erie, res 30 Nebraska [Lulu]
" William F, Co Auditor, res 40 Front [Mary]

Swain, Bennet, res 3 s Lafontaine [Ellen]
" Bert, lab res 151 e Sabine [Bertha]

Swart, Amos M, eng and machinist, res 66 High [Myrie E]
Minnie I, Marie A

Swartz, Wm, lab res 71 w Tipton
" G W, machinist Erie res 66 High

*Swartz, Frank L, emp Withington res c fair ground [Elizabeth] Goldie M, Arthur, Edna, Freddie
"   O E, res 14 Iva
Sweetland, LeRoy, eng Erie, res 63 s Jefferson [Anna] Albert, Frederick
Swihart, Isaac J, tonsorial parlors 156 e Market, res over same [Adelia] Blanche, Ethel, Floyd.
Swinehart, H A, emp Erie round house, res 84 Grayston ave [Nancy] Ezra, Earl S, Lloyd
"   James B, emp Erie shops res 26 Canfield [Mary] Lulu, Ollie, Roscoe, Charles

T

Taflinger, David, yard master Erie, res 99 First [Rachael] Harmon, Arthur, Levetta
Tanzier, Louis, lab res 27 w Washington
Tarlton, J F, brick mason, res 102 Etna ave [Agnes] Walter
Tate, Wm, brakeman Erie, res 158 e Market [Mary] Wm jr, John, Mary, Hazel
Taylor, E M, res 92 e Market [Lizzie A]
"   Mary J (wid Wallace) res 1 Hannah
"   Jennie (wid Edward) res 119 over n Jefferson. Bessie
"   Enos T, pres Citizens Bank, res 19 Etna ave [Emma] Paul, Miriam
"   J W, carpenter Erie, res 14 Allen [Lulu]
* "   Wm, res s Henry [Agnes]
"   Herbert, clk Wabash frt house, bds 41 e Franklin
Teeple, Thos, towerman interlocker, res 49 South [Delana] Hiley M

Teusch, John, gardener, res 65 Hitzfield [Rachael]
"   Jacob, lab, res 65 Hitzfield
"   John jr, lab, res 51 Bartlett [Katie] Edward, Albert, Cecelia, Lizzie, Anna, Katie
The News Publishing Co (O W Whitelock, pres) pubs News-Democrat, daily, weekly and mid-weekly, 20 west Market
Thieme, William, lab, res 108 Walnut
Thomann, E N, cabinet maker, 42 Cherry, res 48 Marshall [Anna], Celia, Albert, Emma, Herbert
"   William, emp E N Thomann, res 48 Marshall
"   Estella, stenographer, res 48 Marshal
Thomas, John, brick layer, res over 114 n Jefferson
"   Wm, (Zahn & Thomas) res over 46 Cherry [Lucy]
"   Frank, clk, res 114 n Jefferson [Ada]
"   Albert J, cond Erie, res 212 e Market [Estella] Ruth
* "   Joseph, lab, res e fair ground [Ella E] Hazel
"   James, book agt, res 24 Sherman [Mattie] Nora
* "   Anna, domestic, res s Etna ave.
"   John J, res 69 Henry.
Thompson, ——, saw filer Griffith & Son, res 60 e Market
"   Miss F S, res 101 Guilford
"   Miss M J, res 101 Guilford
"   Bruce, student, res 33 e Tipton
"   Chas, machinest Erie, res 13 Iowa.
"   Anna (wid Adolphus), res 13 Iowa
Thompson Ice Cream Co (Wm L Thompson, Levi Anglemyre) 18-22 Frederick
Thomson, Mary, teacher public schools.
Thorn, Elizabeth, (wid Warren), res 47 Wilkerson. Chas
Thorne, Abraham, lab, res 43 Frederick [Sarah A]
Thornton, Edward, eng Erie, res 3 Briant [Ella]
Thrasher, B G, res 292 e State [Lizzie] Mabel
Thurman, Minnie, (wid) res 1 Hannah
"   Clara, res 1 Hannah

Ticer, Mrs Hattie, res 25 e Tipton   Winifred F,   Lucile

Tierney, Alex, emp Briants, res 164 e Franklin [Louise]
     Martha

"   J F, switchman Erie, res 84 Wilkerson [Rose]

Tillman, Sanford, carpenter Erie, res 16 Leopold [Savilla]
     Hazel

"   Benj, btchr, res 8 Leopold [Elizabeth]   Chester A

"   Jesse C, emp Wabash Ry, res 8 Leopold

"   William, butcher, res 9 w Sabine [Ella]   Charlie

Tisroe, Frank, barber, res 57 w Tipton   Esther

"   Esther, res 39 Everett

Tobias, Oscar, carpenter, res 41 Mayne [Mattie]   Leon,
     Russel

Tobias & Conkle (Ed Tobias, Norman Conkle) photographers
     over 58 n Jefferson

Tobias, Edward (Tobias & Conkle) bds Star restaurant

Todd, Cyrus, harness maker, res 126 Condit [Belle]   Ger-
     trude,   Clodie

Tompkins, Robt, cook Star restaurant, res 87 e State [May]

Toohey, Della, (wid John), boarding house, res 17 e Tipton
     Mary M,   Kate

Toopes, J E, brakeman Erie, res 67 High [Cora B]   Marie

Torborg, Theodore, teacher and organist Catholic church, res
     93 Cherry

Townsend, Frank D, supt H L & F Co, res 38 w Matilda
     [Nettie]   Georgiana

Tracy, B L, res 30 Frederick [Maria]

"   T D, lab, res 12 Glenn [Clara E]   Loyd,   Emma

Trammel, W H, attorney, res 58 e Market [Laura F]   Chas

"   Pat, res 47 e Washington

Tremain, M A, (wid Levi T), matron Orphan's Home

Trixler, Lewis G, tonsorial parlors, 58 n Jefferson, res 7
     Roach [Clara]   Leo

Trovinger, Bert, lab, res fire engine house

"   David, carpenter, res 20 Warren [Mary J]   Laura

Truax, Herbert, fireman Erie, res 39 High [Rebecca] Cora, Eugene

Truman, Nelson, teamster Briant, res 45 South [Isa] Everet

" L F, eng Erie, res 35 High [Alice] Mary, Fred L, Harold, Ralph

† Trusler, T F, agt, res Catherine st [Susan] Dessie

" Frank, bartender S H Lipinsky, res 46 w Market [Belle] Garnet

" Meda, res 24 Cherry

Trutt, Carrie, (wid) res 215 e State

Tschechtelin, Alois, emp Erie, res 60 Zahn [Lizzie]

Tucker, E, lab, res 43 Superior [Martha]

Tumbleston, Nathaniel, res 58 Frederick

Turner, Elihu, (Turner & Henry, res 57 Frederick

Turner & Henry, (Elihu Turner, J R Henry), cabinet makers, 7 Frederick

Tuttle, Morton, bookkeeper Shoe Factory, res 35 Henry [Alice J] Melville W

" Chauncey C, res 35 Henry

Tyler, J J, lumber dealer, res 67 e State [Elizabeth]

U

Ufheil, John sr, carpenter, res 165 n Lafontaine [Martha]

" John jr, carpenter, res 165 n Lafontaine

" Edward, lab, res 165 n Lafontaine

" Henry, contractor, res 143 Poplar [Margaret] Mary, Cecelia, Edith, Clara, Agnes

Ufheil, Frank, carpenter, res 143 Poplar
"   Peter, barber, 92 n Jefferson, res 143 Poplar
"   Joseph, carpenter, res 123 Poplar [Louise] Nicholas,
            Lena, Johannah, Harmon, John, Herbert
"   Constantine, carpenter Erie, res 51 Buchanan [Mary]
            Joseph, Julius, Helen
Ulrich, Laura, asst cook Star restaurant, res 11 e Market
Underwood, Homer C, attorney, res 44 Elm [Anna] Leah
United Telephone Co., (J H Hessin, mgr), Bippus block
United Brethren College, (C H Kiracofe, pres), n Byron st
Unger, Chris, blacksmith Erie, res 33 Iowa [Fannie] Edw
Urich, Mrs W F, (wid Wm), res 149 e Market. Amy, Stella
*Urschell, John, emp Erie round house, res Stults pike
            [Alice]
"   Christena, (wid Chas), res 26 William. Louise

*Do you fear Consumption or Heart Disease?
You can get a cure at Albert Frech's
drug store.*

V

Vampner, Wm E, lab, res 35 Nile
"   Frederick, wood peddler, res 35 Nile [Mary F]
VanAntwerp, Thos, clk Theo VanAntwerp, res 38 Elm [Ella]
            Helen
VanAntwerp, Theo, groceries, provisions, etc, 8 e Market, res
            73 Etna ave [May] Lewis G, Nellie
VanAntwerp, Rebecca B (wid L W) res 73 Etna ave
VanArsdol, J W, merchant tailor over 52 n Jefferson, res 85
            Frederick [Martha B] Ervin L, Mary E, Wil-
            bur G, Glenn W
"   Curtis M, tailor J W VanArsdol, res 85 Frederick

VanArsdol, Lois (wid) res 85 Frederick
VanCamp, J L, painter and paper hanger, res 92 s Jefferson [Sarah C] Nellie M
Vance, Nathaniel, lab, res 19 Salamonie ave
" Mrs Caroline, res 19 Salamonie ave
VanDevender, Lulu, res 25 Buchanan
" Guy C, clk, res 25 Buchanan
Vandewater, Nicholas, brakeman Erie, res 32 Sabine [Alice] Bessie, Florence
†Vandyne, Chas, emp Perrine & Bartlett, res shoe fac addition [Ella] Cora, Laura
† " Pearl, emp Perrine & Bartlett, res shoe fac add.
VanHolten, John, boiler maker Erie, res 122 Grayston avenue [Myrtle] Dorman
" Anna, dressmaker, res 41 Hartman
" Elizabeth, clk, res 41 Hartman
" William, lab, res 41 Hartman
*Vaughn, R W, supt Withington factory, res e Front [Eliza]
Vawter, O D, blacksmith Erie, res 28 Nebraska [Lillie] Clarence
Vendricks, James, blacksmith rear Whitelock & Son, res 183 William [Anna] Vivian, Fred
Venard, Mrs Belle M, dressmaker, res 71 Henry. E Dott
*Vernerder, Chas, bill poster Wallace circus, res 351 e State
* " S W, postal clk Wabash, res 351 e State [Lillie] Mary, Minnie, Earl, Carl
Vernon, J B, civil eng, res 73 Henry [Josephine] Inez, Florence, Gladys, Aubrey W
† " Elvira, domestic, s Salamonie ave
" Isaac, fireman Erie, res 36 Superior [Lottie] Oliver, William
" Amanda, res 28 Taylor
" Lizzie, res 28 Taylor
" Henry, emp Briant, res 34 Superior
Velters, Godfrey, teamster, res 50 Grayston ave [Mary] Edith, Mamie, Carrie

* Vielhauer, Henry, hostler, res 206 Guilford [Mary] Macy, Ernest, Clarence

Vincent, Mrs Cora B, res 117 Elm. Grover C

Voght, Ed, paper hanger, rms over 20 e Market
* " Albert, emp brick yard, res n Guilford [Minnie] Mason
  " Jacob, res 105 Warren [Louise] Anna, Clara
  " Wm M, moulder, res 105 Warren

Volz, Jacob jr, emp Western Lime Assn, res 111 Broadway
  " Louisa, clk John Strodel, res 111 Broadway
  " Jacob sr, emp lime kilns, res 111 Broadway [Katharine] Katharine, Caroline, Valentine, Sophia

Voris, J H, teacher public schools, res 191 n Jefferson

W

Wagner, John, clk M Luber, res 169 William [Mary] Hazel, Paul
  " Fred, emp lime kilns, res 169 William

Wagner, A H, dentist over 59 n Jefferson, res 14 Randolph [Grace] Arthur

Wagoner, Clyde, student, res 96 w State
  " Henry H (Pearl Steam Laundry Co) res 96 w State [Mary] Harry, Ruth, Harmon, Walter
  " Austin E, car repairer Erie, res 172 e Franklin st [Catharine] Florence

Walburn, Robert, teamster, res 91 Grayston ave [Sarah]
  " Edward E, emp Erie section, res 91 Grayston ave
  " Samuel F, emp Briant fac, res 91 Grayston ave
  " Lee, emp Briant fac, res 91 Grayston ave

Waldron, Charles, emp Erie section, res cor Sabine near Erie
    shops [Martha] Eliza
  "   Wm, lab, bds cor Sabine near Erie shops
Walker, Albert, painter, res 170 Byron [Emma J] Charles
  "   Jay, res 3 High
  "   Mary (wid Milton) res 40 Canfield
  "   C W, emp Griffith & Son, res 248 e State [V] Lucile
  "   John, emp Perrine & Bartlett, res 85 Condit. Nettie,
    Marie
  "   Grace, res 30 Nile
  "   Lillie, res 30 Nile
Walknetz, Ed, fireman Erie, res 48 Condit [Mary] Mildred
Wall, Hallie, res 89 Whitelock. Tessie A, Drucy B
Wall, Harry, barber, res 121 Byron [Bertha] Grace
Wallace, John, emp Erie, res 52 Grayston ave [Arcaney]
Walter, Chas A, druggist 74 n Jefferson, res 37 w Tipton st
    [Cecelia] Helen, Gertrude. Anna
Walter, John, lab, res 76 Elm [Phoebe] Denis, Firman,
    Myrtle, Boyd, Agnes
  "   Lizzie, res 115 Cherry
  "   Gottleib, res 94 Buck. Maggie
  "   Gottleib jr, teamster, res 94 Buck
  "   Daniel, emp J M Bronkar, res over 32 Cherry
Ward, Mary (wid Patrick) res 39 w Tipton. Emma
  "   Pat, machinist Erie, res 39 w Tipton
  "   John W, pressman Herald, res 103 Court [Floyd] Paul
  "   William, clk McCaffrey, res 39 w Tipton
  "   James, emp Erie car shops, res 17 Erie
  "   W, carpenter, res 327 e State [Eliza J] Ora
  "   Elizabeth (wid Geo) res 30 e Matilda
  "   John, brakeman Erie, res 25 Second [Martha] Ger-
    trude, Mamie, Albert, Everet
Ware, Harry F, res 47 s Jefferson
  "   Ada, milliner, res 47 s Jefferson
  "   Morgan, res 47 s Jefferson [Mary] Raymond C, El-
    don W, Albert D

160   DIRECTORY OF HUNTINGTON.

Warner, Frank, emp Withington fac. res 50 Superior
"   Wm, emp Withington fac, res 50 Superior
"   Jacob, fireman Withington fac, res 50 Superior [Jennie] Bertha
"   C C, res 119 Cherry [Nora]
"   D R, res 138 First [Emma] Cleo
+Warren, W T, clk Wm Mardenis, res 52 Swan [Elsie] Elvie, Jessie, Mary, Leota
Wasson, Mrs A V (wid Francis) res 78 e State
"   Chas, emp fire dept, res 78 e State
Watkins, Hon C W, judge 56th judicial circuit. res 48 Etna ave [Irene] Cosie I, Grace A
Watson, Samuel, teamster, res 47 Zahn [Clara] Alice
"   Mabel (wid James) res 26 Grayston ave. William C, Clarence, Anna S
"   Orien, emp Midway restaurant, res 10 Frederick
Watt, Sarah (wid Michael) res 12 Iowa. Clarence
Watt, Ed, lab res 12 Iowa
Watt, Emanuel, lab res 12 Iowa
Watt, Harvey, lab res 12 Iowa
Watt, Lee, lab res 12 Iowa
Watters, Matthew, res 41 Everet [Nancy] Lydia
"   Benj, lab res 41 Everet
"   Joseph, lab res 41 Everet
"   John, emp Briant, res 1 Bechtol [Jane] Jacob M, Nancy A
Wasmuth, A D (Hamer & Wasmuth) rms over 37 n Jefferson
Waymack, Fred, cond Erie, res 140 e Market [Lucie] Clara, Leota, Fred
Weaver, Daisy, res 41 e Franklin
"   Alice K, teacher public schools, res 60 e Franklin
* "   Amanda (wid Jacob) res n Jefferson. Emma, Mabel
Weber, Peter, blacksmith Erie, res over 129 n Jefferson [Esther] Josephine, Estella, Lawrence
"   Julia, domestic 70 First
"   H, lab res 46 Grayston ave

Weber, William, lab res 46 Grayston ave
"   Anthony, lab res 46 Grayston ave [Rebecca]
"   Anthony A (Bucher & Weber) res 53 s Jefferson [F C]
        Lillie. Wm M, Grace G, Maggie R, Paul G.
        Mary M
"   Julia Belle, domestic, 131 e Sabine
"   Daisy V, domestic, res 131 e Sabine
"   John, lab res 131 e Sabine [Delilah B] Ray Robt.
        Farie Ferl, John Albert
"   Fred, eng lime kilns. res 131 Broadway [Catharine]
        Blanche, Katie. Carl, John, Ruth
"   Frank, bartender Jacob Weber, res 60 w Matilda
Weber, Jacob, saloon 50 Jefferson, res 60 w Matilda [Lena]
        Hattie, Julius. Harmon, Edith
Webster, H A, teamster, res 65 Whitelock [Cora] Harry,
        Ruth, Maude, Mary
Webster, Wm, emp Erie section, res 187 William [Eva F]
        Mony G
"   E A, butcher, res 46 Buck [Sarah] Homer
Weekley. Henry, lab res 34 Briant [Mary A]
Weese, Mary E (wid John R) res 36 Green. Clarissa N, Don-
        ald E
"   Peter, res 37 Superior [Auzaletta]
"   H G, traveling salesman, res 15 Fredericka [H A]
        Lucy F, Joseph R, Rosanna E,. Robert P.
        Mildred P
"   Harry E, mail clerk Wabash R R, res 15 Fredericka
Weis, Michael, groceries 125 n Jefferson, res 97 west Tipton
        [Amanda]
Weis, Fred, emp M Becker, bds 173 n Jefferson
Weis, Henry, saloon 82 n Jefferson, res 23 n Lafontaine
        [Julia] Albert, Anna, Bertha
Weisman, B F, fruit tree agent, res 49 Kintz [Susan] Oma.
        Lucile
Weist, John, crayon artist, res 99 e Tipton [Caroline] Geo B
Weiford, H C, train despatcher Erie, res 5 Elm [Kitty] Ben-
        jamin O, Florence

Welch, John, emp Collins Ice Cream Co, bds 22 Elm

Welches, Jacob, lab res 44 Cline [Eliza] Herbert, Howard, Goldie

Welker, Sarah, (wid) res 59 s Briant Olive

Weller, George, teamster, res 74 Henry [Emma]

Wells, Herbert L, train despatcher Erie, res 83 Etna ave [Anna] Leota H, Weldon

* " Chas S, ass't sup't water works, res e fair ground [Anna]   .

* " Anna (wid) res e fair ground

" Homer, fireman Erie, res 56 Superior [Lillie] Roy, Clark, Mildred

Wells, H S, millinery and notions 78 Jefferson

Wells, H S, bkpr Griffith & Son, res 158 Guilford [Clara]

Wells, Fargo Express, (Geo Reynolds agt) 26 n Jefferson

Welsheimer, E I, brakeman Erie, res Windsor Hotel

Wensley, Joseph, clk H H Arnold & Son, res 107 Etna ave [Addie] Earl, Hazel

Werner, George, butcher, res 75 e Matilda [Lizzie]

West, David, compositor Farmer's Guide, res cor Kintz and Byron

Harlan, emp Erie, res cor Kintz and Byron

Anderson, painter, res 65 Division [Anna] Ezra, Melvin, Mary

Allen M, lab res cor Kintz and Byron [Maggie M] Carrie, Ernest

Western Union Telegraph Co (Mrs J E D Anderson, mgr) office Wabash depot

Western Lime Co (Peter Martin, pres and treas) office corner Court and Warren

Westley, George, clk Star restaurant, res 66 e Market

Weston, Boston, emp shoe factory, res cor Buck and Etna ave

" Orvilla, emp G L Newcomb, cor Buck and Etna ave

" John, teamster, res cor Buck and Etna ave [Amanda] Bessie

Wetter, John, carpenter Erie, res 21 Wilkerson [Elizabeth]
    Rebecca, Ida
"   A W, carpenter, res 21 Wilkerson
"   Mary E, teacher, res 21 Wilkerson
Wharton, John T, eng Erie, res 119 First [Elizabeth] Walter
"   E J, eng Erie, res 26 Leopold [Lou]
Wheeler, Frank, cond Erie, res 149 e Franklin [Ida] Evola,
    Pearl
"   Boyd, emp Perrine & Bartlett, res 19 Briant
"   Harry, brakeman Erie, res 19 Briant
"   G C, res 19 Briant [Henrietta] Bert, Jessie
"   J D, book agt, res 4 s Lafontaine [Ellen]
Whitacre, Walter B, emp Allman & Bash, res 68 Grayston ave
"   Elmer, emp Erie, res 25 Nile [Bertha] Hazel
"   Conrad, emp Erie round house, res 9 Iowa [Mary]
    May, Ruth
"   Geo W, res 13 Etna ave [S Jennie]
Whitaker, Minnie S, teacher public schools, res 95 e Market
White & Smith (I W White, W H Smith) cabinet makers 27
    Guilford
White, Isaac W (White & Smith) res 46 e Market [Lizzie]
    Baby
"   R A, brakeman Erie, res 144 Byron [Ella]
Whiteley, William, res 29 Buchanan [Louisa] Laura, Lil-
    lie, Frank
Whitelock, O W (Milligan, Whitelock & Cook) res 68 s Jeffer-
    son [Jennie M] Wilfred J, Etta, Clarence J,
    Charles M
Whitelock, W T (Whitelock & Son) res 80 s Jeff'son [Artalisa]
† "   D D, carpenter and contractor, res Wright street
    [Mrs D D] Frank
"   Geo G (Whitelock & Son) res 2 Salamonie avenue
    [Emma] Paul W, Gladys
Whitelock & Son (W T, G G) groceries 17 s Jefferson
*Whitelock, Jonathan, res s Jefferson [Elizabeth]

Whiteside, Harry, tinner Erie, res 63 Briant
   "   Jennie (wid Geo) res 63 Briant. Emma
Whitestine, Mattie, expert accountant, res 57 Court
   "   Ora, veterinary surgeon Harter barn, res 80 e
        Franklin [Minnie]
   "   John A, carpenter, res 50 Webster [Elizabeth]
        Gladys
   "   Geo B, clk postoffice, res 50 Webster
Whitmore, Frank, res 48 w Tipton [Lizzie] Roy, Wallace,
        Isabella, Sarah, Hester, George
Whitney, J L, fireman Erie, res 90 Superior [Ella]
Wickenhiser, F E (Reichenbach & Wickinhiser) res 93 Guil-
        ford [Bessie]
Widener, Wm, emp Griffith & Son, res 61 High [Lizzie]
Wilbur, Marion, eng Erie, res 8 Guilford [Kate]
Wilcox, Cora, res 32 Sabine
Wilder, Newton, brakeman Erie, res 156 e Tipton [Cora]
        Vivian
Wiles, Wm F, emp H L & F Co, res 57 Frederick [Ella]
   "   John, stone and brick mason, res 2 s Lafontaine [Dora]
   "   Luke, lab res 49 Briant [Margaret]
   "   Jennie, domestic 26 w Matilda
Wilhelm, Mary (wid James) res 64 e State. Jackson, Edith,
        Grace, Emma
   "   Lida, clk C W Goble, res 64 e State
   "   Susannah (wid Michael) res 12 William. Flora, Kate
   "   Mary, cashier John Frash, res 12 William
Wilhelm, John F, grocer 69 e Sabine, res same [Caroline]
        Herbert
Wilker, Sarah (wid) res 59 Briant. Olive
Wilkerson Bros (A C, G N) lumber dealers
Wilkerson, A C (Wilkerson Bros) res 42 s Jefferson [Amanda
        E] Effie, Bertha
   "   G N (Wilkerson Bros) res 22 Henry [Tennie] Eva,
        Frank B
   "   Hazel, res 134 Etna ave

Wilkins, Hattie, res 132½ e Market
"   J C, lab res 13 Marshall
"   W M, brakeman Erie, res 13 Marshall [Bertha] H S
"   A S, cond Erie, bds Marchaneil restaurant
Will, Adam, lab res 91 Whitelock [Mary S]
Willetts, Wm, eng Erie, res 88 s Jefferson [Lorena] Harry
Williams, Frank, teamster Griffith & Son, res 32 s Briant st
        [Elizabeth] Ernest, Howard, Everet
"   Rhoda, res 156 First
"   James, contractor, res 91 e Tipton [Elizabeth]
        Chas, Iva M
"   N M, lab res 63 e Market [Louisa] Samuel, Ed-
        die, Lizzie
"   Adam, emp Stults livery, res 63 e Market
Willis, H F, res 12 Arthur [Mary J] Ella C
"   L C, transfer agent Erie and Wabash, res 69 e Tipton
        [Sadie] Ray, Lyle
Willis, Ed, bakery 123 n Jefferson, res 44 w Matilda [Sydney]
        Carl
Wilson, Mat, janitor Erie depot, res Windsor hotel
"   Mary (wid Chas W) res 30 Nile. Virgil
"   James R, emp Erie, res 122 Condit [Sarah R] Mary
        C, Nettie V, Samuel E, Grover W, Ernest,
        John C, Frank
"   J R, eng Erie, res 148 First [J A] George, Vera
"   E C (wid) res 150 Guilford
"   J T, carpenter, res 274 e State [Cora] Claude R
"   Ira, operator Erie, res 147 Etna ave [Agnes] Inez,
        May, Gladys
*Wiltfong, B Frank, hedge fence agt, res s Etna ave [Ella]
        Lillie A, Earl
Wiley, J E (wid) res 108 Byron
Winal, Mary C (wid Henry) res 96 Oak. Katie
"   Joseph H, emp Erie shops, res 96 Oak
"   John J (Winal & Marks) res 200 e Market [Susan]
        Mary, Cecelia, Agnes

Winal & Marks (John Winal, L C Marks) blacksmith and wagon-maker 25 Guilford

Windle, F M B, chief clerk Erie Supt, res 69 First [Jessie F] Woodward K, Camile

"   Wm, chief clerk Erie Roadmaster, res 112 Guilford st [Georgia]

"   W K, res 112 Guilford [Mary]

Windemuth, Wm, emp Huntington Mill Co, res 86 Clark street [Amelia] Mata, Rosa, Harmon, Paul

Windemuth, N, meat market 114 n Jefferson, res 93 William st [Caroline] Julia, Henry, Hannah

Windemuth, Henry, butcher, res 102 Cline

*Winebrenner, David, teamster, res e fair ground [Belle] Ella M, Laura A, William C, Jacob R

Winkleman, Henry, emp Erie section, res 101 Dimond street [Sophia] Arthur

Winkleman, Fred, section foreman Erie, res 157 Court street [Louisa] Minnie

Winans, Rev C S, pastor Tabernacle Baptist church, res 261 e State [Margaret] Donald, Paul, Rosabella

Winans, Miss Francis, res 261 e State

Winter, Rev J F, pastor Reformed church, res 6 Henry [RA] J C, E M

"   Cyrus, canvasser, res 62 Webster [Rebecca A]

"   John, res 62 Webster

"   James, brakeman Erie, res 62 Webster

"   A J, emp Briant, res 4 Mayne [Dora F] John S, Princess E, Mabel I

Wintrode, Jacob, res 83 e State

"   Alfred H, traveling salesman, res 83 e State [May] Eddie

"   C E, traveling salesman, res 83 e State [Jessie A] Mary W

"   Wire, James P, teamster, res 134 Etna ave [Catharine] Dessie, Aldona, Blaine, Charles

Wise, Adam, tailor, res 23 Harris [Elizabeth] Martha, John
Wisner, John, prop Hoosier Steam laundry, res 13 Frederick
    [Mary J]
Wiswell, Mrs Mamie, res 54 First. Ernest
*Withington Factory (W H Withington, pres; P H Withington
    vice-pres; T H Russell, secy-treas; R W Vaughn,
    mgr) handle manufacturers 150 Front
Withrow, D L, carpenter Erie, res 147 First [Eva] Ralph,
    Eldon
Witzerman, Fred, brakeman Erie, res 17 Briant
Woehnker, Barney, lab, res 79 e Market [Anna] Vannessa
Wolf, Chas H, lab res 103 Walnut [Rena]
  "   S C, brick mason, res 132 George [Clara]
  "   Fred, watchman Griffith & Son, res 143 e Franklin st
      [Elizabeth]
  "   Chas, paper hanger, res 143 e Franklin
  "   Mary, res 79 n Lafontaine
Wolsoeffer, Jacob, emp shoe fac, res 28 Elm [Emma] Min-
    nie, Fred
Wolter, Chas, clk Neuer & Eisenhauer, res 133 Oak
  "   Elizabeth (wid Jacob W) res 133 Oak. Katie, John
Wonderly, John, eng Erie, res 140 Guilford [Kate] Georgie,
    Mabel, John, Paul, Joseph
Woods, Patrick, fireman Erie, res 132 First [Minnie]
  "   John A, justice of the peace over 58 n Jefferson, res
      90 Whitelock [Maria J] John C, Glenn D, F G
  "   James F, emp Briant fac, res 23 Harris [Dora]
  "   Elsworth, lab res 173 n Jefferson
  "   John, lab res 29 e Matilda [Bridget]
  "   Ervin, cutter shoe fac, res 86 Henry [Lucy]
Worcester, H S, despatcher Erie, res 23 Henry [Bessie]
Worden, Harry, traveling salesman, res 123 Cherry
Wright, Ervin, physician, office and residence 54 e Market st
    [Laura V] Rhodes
Wright, W H, clk J M Wright, res 49 e Market [Marie] Anna
Wright, Rosetta, res 36 William

Wright, **Chas L,** physician over 1 s Jefferson, res 11 William
[Kate]
"   Wm T, dpty co clk, res 84 Frederick [Sadie M] Carl
R, Clyde H
"   Harvey, tinner Erie, res 161 Byron
"   C W, carpenter, res 161 Byron
"   Wm I, bridge carpenter, res 161 Byron. Dora, Harry, Frank
Wright, J M, grocery 63 e Market, res 107 w State   [Maggie]
Wright, Loranna (wid Geo W) res 61 e Washington.   Edith B,
Eliza A
"   Albert G, clk Koh-I-Noor, res 61 e Washington
"   Marshall (Wright & Son) res over 27 s Jefferson street
[Mary]
Wright & Son (Marshall, M G) druggists 27 s Jefferson
Wright, Marion G (Wright & Son) res 12 Salamonie ave   [Agnes J] Dudley R, Dessie, Clarence, Lucy
"   J J, plasterer, res 8 Canal
Wyman, Chas E, eng Erie, res 19 High   [Mary E]
Wyman, A H, eng Erie, res 147 e Franklin   [Mrs A H]
Wysong, Wm, carp Erie, res 52 Grayston ave   [Maggie]
Wyss, Victor, emp Briant, res 117 w Tipton
Wyss, Constantine, emp Erie shops, res 117 w Tipton   [Anna
R] Francis, Anna, Agnes, Julia A
Wyss, Arnold, saloon 97 n Jefferson, res over same   [Anna]
Joseph, Louisa, Paul, Baby

Y

Yager, Wm, lab res 42 Mayne [Emma] Lulu, Cora, Jesse, David, Sarah

Yahnke, Wm, emp lime kilns, res 105 Dimond [Dora] Fred, Gusta, Willie, Carl, Harmon, Ferd

" Rudolph, painter, res 105 Dimond

Yaney, John, lab, res 147 e Sabine [Kate] Florence, May

Yant, Eli, ret, res 9 William

" Howard, teacher, res 9 William

Yates, Edward, painter, res 42 Mayne [Della] Pearl

Yeater, Wm, lab, res 10 Edwin [Sarah] (Chas A Slusser) (Goldie Slusser)

Yerman & Eisele, (Frank Yerman, John Eisele) Bottling Works, 83 Dimond

Yerman, Frank (Yerman & Eisele) 69 Dimond [Rose] Frank jr

" John, cigar mfg over 97 n Jefferson, res 129 w Tipton [Dora] Delia, Edward, Fred, Cora, Albion

Yetter, Albert, brakeman Erie, res 14 Indiana [Carrie] Glendora

Yingling, Daniel, physician over 2 w Market res 63 Cherry [Corrilla] Clara

Yopst, S E, (wid John) res 33 e Matilda

*Yopst, Geo A, attorney over Koh-I-Noor, res Stults pike [Minnie E] Mabel A, Willis J

Young, B F, carpenter, res 124 w Matilda [Emma] Francis, Lulu

" Frankie, domestic, res 88 s Jefferson

" Henry, fireman Erie, res 23 Dimond

" Dietrich, stone mason, res 23 Dimond [Minnie]

Young, W W, prop Grand View Hotel, 10 e State res same [Anna] N Pearl

" Miss Emma, stenographer, res Grand View Hotel

" John F, painter S Hall, res 35 Byron

Young, Geo, meat market cor Briant and State, res 161 e State
    [Nettie] Paul, Susan
  "   Chas P pressman, res 35 Byron
  "   Harry A, shoemaker, 28 e Market, res 35 Byron
       [Esther] Anna, George, Gertrude, Francis,
       Delbert A
  "   Theo, carpenter Erie, res 251 e State   [Clara B]
  "   Ina, dressmaker, res 239 e State
  "   William A, emp Withington res 239 e State [Mary E]
       Eldon, Ora, Verda, Blanche, Hazel
  "   Amos, res 10 Jackson [Anna] Howard, Boyd
  "   M F, (wid) res 10 Jackson
  "   Mary, domestic at 41 s Jefferson
  "   Harry I, emp Withington, res 78 Henry
  "   Jerry, timber buyer, res 78 Henry   [Martha V]
  "   Harry J, caller Erie res 23 Faust
  "   John B, harnessmaker J Kindler, res 105 Cherry
       [Mary] Carrie, Hubert
  "   Edward, clk A Kindler, res 105 Cherry
  "   Philip, clk H C Snyder, res 111 Cherry [Catharine]
       Mary, Nicholas, Jacob, Harmon, Monic, Frank
  "   Geo, clk Boston store, res 111 Cherry
  "   Tillie, clk Boston store, res 111 Cherry
  "   N W, painter, res 37 Division [Rose E] Margaret,
       William, Bessie
  "   Chas, car inspector Erie, res 122 First [Leona] Earl
  "   Geo D, machinist Erie, res 23 Faust [Margaret]
Youngblood, John, res 112 Byron [Catharine] Lena, Lulu,
    (Elmer Shaffer)
Youngblood, William, fireman Erie, res 166 e Franklin street
    [Louise]

Z

Zahm, L V (Fowerbaugh & Zahm) res 88 Oak [Maggie] Geo
  J. Eugene F, Wm M. Morris A

Zahn, Jacob (Zahn & Thomas) res 47 w Tipton [Emma]
  Ruth., Joseph, Mary

Zahn & Thomas (Jacob Zahn, Wm Thomas) fish dlrs 102 n
  Jefferson

Zahn, Geo. jeweler, res 47 w Tiptou
  "   Peter, tailor over 5 e Market. res 47 w Tipton [Caroline]
  "   Harriet, res 60 w Matilda
  "   Elizabeth (wid Geo) res 41 Byron
  "   Philip, cigar maker. res 41 Byron
  "   Herbert J, cashier McCaffrey, res 292 n Jefferson
  "   Peter H, clk McCaffrey, res 292 n Jefferson [Antonia
            M, Cecelia F
  "   Andrew, dlvry clk McCaffrey, res 128 Cherry [Emma[
            Odelia, Marie, Arthur

Zehringer, Rose (wid Martin) res 143 n Lafontaine

Zell, Henry, blacksmith W H Shank, res 98 e Market [Emma]

Zell, Teua, blacksmith, res 98 e Market

Zell, Almond, emp Briant, res 10 Kocher [Eunice A] Wm F,
  Gertrude A, Minnie M

*Zell, Isaiah, lab res fair ground. [Mary E] Allan, Chas

*Zell, Jacob, lab res fair ground

Zell, Page, lab rms over 92 n Jefferson

Zelle, Pique, operator United Telephone Co, res 98 e Market

Zeller, William A, boots and shoes 56 n Jefferson, res 38 William street [Francis] Lena C

Zeller, Anna B, bkpr W A Zeller, res 38 William
  "   Edwin S, barber, res 38 William
  "   Henry A, bookkeeper, res 38 William

Zeller, W A jr, reporter and bookbinder, res 46 Elm [Eliza-
  beth M] Clair V A, Vera H

Zent & Son (Peter W, Howard) buggies, carriages, harness, etc, 45 Warren st

Zent, P W (Zent & Son) res 89 e Franklin [Catharine H]
"   Howard F (Zent & Son) res 85 e Franklin [Lou] Walter H, Herbert R

Zigerli, Mary (wid Gabriel) res 66 w Matilda
"   Edward, clk E Hewitt, res 66 w Matilda

Zimmerman, Henry, brakeman Erie, res Windsor hotel

Zink, John, teamster, res 45 Kirtz [Alma] Ray, Maude

Zink, Chas, lab res Grand View hotel

Zitzer, Geo J, blacksmith M Highland, res 52 William [Elizabeth] John

Zitzer, Maggie (wid John) res 11 Hannah

|Zoller, Geo, emp Withington fac, res e State near Broadway. [Hattie] Lulu, Otto

---

Supplemental List.

(Names omitted in original canvass)

Adams, Melvin, res 31 Green

Adams, John O, res 31 Green

Amos & Sheridan (Chas A Amos, Elmer F Sheridan) abstractors over 52 n Jefferson

Amos, Chas A (Amos & Sheridan) res———— [Agnes] Harry

Bensing, Katie, res 155 Poplar

Barnaby, A P, teacher U B college, res 43 Milligan [Lillian] Paul, Ruth, Naoma

Bradley, O E (Bradley Bros) res 117 Etna ave [Nellie] John H

Bruner, W M, prof bookkeeping Business University, rms 85 Railroad, bds Marchaneil restaurant

Beebe, Laura, res 28 Taylor

Bash, Philip P, res 38 e Washington

Boston Store (T Stewart, prop) dry goods 55 n Jefferson

Brunswick Billiard Parlor (S F Nave, prop) 18 e Market

Conkle, Norman (Tobias & Conkle) res 20 Madison

Chicago & Erie Ry, yards, shops and office e Market, between Third and Condit sts

Cook, C W, eng Perrine & Bartlett, res 55 s Briant [Lizzie] Pearl, Ralph.

Collins, Mamie, milliner over 55 n Jefferson

Carll, Lizzie, res 221 e State

Carll, Robt, lab res 221 e State

C & E Eating House (C C Kirk, prop) end e Franklin st

Collins, Chas, res 90 Etna ave

Coy & Dolan (Harvey Coy, John Dolan) confectionery and billiard hall 13 s Jefferson

Davidson, Sadie, milliner, res 9 Allen

Deemer, Peter, lab res 2 Herman st

*Ellett, Wm, emp Erie, res e fair ground

Economy Store (Steinfeld & Van Baalen, props) department store 52 Jefferson

Everding, Mrs Ida, res 124 e Market. Minnie

Ellerman, Chas jr, res 9 Gay

Eagle Bakery (E W Stover, prop) 17 w Market

Freel, Mary (wife of Lewis) res 40 Whitelock

Freel, Wm, lab, res 40 Whitelock

†Fauth, Richard, emp shoe fac, res 42 Salamonie ave   [MrsR] Willie, George, John, Lena

Fahrnow, Fredericka (wid) res 105 Bartlett

Gift, Daniel, lab bds 173 n Jefferson

Gibson, Bonnie, res 92 Condit

Globe Clothing House (Chas A Edwards, prop) 33 n Jefferson

Hammond, F C, emp Erie, res 143 Byron   [Ellen]   Harry

Highland, Jesse, res over 26 Cherry.

Highland, Robert, res over 26 Cherry

Hoover, Nellie (wife of Eph) res 99 Oak

Kunce, Ammon R, res 165 William

McClure, Elmer, res 90 Front

Stanton, Mrs Lizzie, res 79 w State.

Stults, Mary (wid John) res 5 Water

Shurtleff, Zua (wife of Chas) res 8 Iowa

Shutt, L A & Co (L A Shutt, J L Brown) sewer pipe and fittings, cor Third and Faust sts

Steinfeld, Harry (Steinfeld & Van Baalen) bds Exchange

Truman, Nelson jr, res 45 South

Van Baalen, Phil (Steinfeld & Van Baalen) bds Exchange

Whitten, Ben F, blacksmith 7 Front, res 82 Henry